The shower curtain was pulled back

Shanna felt the gust of cool air. She heard Derek step in behind her. He pressed her tightly against him, the pressure of his lips upon her neck merging with the spray.

Suddenly Shanna pivoted around and pushed him away. Water streamed down her face and beat against her back. "You can't keep doing this to me!" she cried.

"Shanna—"

"I can't be here for you whenever it suits you. Emotions aren't like toys or games—"

"Shanna, I love you." He whispered the words into her moist lips. "I love you." Into her ears. "I love you." His fingers gripped her glistening shoulders, her arms, her hips. "I love you."

Shanna had waited so long to hear those words. "I love you, too, Derek," she admitted for the first time....

ABOUT THE AUTHOR

"This story grew from a desire to write about the experience of motherhood," says Lauren Bauman, whose own son was born soon after the completion of her first Superromance novel. "I decided to make the heroine a widow with a newborn baby; she meets a man who *seems* a very unlikely future partner." *Circles,* Lauren's second Superromance, is set in the Kitchener-Waterloo region of Ontario, where the author lives with her family.

Books by Lauren Bauman

HARLEQUIN SUPERROMANCE
354—SEASONS

Circles

LAUREN BAUMAN

Harlequin Books

TORONTO • NEW YORK • LONDON
AMSTERDAM • PARIS • SYDNEY • HAMBURG
STOCKHOLM • ATHENS • TOKYO • MILAN

Published April 1991

ISBN 0-373-70447-X

CIRCLES

To my far-reaching family,
especially Mom, Dad, Mary and Gerry,
for all their love and support.

And in grateful acknowledgment
to Theresa Macpherson, LL.B.
for her legal assistance.

CHAPTER ONE

"WELL, AREN'T YOU going to introduce us?"

Drowsily, Shanna turned from the view out the hospital window beside her bed. She hadn't really been focusing on the adjacent wing of brick, concrete and glass or the patch of blue sky that peeked through. Her thoughts had been turned inward, marveling, trying to fathom the miracle of birth.

She met the suspiciously watery gaze of her father just before he set down an armload of parcels. "Hi, Dad," she murmured as he bent to kiss her cheek.

"I was so excited when you called this morning that I forgot to ask her name."

They both looked over at the small red-faced bundle fast asleep in her glass-sided crib. Her cheeks were puffy, scrunched-up, surrounding the tiniest buttonlike nose and rosebud mouth Shanna had ever seen. She still couldn't believe the child was hers. All healthy eight pounds of her. The traditional pink card proclaiming It's A Girl blurred before her eyes, giving the scene an additional sense of unreality.

"Meet Alicia Michelle," she announced softly, proudly, still trying to associate the name she'd chosen with the child.

"Alicia Michelle," Ned Bennett said in a choked voice. "Your mother would have been very proud to share her name with such a beautiful granddaughter." He rarely spoke of Michelle Bennett, who had passed away two years ago of leukemia. "And how's my other little girl? Did...everything go okay?" he added with a touchingly shy concern.

"Everything went fine." Shanna didn't elaborate on her relatively fast, complication-free labor, although it hadn't been without its difficult moments. Her body was exhausted, since she'd been up most of the previous night, but her mind was so exhilarated that she hadn't been able to sleep yet.

"You're happy with your room?" He looked around skeptically at the cramped space, functionally furnished and decorated in pale earth tones.

"It's not the Ritz, but I'm just lucky one was available so that I could have rooming-in privileges with Alicia."

"I would have been here sooner, but I wanted to let you rest up. And I was out, picking up a few things...."

He handed her the assortment of parcels and watched as she pulled out two teddy bears, one pink, one white, a bunny rabbit twice the size of Alicia, the tiniest pink frilly dress Shanna had ever seen, a knitted sweater set and a few rattles and bibs. On the windowsill already sat another of his gifts: a huge bouquet of red and white carnations that had been delivered so promptly that Shanna feared the florist had been bribed.

"Dad, this is more than enough..."

"I couldn't decide what *not* to get," he said sheepishly. "And the salesclerk was so helpful. Luckily the store closes at six on Saturday, or I'd still be there."

Shanna just shook her head. "You're not planning to spoil my daughter now, are you?"

"Just a little..."

"Well, thank you for everything." And Shanna started sniffling, crying and laughing on a sudden wave of emotion. "Sorry, I'm a bit out of sorts today."

He cleared his throat. "I think you're a real champ, managing on your own at a time like this . . . without Michael."

Shanna hesitated, then spoke. "I felt him there, Dad. At the toughest times. And at the end. It—it helped."

His eyes crinkled in understanding as he thought of the many times since his wife of thirty-four years had died that he'd been comforted by her loving spirit, almost as if it were a tangible force.

What Shanna couldn't express to him, though, was how she'd felt when she'd been alone for the first time with her baby, a few hours ago. Throughout her pregnancy it had taken a supreme effort not to let her grief and anger over Michael's sudden death overpower her, for the sake of the child growing within her. She'd secretly feared, though, that once their baby was physically separated from her, Michael's loss would strike her uncontrollably, releasing all her bottled-up emotions. Instead, she realized, she'd managed to survive the worst and she knew she was going to be okay. Her sorrow was still deep, jagged-edged, but somehow more bearable.

And her new, indescribably wondrous love for her daughter was already reaching into the void. . . .

"If there's anything you need down the road, anything at all, Shanna, just ask for it. You can count on me," Ned said with fervor. "You and I have to stick together."

A wail from Alicia reminded him that he'd forgotten someone very important indeed.

"You can hold her," Shanna suggested.

Instinctively Ned drew his hands behind his back. "Oh, no, I couldn't."

"Sure you can, Gramps. Just wash up and put on that extra gown."

"Well, just for a minute..." Ned prepared himself, then, as if Shanna had asked him to pick up a time bomb, gingerly lifted the tightly wrapped infant into the cradle of his arms, carefully adjusting the warming cap she still wore. "Hello, sweetie, aren't you something? My goodness, it's been a while since I held someone as tiny as you." He rocked his whole body back and forth, his elbows freezing into position. Gradually he loosened up when he saw that Alicia wasn't going to explode in distress.

Like Shanna, Ned Bennett was not overly tall, but his large hands made the baby seem even more diminutive. He had a kind, square-shaped face—so honest-looking he would have made a good used-car salesman, Shanna's mother used to tease. With his full head of lightly graying, reddish-brown hair, his spare body and his meticulously neat style of dressing, he was a handsome man, in an understated way. His air of reserve, his habit of not looking directly into other people's eyes and his quiet-spoken manner made him appear shy. Hardworking, but not one to flaunt his accomplishments, Ned Bennett preferred not to clutter his life with unnecessary complications.

As Shanna watched her father's beaming face, she knew that the baby was going to be good for him. Since he'd been practically forced by the new, younger management to take early retirement from the bank a few months ago, he'd been at loose ends, brooding too much over his wife's absence.

"Looks like you two are going to get along just fine," Shanna said spiritedly, her eyes filling again. "And I'll certainly be able to use all the help I can get."

"Well, I wasn't around much when you were this young—back then I was too busy earning my paycheck and your mother seemed to be doing a fine job without my interference. But I'll certainly give it the old college try, at least."

"You probably know more than I, though, about raising a child." She subdued her rush of panic at the thought of the incredible responsibility she faced. "Somehow I made it to thirty-five without even changing a diaper—a nurse was in earlier to give me my first lesson. And then, before I know it, there'll be *boys* calling her."

"Just take one day at a time," her father said with a knowing smile.

"More like one hour," Shanna corrected him as Alicia informed her, in her no-nonsense way, that it was already time for another feeding.

Ned quickly transferred the crying baby to her mother's arms. "I should be heading out now, anyway...."

"You don't have to yet, Dad. You can wait while I feed her."

"No, no, you do what you have to." He kissed her goodbye and quickly exited, clearly not comfortable yet with the idea of watching her breast-feed.

It wasn't until much later, after Alicia had been taken from her to spend her first night under surveillance in the nursery, that Shanna was aware of yet another unfamiliar feeling on a day that had mercilessly depleted her emotional reservoir. Guilt. Because of Michael. It was as if she were betraying their love somehow by not mourning for him long and hard enough. But tonight she was just too drained to dwell on it all....

"JUST GIVE ME one good reason why I should do it, Ray."

"Do it for Terry. Do it for the girl. I don't care. Someone's got to pay a courtesy visit. I sort of promised her. You've at least met her, haven't you?"

"Once or twice with Terry at the bar where she worked, but Terry was pouring on the charm to her so much that I restrained my own charming self." Derek propped himself up in his bed, the phone cradled between his neck and bare shoulder, and glanced at the time on the clock radio. Nine o'clock. Sunday morning. His one day to catch up on a week's worth of insufficient sleep.

"Well, she was in rough shape when she called me at work yesterday, trying to get hold of Terry. Seems the baby was coming early."

"And it took you until today to pass the buck...that's real crisis management, Ray."

"You know damn well I've been up to my eyeballs in disaster all week. I've got two drivers out on Workers' Comp, a backlog of orders, customers driving me crazy, a loading dock that's crammed tighter than hell and a fuse shorter than—"

Derek didn't wait to hear who would be the victim of his older brother's unflattering comparison. "And you don't think I've been just as busy? I need my day off as much as you. If I'm lucky I might get a chance to open a newspaper and see what else is going on in the world, besides *your* never-ending operations problems."

Ray and Derek were each vice presidents at Morgan Cartage, the transport company owned by their father,

Leo Morgan, who was still an active president. Ray was in charge of operations, while Derek handled the financial side of the successful Canada-wide transport firm.

"Look, Derek, I can't get away today. Brenda's upset that I'm never around and not spending enough time with the kids. You know I'd do anything for those kids. At least you don't have a family—or anyone besides yourself—to worry about."

"I worry about myself more than enough, thank you."

"Come on, you know what I mean. It doesn't hurt to put yourself out once in a while."

"Like you did with Carol?" He couldn't resist the barb. Ray, who'd probably been unfaithful to his wife more than the one time he'd gotten caught, was the last person who should be lecturing him about selfishness.

"I told you," he replied swiftly, lowering his voice, "I'm trying to make it up to Brenda, and you're not helping any."

"I've got as much right to my free time as you do, Ray. Who's to say that how I spend it is any less *significant* because I happen to like living on my own?"

"I'm not saying that. It would just be a heck of a lot easier for you to rearrange your squash game at the club, or whatever else of *significance* you've got planned, than it is for me to get out of my commitments to three people who are depending on me."

Derek ran his fingers through his hair. "So you expect me to just put aside everything and rush to the hospital to see a teenager I barely know, casually say, 'Oh, I'm sorry my brother got you pregnant, he's disappeared somewhere—and probably wouldn't want to be around anyway, heartless soul that he is—but we Morgan fellows stick together, so here I am instead. Here's a token gift for the baby.'"

"You're on the right track," Ray replied with an infuriating seriousness. "Just try to act as decent as possible, if that's not too hard for a cool dude like you." There was a riot of voices in the background. "Geoffrey, get that hockey stick out of the living room. Okay, okay. Look, I gotta run," he directed back at Derek.

"She's at Kitchener-Waterloo Hospital?" Derek asked on a sigh of resignation.

"Uh-huh. You'll get your reward in heaven. Or maybe Terry will find you a new lady now that you're single again. He always seems to have an excess."

"No thanks..." Derek murmured, but Ray had already hung up after a clipped goodbye.

This certainly wasn't the first time he'd bailed his renegade younger brother Terry out of trouble, but Derek swore it would be the last as he swung his legs out of bed and just sat there for a few precious moments longer.

Terry, a professional tennis player, had lost a match in France early in the tournament, according to the media reports, and no one had heard from him since. Although he'd been a rising Canadian star in men's singles in his early twenties, the thirty-year-old had been on a losing streak for about two years now. Derek suspected Terry was involved in some decidedly unhealthy pursuit to soften the blow of this latest defeat and to escape the pressure from his coaches and sponsors.

Unfortunately, Terry's impending fatherhood was probably the last thing on his mind. Derek felt sorry for this Megan. She was far too young to handle such an expert philanderer as Terry. She'd said she was nineteen, but Derek suspected she'd probably lied about her age to get her barmaid's job and to entice Terry. She'd been impressed when she'd found out Terry was something of a celebrity in the sports world. Terry had always been a sucker for that kind of adulation, not to mention her ample cleavage and vulnerable, come-hither look. He'd once joked that Megan was like candy to him, but once his sweet craving was satisfied, he wanted no more. Well, the savoring of the so-called candy had brought him more of an aftertaste than he'd anticipated. A distraught Megan had later informed him she was pregnant, having forgotten to take a pill or two that month.

Terry had felt minimal responsibility for the accident and had given Megan halfhearted support during the pregnancy that she'd refused to terminate. He'd seen Megan on the rare occasions when he'd been in town, but, as he'd admitted to Derek before he'd left for France, "There's nothing there anymore...not that there ever was much. At first, she was the perfect blond fantasy, my Monroe." He'd grinned self-consciously. "But that wore away all too soon, you know?"

Derek knew. His relationships usually lasted longer than Terry's, and he found it simpler never to date more than one woman at a time, a practice his brother didn't always follow. Still, he couldn't seem to maintain a "meaningful relationship," as Rachel had recently put it—he'd dated her for a record eighteen months before things had turned sour. But he hadn't wanted to admit all that to Terry. Instead, he'd asked if Megan was aware how Terry felt about her.

"I've tried putting it to her nicely. But she's turned out to be a real clinger. Keeps hoping I'll come around once the baby's here."

"Maybe she's right."

Terry had just shaken his head. "Megan has a tendency to get hysterical...must be being pregnant or something. Maybe after, when it's all over, she'll see I'm just not the domestic type."

"You should see this thing through, somehow," Derek had heard himself saying. He'd hated sounding so preachy, especially since he hadn't led such a saintly life himself, but Derek had always felt more fatherly than brotherly toward his youngest sibling, even though only six years separated the two.

"Yeah, yeah..." Terry had said dismissively, then added in a rare moment of self-analysis, "I'm just a big kid myself. What do I know about raising another kid? I do know it would be a big mistake to marry someone I don't love. But don't worry, I'll pay my share of the bills. And whatever you do, don't tell Dad. Why add fuel to the fire?"

No one in the family had ever spoken of why Leo had always been so hard on Terry. It seemed Terry's achievements were never quite good enough for Leo. As Derek had matured, though, he'd realized that Leo probably blamed his youngest son for his wife's sudden death soon after Terry's birth, as if he believed God had traded one life for another. However, no one had dared point out to Leo how unfair to Terry his attitude was.

Derek was definitely not looking forward to handling this delicate situation with the near-stranger. He waited until mid-afternoon, an appropriate visiting time, he figured, then drove to the hospital in his new 911 Speedster Porsche. He stopped at the gift shop and pondered the selection of baby items longer than he'd intended. Finally he bought a plain white teddy bear because it bore a Gund label that the clerk assured him meant quality in the world of stuffed animals. Derek believed one could never go wrong with a good label. He signed a congratulations card simply, The Morgans, and made his way to the elevator.

Derek's unease increased as he stepped onto the maternity ward. What on earth was he going to say to this Megan? He refused to make excuses for his brother's irresponsible behavior and he had absolutely no experience with babies, pregnancy or labor. If ever a man was out of his depth, he was.

Taking a deep breath, he approached the counter of the nursing station. An attractive young woman in a light yellow pantsuit looked up at him.

"Hi. I'm here to see Megan Tucker. Apparently she just had her baby... yesterday, I think."

"Oh..." The nurse gave him a curious stare. "Are you family... or perhaps the father?"

"No, no. I'm the father's brother." He thought it nobody's business to elaborate.

"I see. Please wait here a moment."

She disappeared into an adjacent office, leaving him feeling ridiculous standing there, clutching the teddy bear. And why should he care that there'd been a note of disapproval in her voice because of his association to the absent father?

Another older nurse, wearing the traditional white uniform, emerged. "Hello, I'm Mrs. Thornton, the head nurse. And you're—"

"Derek Morgan."

"I understand you're here to see Megan Tucker."

"Yes." Why couldn't he just have made a quick, unobtrusive visit?

"Do you know her very well?"

"Not really. But I'm visiting on behalf of my brother who knew... knows her," he added, anxious to get this interview over with.

"Megan wouldn't let us contact anyone," she said, softening her voice. "She had a hard time and there were some complications. You should know that, unfortunately, her baby was stillborn."

CHAPTER TWO

DEREK HESITATED OUTSIDE Megan's room for several long seconds before he tapped on the closed door. There was no reply. He tapped again. From down the hall, the head nurse gestured for him to enter, which he finally did. Tentatively.

He would not have recognized the hazel-eyed girl who stared up at him listlessly from the bed. The last time he'd seen her many months ago, her white-blond hair had been moussed into a controlled disarray around her face. She must have been wearing lots of makeup because he remembered a black raccoonlike outline to her eyes and cherry-red lips. But now her hair was an ordinary shade of brown, shorter, pulled back from her pale, puffy face. The nurse had warned Megan he was coming, yet no welcome shone from her eyes.

"Hi, I'm Derek," he began, cursing the false brightness in his voice, not knowing what other approach to take. "We met awhile ago, the night you were working—"

"I remember." The abruptness of her reply preceded a long silence.

"Look, I'm sorry about what happened," he said at last, meaning it. "How are you feeling?"

"Lousy. But why should you care?"

He ignored her hostility, suspecting she was using him as a scapegoat for his brother. "We haven't been able to reach Terry."

"What else is new?"

"He was defeated in his match. It's probably the end of his career. He seems to have lost his edge. He's facing up to that—or likely not facing it yet. Somewhere he can be anonymous." He didn't add that his brother was no doubt indulging in a sport he always excelled at with a faceless partner who made no demands on him.

"Poor Terry..." Her eyes filled as she turned away, and Derek knew she was really feeling self-pity.

"Your...labor was so early. He'll show up eventually and you two can work everything out." She said nothing, distractedly tightening the crisscross of her bed jacket over her full figure. Feeling increasingly helpless, Derek said quickly, "You must have family to talk to at a time like this."

"I haven't spoken to my mom or stepdad since he came on to me over a year ago. He denied it and she believed him," Megan stated flatly. "I hated living there with them, anyway. I quit school, got a job and found my own place." She snorted in self-deprecation. "I was worried about the place being so cramped, such a dive, with the baby coming and all, and now..." The hands that swiped at her eyes were shaking, and when she could talk again it was in a small, vulnerable voice that suddenly reminded Derek just how young and unequipped she was to deal with a birth and death on the same day. "I'm not up to company right now. Could you leave, please?"

"Sure. But first..." Derek reached in his wallet, picked out one of his business cards and wrote his home number on it. "Call me if you need anything. I don't know if I can help, but I can try, okay?"

She shrugged, sucking in her breath in an effort to regain control. She took the card. "Vice president, Finance," she read out. "You must play around with a lot of money. Like a giant, real-life Monopoly game."

"Yeah, with a few sixteen-wheel trucks thrown in instead of hotels." She cracked the faintest smile. "I brought you a little something." He handed her the stuffed toy, but didn't reach into his pocket for the inappropriate card.

"Thanks."

"Just pretend I won it for you throwing darts or spinning wheels at the midway," he said, hoping to coax another smile out of her. When all else failed, humor had always been his salvation.

But tears welled into her eyes again, further evidence of her precarious emotional state. "Nobody ever did that. I never had much luck with guys. Guess I scared them off by wanting it all too badly. I—I thought that maybe this time . . . with the baby . . ."

When she buried her face into her pillow on a long vibrating sob, Derek didn't linger. He murmured, "Goodbye, Megan. Take care," then left, empty-handed, unexpectedly heavy of heart.

His head was bent as he walked down the corridor, so a door swinging open ahead startled him. As he stepped back to avoid a collision, he looked in annoyance at the cause of the disturbance. A woman, clad in a mint-green robe, a shade lighter than the cool color of her eyes, stared back at him, equally startled.

It took a few seconds to place her. With recognition came a welcome memory of a simpler time, long past.

FOR SHANNA, RECOGNITION WAS instantaneous. Although his perfectly styled hair was sprinkled with some gray and his face had a more rugged cast, Derek Morgan had retained his youthful good looks. And if his trim, solid physique was any indication, he was still as athletic as ever.

Derek Morgan had always seemed taller to her, larger-than-life. Maybe because he'd been such a popular, prominent figure at the high school they'd both attended in the late sixties and early seventies. But now, Shanna saw that he was probably about five-ten or so, just a few inches taller than herself. Actually, she was so conscious that they were practically at eye level because of the strong visual impact of his eyes—an exceptionally bright, heart-stopping blue, all the more magnificent in contrast to his jet-black hair and long dark lashes.

He seemed distracted, self-absorbed, so she was the one who said hello first. He assessed her a few seconds before responding, giving her time to notice what he wore. His black trench coat, trailing behind like a cape, gave him a rakish look, punctuated by the sun shades perched sportily on his head. He wore khaki-colored, pleated pants with a perfectly coordinated sweater, and Shanna had the distinct impression he would never be caught in public in old jeans and a sweatshirt. No question he was attractive, but he probably knew it.

Even at first glance, it was apparent that he carried himself with aplomb, giving the impression that whatever he did for a living he did successfully, easily. Then Shanna noticed that he carried a black felt baseball cap in his hand, of all things—an irreverent, zany, but somehow elegant touch, that suited the Derek Morgan she remembered—the well-liked class cutup who used to charm teachers into the most outrageous concessions.

"Twelve C!" he finally exclaimed. "Sharon . . . ?"

"Shanna. Shanna Rhodes, formerly Bennett." She waited, but her married name held no significance for him; thankfully, because she didn't feel like launching into long explanations about Michael. Because they'd hung around in different crowds, Shanna couldn't recall ever having spoken to him before. It felt strange to be acting familiar. He was probably a year older than her, along with many of her classmates, because she'd skipped a junior grade. "And you're Derek Morgan, right?"

"Right. You've got a good memory."

"And you were rather visible." Her mind raced through all she remembered: star athlete, looked up to by his male peers, sought after by an elite segment of the female student body—the pretty, generally well-endowed ones who liked to huddle under blankets on bleachers, watching games they barely understood. Shanna hadn't wasted her time that way. But she didn't want to get into any of that. "Didn't you run in some student election, with banners all over the place and some weird slogan?"

He rolled his eyes in mock embarrassment. "My first and last foray into politics. That was the year I ran for sports rep. I cleverly decided to advocate nonviolence in sports as my election platform and came up with some propaganda nonsense along the lines of 'Vote DM for No SM.'"

Shanna grimaced. "Ouch. But it worked, didn't it?"

"Of course."

He possessed the same air of self-assurance as before, or maybe it was conceit. She couldn't decide whether his understated, full-lipped smile reminded her of Tom Cruise or Kevin Costner, but the same charisma was definitely there.

"And you always got good marks," he surprised her by remembering. "You actually studied and used the library for more than a meeting ground. A real—'' He stopped.

"Browner?"

He grinned. "Yeah. Ah, but we were a cruel bunch."

It had been no secret that Shanna's more studious friends were referred to less than flatteringly as "browners," with all the implications of being boring human beings who brown-nosed teachers for higher marks. Her crowd, however, had considered themselves both intellectually and creatively superior to crass sports types like Derek and his cronies. Each group had held a disdain for the other with all the self-righteous snobbery of youth.

Suddenly Shanna felt awkward as she faced him, the surprise of running into him having made her temporarily forget her present circumstances. She crossed her arms over her tight-fitting housecoat, painfully conscious of her roundness. What's more, she'd just showered and her long auburn hair hung in damp tendrils below her shoulders.

He must have sensed her self-consciousness as the present superceded their brief journey into the past. His eyes darted into her room, then back to her, carefully avoiding looking at her shape, but whether out of shyness or respect for her discomfort, she couldn't be sure.

"You just had a baby?" Derek asked tentatively, assuming nothing after learning of Megan's situation.

"Yes...a baby girl. A beautiful baby girl, I might add."

And her face immediately shone with a proud glow that was a far cry from Megan's despondency. He'd never seen eyes of such a lovely green shade, peppermint-cool, spring-fresh, Nile-deep. He was barely aware of the rest of her, so captivated was he by those unusual eyes. And on her pale, milk-white complexion the faintest apricot colored her prominent cheekbones.

"Congratulations," he murmured, his mind scrambling for all the typical questions he was supposed to ask. But she changed the subject.

"And you? Are you delivering real or chocolate cigars?" At his taken-aback expression, she added, "You know, proud papa and all that."

He sputtered. "Me? No, no, no. I'm just visiting a friend," he hastened to explain.

Shanna couldn't resist a smile at his utter panic at the thought of paternity. Her smile prompted him to elaborate. "I'm not even married, let alone willing to do my bit for the baby boom. Did you see the movie *Three Men and a Baby?*"

"Yes..."

"Well, I don't think I'd fare nearly as well as those bumbling guys when it comes to kids, especially young, toothless ones." He spoke lightly, feeling himself begin to relax after his tense encounter with Megan. "I've negotiated multimillion-dollar contracts, but I'd be a complete idiot if I had to change a diaper. Nor am I eager to learn."

What an odd comparison, Shanna thought, but his lightness was contagious, just what she needed after the intense emotion of the past few days. "Oh, come, *everyone* has a soft spot for a baby. Do you want to see the most special child in the whole world?"

Derek hedged, tried to glance surreptitiously at the expensive-looking watch peeking out from his sweater. "I should be getting home. Debits and credits await...."

"On a Sunday?" She hadn't been able to hide her disappointment.

"There's no rest for the wicked or for those in their own business."

"Where do you work exactly?"

"Morgan Cartage. My father started it up. In fact, it's *his* favorite baby. Or at least the one area of his life he'd never neglect."

Shanna detected a hard edge to his sarcasm. "I've heard of Morgan's. In fact, I've probably cursed getting caught behind one of those trucks on the highway many a time."

"Well, next time just give a big wave and think of the great service being performed for our customers and the tidy profit in our pockets."

She smiled dryly. His eyes had briefly exhibited the raw-edged gleam of someone who enjoyed making money, and enjoyed the power money provided. "Well, if you can't come along, I'll have to say goodbye. I was just on my way to pick up Alicia from the nursery. She usually stays with me, but I left her there while I had a shower."

He was staring at her as if he didn't really want to leave yet, then to her surprise he did an about-face. "Actually I *am* curious to see the youngest baby in the world who possesses her own library card, if she's truly her mother's daughter."

"*And* a complete set of *Encyclopedia Britannica,* of course," Shanna rallied back, unexpectedly pleased at his change of heart, perhaps because she'd developed an unabashed desire to show off her baby to anyone available to admire her.

Derek adjusted his pace to her shuffle as they made their way down the corridor. The curtains were open at the viewing window of the nursery. Shanna waved at the attending nurse, who remembered her and wheeled Alicia's cart out to the hallway.

Derek watched the softening of Shanna's face and her little shake of incredulity as she saw her daughter again. He looked at the baby, her fists ramming her chubby cheeks out of proportion as she slept, breathing noisily, wrapped tighter than an ancient mummy, and something kicked over inside himself, something profound, life-affirming. It was all the more powerful, because a few minutes ago with Megan he'd been confronted with a loss of life.

Shanna was looking up at him expectantly, her sparkling eyes lighting up her whole face. "She's . . . sweet," Derek murmured, thrown off balance. He reverted to humor to get back on track. "But I hope she grows out of that snoring habit—it won't endear her to the opposite sex in a few years."

"Good, then maybe I won't have to lock her up until she has a good education, a reputable career and enough sense to marry with her heart *and* her head."

"Like mother, like daughter?"

"I suppose," Shanna said vaguely, turning away, looking down at the baby.

Derek wasn't sure if he'd imagined the catch in her voice. He followed her eyes to study her offspring more closely. "Well, one thing she doesn't have is your coloring. What little hair she has is definitely blond. She must take after her father in that respect." The comment was really a question.

This time there was no mistaking the pain behind Shanna's affirmative reply. "I married Michael Rhodes," she added distractedly. "Maybe you remember him."

Derek nodded as his eyes widened in surprise. "Yeah. Tall, intellectual guy. Kept to himself. Very..." He extended his fingers as he searched for the right word.

"Intense."

"Right. Didn't go in for sports much, I remember that."

"He wasn't very good at them, that was all." He was watching her closely, but she wouldn't meet his eyes as she struggled with the maelstrom of emotion the conversation was provoking.

"What did he end up doing, jobwise?"

With a familiar searing grief, Shanna thought of the introverted man she had lived with for nine years and loved for much longer. Michael had been extremely single-minded, whether in his love for her or his drive to become a lawyer, not just any lawyer, but the best. Unfortunately he'd only been able to focus on one priority at a time.

She answered slowly, "He worked at a legal publisher's for a while, editing, then decided to go back to school to become a lawyer, while I worked." Derek was nodding, as if her words confirmed what he'd suspected, as if they were playing some sort of guessing game with her life.

"And what were you working at?"

"Maybe you could tell me," she said, suddenly annoyed.

He assessed her momentarily, then the teasing gleam was back in his eyes. "How about school marm?"

"As a matter of fact, I *do* teach English as a Second Language to new Canadians."

"Now, why doesn't that come as any surprise, either?"

"Maybe because you make snap judgments about people," she said hotly, knowing she should tell him the truth about Michael, but not wanting to bare her soul to him.

"Hey, I didn't mean to imply that your husband wasn't an okay guy, if that's what's upsetting you. I just didn't know him very well, that's all."

"He *was* okay," she said as soft as a whisper, as sharp-edged as a cry.

"I saw you walking by," a stranger's voice suddenly said none too quietly. "I thought you came to see *me*. Or are you just making the rounds?"

A maternity patient whose light brown hair was pulled back carelessly with an elastic band was standing beside Derek, staring up at him accusingly.

"I ran into an old acquaintance," he swiftly explained to her, annoyance at her rude tone flickering through his eyes. "Shanna, this is Megan Tucker, the young lady I came to visit."

His own tone had suddenly softened, become more compassionate, but not without an effort on his part, Shanna noticed. Relieved to have the conversation shift direction and pleased to meet another new mother, Shanna said, "Hi. Have you been here long?"

"Long enough." Megan was staring hard at the baby, chewing on her lip. "What's her name?"

"Alicia Michelle."

"Mine was a girl, too."

"Really? Congratulations. How big?"

Megan smiled crookedly and finally mumbled, "Smaller."

Shanna went on blithely, unaware that Derek was trying to make eye contact, "Is she here in the nursery?" Megan shook her head. "We can stop by your room on the way back then. I'd love to see her, swap stories with someone who's been through—"

Derek's fingers dug into her arm like daggers of warning as Megan's pasty countenance crumpled. She let out a heart-wrenching sob, then turned and ran down the corridor, brushing against a surprised orderly.

Shanna's eyes locked with Derek's and his words confirmed what her knotted stomach was telling her brain. "Her baby died."

Her lids squeezed shut for an extended second. "I'm so sorry. I didn't realize..."

But he was gone, after Megan. Shanna walked back to her own room, cart in tow, even more slowly than usual.

About half an hour later, Shanna was rocking a full-tummied but fussing Alicia. She'd discovered that the more vigorous the motion, the more effective the results. Alicia's eyes were just growing heavy when a creak from the swinging door behind them jolted her awake and caused her screeching to begin again.

Shanna met the apologetic gaze of Derek Morgan. She mouthed, "Shh," but she needn't have bothered. He stood rooted to the spot until Alicia grew still once more. After she'd gently laid her down, Shanna turned to her guest.

"Sorry about that," he whispered.

"You can talk normally now that she's asleep." Already, Shanna thought, she was starting to know some of her child's quirks and patterns, although they were bound to change, and she still had so much to learn.

"And you can stop rocking."

She matched his grin as she realized she was swaying in the same rhythm she'd adopted for the past several minutes. "Mothers need comforting, too." Her expression instantly sobered. "How's Megan?"

He shrugged wearily. "Not great. I did what I could, but what do I know about these kinds of things? Anyway, I relayed what happened to the head nurse and she assured me that Megan's doctor and the staff psychiatrist would look after her. She said something about postpartum depression.''

"I think it's more than that." Shanna supported herself on the edge of the bed, suddenly aware of how tired she was. "Losing a baby would be like losing a part of yourself. Even worse than—" She stopped. "Where is Megan's husband?"

Briefly Derek filled her in on the situation with Terry and his own reluctant last-minute involvement. Shanna's eyes filled with caring as he talked; she studied his face intently, and he had the uncanny feeling that she understood more than he'd expressed.

"I am *so* sorry I was such a blithering idiot in front of Megan," she said when he'd finished.

"You couldn't have known. I should have said something myself earlier." He looked past her, at the floral pattern on the curtains. "I didn't want to leave today, letting you think it was your fault."

"I should have been more in tune, but I guess I was too full of myself, my own good fortune."

The room was quiet for a few moments. Derek glanced at the child, then back at her. "Yes, you and your husband must be very proud."

Shanna knew she had to be honest, but she had difficulty saying the words that still rang false to her. "Michael died over eight months ago," she said quietly, fuzzily. "I should have told you before, but...it's hard."

For the second time that day, Derek felt the chill of shock run down his spine, and he was forced to look at the facts in a whole new light. "Oh . . . I'm sorry. Was he sick or—"

"A motorcycle accident. He was the passenger. His friend only broke a few ribs."

"Were you married long?" Hell, what did that matter, he thought, but she didn't seem to think it was an irrelevant question.

"Nine years. The proverbial nine years that finally ran out," she said with a humorless laugh.

"Hmm, I've never been married, but I can imagine how hard it must be for you, with the baby and all...."

"He never even knew I was pregnant," she murmured softly, but the words seemed to echo louder with a poignancy of their own. Bitterness laced her voice as she went on, "For so many years we were both so busy, all the fun things were on hold, for the future—and finally everything should have been coming together. Michael had gotten a good position in a small law firm, we had just bought a house, when..." She had spoken in a rush, shakily, but she finally ran out of momentum and stopped to draw a deep breath. "I have a lot of good memories. They help me from going over the edge, and I'm sure that Alicia will keep me too busy to dwell on—on what might have been."

She'd only allowed him a glimpse of the vulnerability and grief knotted inside her, but Derek felt them like real entities in the room. He was also struck by the determination glistening brightly in her emerald eyes, and he knew her to be a survivor.

"Can your folks give you a hand?" he asked Shanna.

"My dad's a widower, but he's been great. We're pretty close. And he kind of likes Alicia." She pointed to the mountain of gifts on the window ledge. "Courtesy of the proud grandpa."

"My ever-practical father has always given my brother's kids Canada Savings Bonds, with cards signed

by his secretary,'' Derek found himself admitting to her.
"A hundred-dollar bond got eaten once by my nephew
when he was a toddler. Anyway, speaking of the outside
world, I should be going now,'' he added, despite another strange pull to linger, even though he'd probably
never see her again.

"Thanks for stopping by again. You didn't have to.''

"No problem. I, ah, hope everything works out for
you.''

"No problem,'' she echoed, and her wide, full-lipped
smile was unexpectedly warming, utterly disarming. Her
thick wavy hair, side-parted with a long layered bang, had
dried to a shiny chestnut tumble below her shoulders,
much longer than she'd worn it in high school. He liked
the casual way she swept it back from time to time. She
was pretty, feminine, in a natural fashion. Her features
weren't perfect—the nose turned up a little too pertly, a
few freckles dusted her complexion, but still he wondered why he'd never looked twice at her back then....

"You certainly got more than you bargained for on
your duty visit,'' Shanna said, trying to discern the reason for his disoriented look. She sensed that Derek Morgan didn't usually involve himself in other people's
problems. He was probably most competent at looking
out for himself.

"It's been interesting, to say the least. But before I
tackle paperwork I think I'm ready for a workout at the
club. Have to keep this lean-and-mean bod' in shape, you
know.'' He patted what she presumed was a trim middle
beneath the loose-fitting clothes he wore.

"Didn't you hear? Love handles are in this year,'' she
said dryly.

"Not for this lad,'' he remarked so seriously she had
to laugh. "What's so funny?''

"You're talking to someone who's just glad she can see her toes again. An extra pound or two hardly seems like the kiss of death."

"Well, in my case, a good physique never hurt the average single male. And for double security, a little money always goes a long way, too. Isn't that what the modern, discriminating female is really looking for?"

Shanna refused to answer the question, annoyed at his blatant self-satisfaction. She wondered what it took to really get past his wisecracking. "I suppose you admire Ben Johnson, too. What's a few illegal steroids when we're talking big bucks and big hamstrings?"

"He's mainly guilty of wanting it all. How many of us aren't guilty of that in different ways?"

"But there have to be rules, moral guidelines."

"Have you never bent the rules, rewritten them to your own advantage, Shanna?"

As she was drawn into the depths of his eyes, she was thinking how swiftly they could change from a cool aqua to the dazzling, daring blue that had probably caused many a sane woman's intentions to run in reckless directions.... "Such as?" she asked, buying distance with another question.

He cocked his head and she foresaw mischief coming. "You're not the only one with a good memory. I seem to recall a certain incident in which you and a few friends were suspended for holding the high school version of a summit meeting."

"Hey, we were deeply involved in some sort of grandiose discussion about either world peace or inner peace," she said with a smile and a tilting of her own head that meant touché. "Someone had put together a slide show with music. But it was hard to figure out Leonard Cohen's songs during a brief lunch hour, so we ran a little late. Physics class just didn't seem relevant, you know. Hardly worth a suspension.''

"I don't know. Sounds mighty rebellious to me, especially to someone who later became an upstanding member of the education system.''

"Let's just say I indulged in a little early self-education then.''

"Whatever you say, teach. I do feel as if I should be humming a few bars of *The Way We Were*, though. When life was simpler and all that.''

Shanna thought of her serious attitude to her education, her idealistic desire to make a mark in the troubled world, her tumultuous courtship with Michael, and then she compared all that to the past few years—her frenetic work schedule, Michael's preoccupation with his own career, his withdrawal from her, the upheaval of all her priorities with his death, her pregnancy. "I don't think I ever made life simple. What I do realize, though, talking to you, is how little people really change. You, for example. From football captain to financial wizard. The game may be different, but the stakes are basically the same. You want to win, to get ahead." She didn't know why, but he made her want to challenge him.

"How else can I make the local list of the Ten Most Successful Men?''

"Is that what you really want?'' she asked disbelievingly, despite his cocky but convincing look.

"Of course.''

He was half teasing, half serious. "Do you like your job?'' she threw at him.

"It's a means to an end.''

"What end?''

"Power. Status,'' he said smoothly, too smoothly, as if he were dueling, playing a game. His grin was wide and engaging enough, though, to convince the biggest skeptic that the dollar was worthless or that Elvis was alive. "How am I doing, teach?"

"So-so."

"Phew—you're a tough marker. Okay, here's a few simple facts. I've got expensive tastes. I like the finest things in life—good clothes, luxury holidays, nice digs, a private box at the SkyDome. But why do I have to justify myself to you?"

"You don't, just to yourself."

"You're clever with words, but then that's your forte. One of mine is managing money, making it, spending it. What's wrong with that?"

"Nothing. As long as you're happy. I've always believed in balancing work and materialism with...other things, though."

"Such as?"

This time he was playing devil's advocate. She was thinking about love and its many forms, but she said, "Relaxation. Fun."

"Now you're talking *my* language," he murmured suggestively, then glanced down as Alicia let out a small cry.

"And family," Shanna added with a firmness in her voice, refusing to flirt.

"So what *do* you do for pleasure?" he asked, crossing his legs and arms as he leaned against the wall, his pose disconcertingly relaxed, all male. Clearly he was enjoying their banter.

"Reading," she asserted quickly. "Modern novels, classics, biographies. I'll have to add Dr. Spock to my reading list. And you?"

He paused to consider his answer. "Oh, *GQ*, the stocks and the swimsuit issue of *Sports Illustrated*." His comment was light, breezy, playful. He backed out of the room then, with a wave and a cheery smirk, accompanied by a quick well-practiced wink. "Have a good life, teach, and better keep your daughter away from guys like me. Unless she wants a life of caviar wishes and champagne dreams."

Derek set his velvety baseball cap on his head, gave it a tweak, then he was gone. In spite of herself, Shanna was left smiling, feeling better than she had in a long time. She was also contemplating the therapeutic effects of the color blue.

With a start she remembered that Michael's eyes had been blue, too. A pale, almost gray-blue that blended with his fair skin and wheat-colored hair. Quite different from the vibrant blue that reminded her of clear skies, tropical waters, lazy summer days . . .

She forced herself to concentrate on reading the many pamphlets on baby care that had arrived in a promotional package. It didn't seem right to compare Michael physically or any other way to the brazen Derek Morgan, a man she barely knew and would never see again.

The truth was that she still felt married to Michael, despite the stark reality of his death, the many forlorn nights alone in their bed, the passage of time. Till death do us part. Intellectually she could rationalize that the vows she'd taken no longer applied. But no amount of rationalizing could sever her deep emotional tie to him. The love she'd pledged and the kaleidoscope of memories of their time together had refused to be buried with him.

Theirs had been a very stormy relationship that had spanned almost two decades. They'd broken up numerous times, but had never been able to let go completely, and after one of those reconciliations had married se-

cretly in a civil ceremony, without any of the fanfare of
a big wedding. Michael had disliked crowds, fuss. He'd
wanted her just for himself. Shanna had never regretted
that decision, because her life was already so entwined
with Michael's, her heart with his. The quiet tone of the
wedding day had set the tone for their marriage. A controlled, dignified harmony that each had been afraid to
upset. A delicate balance that each had needed to maintain.

Despite all the differences in her life now, Shanna still
felt as if a vital part of her were missing. She was left with
so many unresolved feelings about her marriage to Michael, especially the recent years. And he would always
have his hold on her as Alicia's father. That was an in-
disputable fact.

Someone like Derek Morgan, caught up in his self-
centered, money-oriented world, who could clown
around as if he didn't have a care in that world, could
never understand how her heart ached for what she'd
lost, how overwhelmed she was by the hurricane of
change in her life.

CHAPTER THREE

THE NEXT MORNING, Monday, Shanna was dozing after a wakeful night with the baby, who suddenly seemed to have her days and nights mixed up. The shrill ringing of the phone jolted her awake.

"Hello?" she murmured groggily.

"Hi, Mom. How could you do this to me?"

Shanna sat up, immediately recognizing the boisterous, mockingly indignant voice of her best friend. "Sorry, Talia. There's no fooling around with Mother Nature. Alicia just didn't seem to understand she was supposed to wait until you were back from your conference in Montreal. How was it, anyway?"

"Demonstrations of the latest beauty products paled in comparison to some of the Frenchmen I had my eyes on. But, alas, nothing materialized."

Talia, an esthetician at The Hair Moussetique, was divorced two years ago. She was constantly bemoaning the shortage of available unmarried men, but that didn't prevent her from looking hard for one.

"But enough about me. Could you please elaborate on that frustrating message I heard on my answering machine? In other words, tell me everything. First, how on earth did you remember all the breathing without your prize coach?"

"With great difficulty, but the nurses were very helpful," Shanna admitted.

"I can't believe I missed the whole thing after all those weeks of classes. I was practicing our breathing during the train trip and got more than my share of strange looks for nothing. But what's a few misplaced hee...hee... hee...who's? I'm so sorry you were all alone, Shanna. You counted on me."

"Hey, that doesn't matter now. I have the most beautiful little girl."

"I'm dying to see her, but I have to work late tonight."

"I'll probably be discharged tomorrow, so come see me at home in another day or two."

Then Shanna briefly answered Talia's explicit questions about the labor, smiling at the other woman's thorough knowledge of medical terminology. She knew how important it had been for her friend to share the birth experience since Talia had been unable to have any children of her own before the breakup of her marriage. And for her own part, talking to another woman was just what Shanna needed. In the absence of her own mother and husband, Talia was a caring, enthusiastic substitute. In fact, she'd been extremely supportive since Michael's death.

"Give Alicia a big hug and kiss for me," Talia said before she hung up, her voice unsteady. "And make sure everyone who comes within a foot of her has been screened for colds, warts, microscopic viruses, *everything*. We've come this far."

Shanna laughed at her friend's proprietorial concern, but the warning sparked a twinge of fear. If anything should happen to Alicia... After she hung up the phone, Shanna could not resist picking up her daughter and holding her close. Slowly the baby's warmth reassured her.

So absorbed was she as she stood by the window that she didn't hear her door open. Somehow she sensed she was not alone, though, and she turned to see Megan watching her.

"Hi...come in." But the invitation was unnecessary. Megan was already walking toward her. Dark makeup lined her hazel eyes today, and her chin-length brown hair had been styled into a pageboy, as if she were trying for a semblance of normalcy. But she still looked numbed, tired, and Shanna suspected she was on medication to ease her mental anguish.

"I saw my baby briefly," Megan said softly. "But I wish I'd asked to hold her. It all happened so fast. And now it's too late." Reaching out, she touched Alicia's hand, gently stroking the tiny inert fingers as the child slept. "Can I hold her?"

Shanna didn't have the heart to refuse. She slid the blanketed bundle into the arc of Megan's waiting arms. Alicia's eyes popped open at the disturbance, but she seemed content.

"Hello, little one," Megan murmured, then smiled as Alicia gripped one of her fingers. "So strong and healthy, aren't you?"

"She's very special to me."

Megan gave a small jolt as if she'd forgotten Shanna's presence.

"My husband died when I was first pregnant," Shanna confessed quietly. "It's not the same thing, but I can understand some of what you must be feeling."

Megan looked past her, her eyes unfocused. "Terry never wanted our baby. Not really. It's his fault she's gone. Not mine. He jinxed everything, upset me. I did everything right, took vitamins—even drank lots of milk. I hate milk. It's not my fault." She was on the verge of crying, her words coming in semicoherent bursts. Abruptly, she handed the baby back.

"You mustn't blame yourself or anyone else," Shanna said gently. "The same thing has happened to many women. Sometimes it just . . . happens."

"That's what the shrink says. I don't believe it. There has to be a reason. She was so tiny, so helpless . . ."

She looked so vulnerable herself that if Shanna were not holding Alicia, she would have put her arms around the younger woman, which was probably what Megan needed most. "In time, maybe you'll be able to see—"

But Megan wasn't listening. She seemed fired up, hyperactive. "I know everything would have worked out with Terry if he'd only given me a chance. I need to talk to him, explain. But they can't find him. He lost his match, you see. He needs someone who cares, someone who understands. I do. I know what it's like to be all alone. Friends don't really give a hoot. You have to be with someone you love."

Even though Derek had told Shanna little about his brother's brief affair with the young waitress, it was plain that Megan was attributing far more to the relationship than had ever existed. Nevertheless, so soon after her baby's death was no time to help Megan deal with that. But maybe it would be therapeutic for her to talk about Terry with someone less threatening than a psychiatrist.

"What's Terry like?" Shanna asked, trying to ignore Alicia's sudden, red-faced concentration.

"Gorgeous. With a George Michael body. A great dancer. Sweet and romantic when he wants to be," Megan said dreamily, exuberantly, in another mood swing that caught Shanna by surprise. "He had money. And people recognized him at the bar. On the street. Lots of girls were after him, but he picked me. Me! I couldn't believe it. He kept coming back to the bar where I worked just to see me."

Her eyes shone, transforming her wan features. Her animation made her prettier, closer to the girl Terry must have been attracted to. Shanna listened, afraid of interrupting, of bursting the fragile bubble.

"You know, I had friends who used to hang out at rock concerts, hotels, on the off chance that they'd get a chance to meet the guys in the band. They didn't even care which guy sometimes. My friend Jackie actually got lucky once. Like a real groupie, but I never even heard of the band. I would never lower myself like that. Terry came to me. Not the other way around," she said defiantly. "It was special, it really was. And now without the baby to make him come back..."

Her eyes swiftly filled with hurt and disbelief and anger again. "I have to go," she said and was out the door as suddenly as she'd appeared a few minutes ago.

A bewildered Shanna felt as if she'd been caught in both the eye of a storm and the storm itself simultaneously.

TUESDAY MORNING DAWNED clear and bright—a sun-kissed day that seemed to beckon Shanna to emerge from her hospital cocoon and join the world again. Although she'd only been there for a few days, it felt like forever, perhaps because her days and nights had been so unpredictable, so dependent on Alicia's erratic schedule. Exhaustion and euphoria had been constantly at war within her, and she longed for the familiarity of home. A stomach-knotting excitement filled her at the thought of starting her new life with her daughter. She refused to dwell on the fact that there should have been three of them....

Her doctor visited her just after breakfast and proclaimed both her and infant ready to be discharged. Since her father was coming at eleven to pick her up, she only had a couple of hours to sort through her belongings and get both herself and Alicia ready for what seemed like a major journey. Thankfully Alicia was proving to be a good sleeper—in the daytime, at least. Shanna would work at correcting that pattern once she got home.

In the closet she found her forgotten labor bag. Talia had insisted on being prepared; she'd packed nearly every possible pain reliever or attention diverter. Shanna had not used any. She threw away the lollipops, tennis balls and pictures. By ten-thirty she'd managed to repack everything and get herself dressed. She felt restless, though, unable to concentrate on the new pile of post-natal information one of the nurses had dropped off earlier that morning. Suddenly she remembered that she wanted to say goodbye to a fellow patient—a friendly South Korean immigrant whose English had been less than perfect, prompting Shanna to slip into her familiar teaching role and answer some of the woman's questions about the care of her first child. She'd sympathized with Kim Cho Hartly—it was hard enough being a new mother in the strange hospital environment, let alone having to cope with a language problem, so she'd shared some of her own, admittedly limited, expertise.

She poked her head out her door and saw Dinah, one of the nurses who'd been particularly helpful to her, disappear into Kim's room. Shanna glanced at the sleeping Alicia, hesitated, then slipped out the door, closing it carefully behind her. She'd only be gone a few minutes and she didn't want to miss seeing Dinah or Kim before she went home.

She tapped tentatively on the closed door. "It's just me, Shanna," she called out

"Come in, please," bid a softly pleasant voice with a distinctive Oriental accent.

As Shanna entered, she saw that Dinah had just finished taking Kim's blood pressure. The Korean woman had delivered her son, Teddy, by Caeserean, so she was staying longer in the hospital. She was propped up in her bed, her straight dark hair a dramatic contrast to her lacy, pale pink nightgown. Sitting back in the room's only chair was a man who held Teddy in his arms. He kept glancing down proudly at the child, his face splitting into little grins—he had to be the father.

"I hope I'm not disturbing you," Shanna began, eyeing the family with envy. "I just wanted to say goodbye before I left."

"Don't worry," Kim assured her. "Shanna, this is my husband, Roger."

His name came out sounding more like Lodger, but Shanna resisted her impulse to correct the pronunciation. "Pleased to meet you. But don't get up," she added as he went to stand. "You look quite comfortable right where you are. And Teddy certainly looks as if he gets along with his daddy."

"He's a good kid," Roger said in a quiet, deep voice, beaming self-consciously. "I can see already that it might be hard getting tough with him when the time comes."

Dinah nodded knowingly as she jotted down some figures on the clipboard she carried. "It doesn't take long for these squirts to wrap you around their little fingers."

"Roger very happy I give him son. Now he tell me this. He is more like Korean men than he thinks," Kim said, her dark eyes teasing. "Now I know why I stay in this country to marry him." Roger just shrugged, feigning nonchalance, but the glance he stole at his wife bespoke nothing less than adoration.

If the old adage that opposites attracted were true, Kim and Roger fit the bill, at least in appearance. He was a large, heavily built man, while she was fine-boned and much tinier. In contrast to her long black hair, his was a light reddish-blond, short-cropped about his rough-looking, pockmarked face. His deep-set eyes seemed wary, shy, while Kim's manner was more open and gentle.

"So how does it feel to be wearing real clothes?" the matronly Dinah asked, glancing at Shanna's baggy white sweater and royal-blue track pants.

Shanna pulled at her sweater and sighed. "These are still remnants from my maternity wardrobe."

"Don't despair," Dinah said reassuringly. "You'll be thin as a rake, once you're chasing your little monkey around. So today's the big day, is it? Alicia's coming-out party?"

"She's resting up for the occasion. I can't stay long. But I just wanted to thank you for everything. I know how busy you are and you've been a big help to a novice like myself."

"Just doing my job."

Kim turned to her husband. "Shanna was teaching me better English and helping me to understand all this." She pointed to the stack of pamphlets, ranging from breast-feeding techniques to postnatal exercises.

"I'll help you when we get home, too, Kimmie," Roger said, and Shanna sensed that his protectiveness and concern for his wife were integral to their relationship. "When I have time," he added wearily, guiltily.

"It's okay," she told him, looking away, then explained for the others' benefit. "Roger is always too busy with his job."

"Where do you work?" Shanna asked politely.

"At a trucking company. In shipping and receiving."

"Roger very strong," Kim said in admiration. "But I tell him he can't throw Teddy up, like a box."

"Can't throw Teddy *around,*" Shanna couldn't resist clarifying. "Which company, Roger?"

"Morgan Cartage." At her sudden jolt he asked, "You've heard of it?"

"Yes. I know someone else who works there. Actually it's Derek Morgan."

This time it was Roger who looked surprised. "He's not a bad guy. Dresses like a hot shot, for a trucking company, at least. Likes to flaunt his bucks, I guess. His old man, Leo, really cracks the whip. Once you're punched in and he's promised next-day service to everybody and his cousin, you don't punch out until every last truck is reloaded for delivery. Don't matter if it's midnight, two in the morning, or the crack of dawn."

"That's why Roger was visiting me yesterday in middle of night," Kim cut in. "But Dinah tell nurses at desk it's okay."

Dinah put her finger to her lips, but there was a conspiratorial gleam to her eyes. "Hey, not too loud. I could lose my job for helping to smuggle in handsome men after hours in this female dorm."

Suddenly Shanna was reminded of her daughter alone in her room. "Look, I have to run back and check on Alicia. Why don't we exchange phone numbers, Kim, so we can help each other out, and pretend to everyone else that we know what we're doing?"

Kim grinned widely. "So they won't know we are really n-novices."

"Right." Because she'd felt an instant bond of friendship with the other woman, Shanna heard herself offering, "And maybe once things settle back home, you'd like to get together for some English lessons. I have the summer off and life just wouldn't be the same if I wasn't teaching." Plus, she had an inkling of the adjustments Kim faced as a new Canadian because of her own experience teaching young immigrants and their families.

"That would be very nice," Kim enthused, "but who would watch the baby when Roger is not home?" She didn't look at her husband, who had stiffened. "And I must to pay you."

"We'll work all that out," Shanna said swiftly. "But I really have to go now."

"Me, too." Dinah gave a quick wave from the door. "Good luck, Shanna. Just trust your common sense and you'll do fine on your own."

"Thanks again . . ."

"Before you go, Shanna, you must to see these pictures Roger took of Teddy."

And Shanna halfheartedly endured what she could almost swear were a dozen replicas of the same shot. Several minutes later with Kim's number in her pocket, she hurried down the hall. As she pushed open her door, she was thinking that she'd been sadly remiss in photographing her own child's first days of life. She took one step into the room and froze.

Alicia's crib was empty. Her clothes were gone from the bed.

Panic rose in her throat like gall. Knowing her panic could lead to a complete loss of control, Shanna forced herself to think. Calmly. With a supreme effort she told herself, *There has to be a reasonable explanation.* But as she tried to slow down her brain, her legs were moving at racing speed. She rushed into the nursery first, oblivious to anyone she passed in the corridor.

"Is Alicia here?" she gasped as a blur of faces looked up at her and she scanned the rows of carts.

"No, she's going home today, isn't—"

Shanna found herself at the nursing station, white-faced, shaking. "Where's Alicia?"

The nurse on duty was unfamiliar. She looked at Shanna in concern, puzzlement. Shanna didn't wait to explain. *Her father. Maybe he'd come early. The lobby. She'd check the lobby.* But only one young man in a baseball shirt was there, nervously drawing on a cigarette.

"Have you been here long?"

"Twenty minutes or so. They're doing an emergency operation on my wife," he began, plainly eager to talk.

"Did you see a man—an older man, fifties, with a baby?"

"No, I don't think so—"

"Shanna, what's the matter?" Dinah said, grabbing her by the shoulders. "I saw you tearing down the hall as if the place was on fire. And the nurse at the desk said—"

"Alicia's gone. She's not in the room. I can't find her. I left her. I should never have left her." Her voice was growing louder, rising in pitch, starting to ring in her own ears.

"Shanna, listen. She has to be here somewhere. We'll find her. Just take it easy."

But Dinah's calm, firm words had an opposite effect on Shanna. She didn't want platitudes. She wanted her baby.

"Something's wrong," she whispered, barely audibly. "I know it." Several nurses had congregated outside the nursing station by now, next to the lobby. "Do something," she screamed at them, her control snapping, her panic turning to hysteria.

In front of her, the red elevator light went on and a bell clanged shrilly before the doors opened. A wild hope flared in Shanna. Disoriented, she saw a figure in a dark coat emerging, but no baby was returned to her arms miraculously. Infiltrating her consciousness was a memory of a bizarre baby-selling scheme she'd heard about, where healthy babies were switched for sick ones, like changelings in a fairy tale. But this wasn't the nightly news, which always seemed to happen to strangers, and it wasn't fiction. It was happening to her. And it was real. Nightmarish, but real.

"What's wrong, Shanna?"

The voice came from the figure in the dark coat that was drawing nearer. Suddenly bright blue eyes were staring at her. She blinked, focused. Derek Morgan's eyes.

"She's gone. Alicia's gone," she reiterated, chantlike. She went to turn, to run, but Derek's fingers gripped her arms.

"Stay here. I'll look for you."

"No!" She could hardly breathe, so furiously was her heart pounding.

"Shanna, come with me," pleaded Dinah, from her other side. "You need to sit."

"No!"

"I promise I'll find her," Derek was saying, and in that instant she knew instinctively that if anyone could help her, he was the one.

"Please," she appealed to him in a voice grown hoarse with fear, "if anything happens to her, I'll—"

"Nothing will happen to her. Do you hear me? Nothing will happen to her."

Reluctantly, born out of the desperation of the moment, a trust as fragile as fine crystal passed from her to him. Then he was gone and Dinah was leading her away, Shanna's legs barely strong enough to carry her.

ALTHOUGH HE KNEW what he'd find there, Derek checked Megan's room anyway. As he'd suspected, it was deserted, the bed already made up for the next patient.

He stepped into the hall and noticed another man looking out curiously from a room a few yards away. Roger Hartly. Seeing him there in the frenzy of the moment, amidst the dramatic events of the last day or two, failed to surprise him. "Hi, Roger," he said as if they were meeting on the loading dock at Morgan's on a normal working day.

"Hi," the other man answered, plainly more taken aback than his employer at the unexpected encounter. "What are you doing here?"

"Visiting a friend," Derek answered briskly, already starting to move away.

"My wife just had a baby. A son."

"That's great. Talk to you later."

Roger was an enigmatic but hard-working employee who set himself apart from the camaraderie of the other drivers and warehouse workers. Derek made a mental note to congratulate him properly the next time he saw him. Right now, his all-absorbing priority was to find Shanna's baby and Megan. His gut feeling was that they were together.

His impulsive promise to Shanna had been wrenched from deep inside him; it still rang in his ears, like an echo. Exactly when he had changed from a reluctant bystander in their lives to someone who could not turn away, he wasn't sure. He only knew that it was imperative that he do everything in his power to find Alicia for Shanna.

Confusion reigned in the lobby and he slipped onto the next elevator going down before anyone could stop him. He tried to think as Megan would. She'd wanted to get away from the hospital as swiftly as she could. She hated it there. She'd told him as much last night, when she'd called him, sometime after midnight, and begged him to take her far away. She'd said she was supposed to be going home in the morning, but she didn't want to go home. She wanted to fly to France immediately to find Terry.

She'd been so distraught that he'd actually feared she might do something irrational. Maybe that was why he'd immediately connected her with the missing baby. He'd promised to pick her up and see that she got home safely. Now, as his patience nearly snapped with each additional stop of the elevator, he was more determined than ever to find his damn brother and make him accountable for his irresponsibility—first by helping Megan get back on track.

Derek's eyes gave a cursory sweep of the main lobby, but he didn't bother checking the cafeteria, knowing that foremost on Megan's mind would be the desire to escape from the building. He ran toward the waiting taxis outside. The first driver looked at him lethargically when he asked if a woman with a baby had taken any of the preceding taxis.

"I take woman," the driver said in a heavy accent, looking past Derek for the passenger in question.

"Forget it." His eyes scanned the nearest bus stops on busy King Street. Megan wasn't among those waiting for the bus heading west, and the other stop was deserted, so he'd probably just missed a loading. An ambulance siren and two accidental jostlings from passersby increased his anxiety and once more he forced himself to think as Megan would.

He sprinted toward the adjacent parking lot and raced up the stairs, too impatient to wait for the elevator. He needed his car to compensate for Megan's head start if she was travelling on foot or by bus. Never had the traffic seemed so slow or lights so long as he moved toward downtown Kitchener, his eyes constantly on the alert. He passed Victoria, then turned at Charles Street and parked the car, needing to walk, reassess, ward off his growing sense of futility.

He bypassed the King Centre—too big. On King he ran by a row of shops—a deli, a record store, a clothing boutique. He stopped as it registered that the clothes in the window were small-sized. For children. He heaved open the door with a rush of certainty, making the bells at the entry clang noisily. Several customers watched with suspicion as he searched the narrow aisles in vain, heedless that he was knocking down a stream of outfits and hangers.

"Are you looking for anything in particular, sir?" asked a salesclerk sharply.

"A woman and baby."

"I wouldn't want to be either of them," he heard the same voice mutter as he propelled himself back onto the street, deflated that his hunch had proved wrong.

For the first time he faced the possibility that maybe he'd have to return to the hospital alone. Megan could have gone in any number of directions, and he hadn't a clue where she lived. He kept walking, toward the translucent green buildings of Market Square. He spotted a phone booth, bolted to it, and practically yanked the book from its chain as he flipped through to the Ts. But the only Tuckers listed were men's names.

He remembered the look of anguish on Shanna's face. For some strange reason he'd really believed he could help her. He'd wanted to help her. Some asinine knight-in-shining-armor he was turning out to be....

Some benches surrounded Speakers' Corner and he moved toward them, needing to catch his breath before heading back. A few tourists were waiting to listen to the noon hour glockenspiel, but he had no interest in the animated re-creation of Snow White and the Seven Dwarfs, or whatever nonsense would be playing. He briefly contemplated making a missing person announcement from the ceremonial podium in the square, thinking he could only improve on his fruitless efforts so far, but he quickly dismissed the thought.

Overheated from the spring warmth, he took off his trench coat and sat down by some greenery in huge planters. The last time he'd been here had been during the opening Oktoberfest festivities and he'd already downed a few beers with some of the guys from work. That levity seemed part of another life.

A family moved toward the Willkommen pavilion, and then he saw her. On the farthest bench. By the towering, blue-striped maypole with its brightly painted crests and folk dancers. Huddled over a white blanketed bundle, taking up the whole bench with her belongings—a purse and a gym-style shoulder bag, out of which protruded the teddy bear he'd given her. His relief was heady. His first instinct was to rush over to her, but he held himself back. He realized how important it was to handle the situation carefully.

Megan didn't notice him coming up to her, so absorbed was she in rocking the child and crooning to her.
She was wearing a denim smock and a long beige coat-
sweater. Her hair was stringy, her face flushed.

"Hello, Megan."

She stiffened, and several seconds passed before she
recognized him. "What are you doing here?"

"I came to take you home. You asked me to." Pushing aside her bags, he sat down beside her.

"I must have forgotten. We had to leave early, anyway. Before Joy woke up. But she started crying on the
bus, so I got off."

"Megan, whose baby is that?"

"Mine," she said with conviction.

He drew a deep breath. What he wouldn't give for a
knowledge of psychology. He knew she was severely depressed, unbalanced, that reality had become distorted
for her. All that mattered right now, though, was ac-
companying her and the baby back to the hospital safely.
He had to prevent her from losing control, but everything in him balked at feeding her delusion, fantasy,
whatever the hell it was. He would play it slowly, follow
her lead.

"Let's go now, Megan. The baby might be cold. She's
so young."

"I dressed her all cosy in her hat and sweater. They
were ready on the bed. And I wrapped her in an extra
blanket. She likes the fresh air. It makes you sleepy,
doesn't it, pumpkin?" And she tightened her hold on
Alicia.

"Come on, Megan." To his surprise, she seemed to
respond to the authoritative tone he'd injected into his
voice. With him carrying her belongings, they made their

way across the oasislike courtyard at the corner of King and Benton.

But when Derek steered Megan back, toward the distant hospital, she immediately turned the other way. "No."

"That's where my car is parked."

But Megan wasn't fooled. "We can't go back there," she whispered.

"Why not?"

She hesitated then answered slowly, "Sometimes they hurt babies. Make them sick...."

"That's not what happened to your baby, Megan," he said gently, his voice wavering with the gamble he was taking. "The doctor wants to talk to you about it."

"Doctors lie!" Her eyes grew wild, and he kept close to her because he feared she might bolt at any second.

He swallowed. "Your doctor cares about you. We all do."

"No, you don't! All you care about is yourselves. Only a baby loves her mother...exactly as she is. Exactly as she is." Tears started streaming down her face, unchecked because she would not release her hold on Alicia who suddenly woke up and joined her in distress. "Don't cry, Joy sweetie. That's why I named you Joy, so you'll never have to cry."

"She's probably hungry, Megan. She wants her mother. Her real mother."

"Don't say that. I can be her mother. I—I *am* her mother now."

"Her mother is very worried and upset. We have to go see her."

She looked away, blinking hard, then her face seemed to crumple as she faced the truth at last. She stared hard at the wailing child, then back at him. "It's not fair. Nothing is fair. Why not?"

"I don't know," he admitted. He found a tissue in his pocket and wiped her cheeks dry. "Come."

And this time she didn't protest. He let her keep the baby as they walked to his car. Whether it was her soothing sounds or their motion, he couldn't be sure, but after a while Alicia quieted and fell back asleep. He would remember Megan's sad smile of satisfaction for a long time.

HAVING TO WAIT PASSIVELY in her room, listening to the reassurances of Dinah and Mrs. Thornton, was the most difficult thing Shanna had ever endured. All her instincts were screaming at her to search for her child herself, but she'd almost fainted and the two nurses were determined that she stay put.

Security had been alerted and a police officer had been in for a report and description of the child, at which Shanna had nearly broken down completely. Her separation from Alicia, a part of her, was like a physical tearing in two.

When her father finally arrived, she fell into his arms, needing his closeness. "Oh, Dad, the most horrible—"

"I know, they told me. Everything's going to be all right," he murmured, squeezing her hard.

"We'll just be out in the hall," Dinah was saying. "Call if you need anything."

Two heads just nodded dully. Shanna pulled away. "It's all my fault. I left her alone, just for a few minutes, but I was longer—" Her voice caught on a sob.

"You couldn't have known something like this would happen. If anyone's responsible, it's the hospital, for letting strangers roam around." He saw the panic-stricken look on her face. "But I'm not saying that's necessarily the case. There has to be a simple explanation, a mix-up. We'll get to the bottom of it."

"The police were here. They wanted a description. Just routine, they told me. My baby's missing and they call it routine. If anyone should hurt her, Dad, I don't know what I'll do."

"Everything's going to be okay," he said, holding her, the only way he could control her growing hysteria. If only his wife were here, he thought. She'd know what to say, what to do. She'd always been more of a take-charge person than he was. As a parent, even of a grown daughter, he secretly felt as if his right arm was missing without her. And as a single grandparent—well, he felt just as inadequate. "Your mother will watch over her little Alicia Michelle," he suddenly added, fervently, like a prayer. "That much I know."

And father and daughter waited silently, perched side by side on the edge of the narrow bed.

Shanna lost all concept of time, and the room was starting to grow claustrophobic. "How long do they expect us to just sit here, like good little children?" she finally asked on an outburst of tension.

"At least until they search the hospital and grounds, they told me."

"I can't stand it anymore. I have to find out what's going on." Despite his effort to restrain her, she flung herself out the door and hurried down the hall toward the lobby.

A baby was crying. Shanna let out a strangled sound and the circle of bodies there parted. As if in slow motion, she witnessed Alicia being passed from Megan to Mrs. Thornton. Shanna's eyes met Megan's. She saw tears there, but she felt no sympathy. Just the shock of relief ricocheting through her whole body and a deep blinding fury.

She reached for her child and clutched her as if she'd never let her go again. The baby and her blanket smelled differently, like clothes that had been hanging outside in fresh air all day. Instinctively she stepped back, needing to put as much distance as possible between herself and the other woman. If only she'd been thinking clearly, she might have connected the baby's disappearance with the depressed Megan earlier.

"How could you do this to me? To her?" she whispered hoarsely, keeping her voice low so as not to disturb Alicia any more. Already she was rocking back and forth in the familiar rhythm.

"I thought she was mine," Megan said clearly, defiantly.

Shanna's rage flared. "You're crazy!"

"Shanna, please let her be. She needs help."

Her eyes flew toward the deep, familiar voice, and for the first time she noticed Derek Morgan beside Megan, carrying her bags. By virtue of association he was as much to blame, Shanna suddenly thought in her shaken state, as the hospital system that had not been able to prevent this calamity. "Get her help, then!" she told him with undisguised hostility. "All of you," she added to the sea of faces around her. "Just leave me and my baby out of it."

Her father's arms encircled her then, supporting her. She couldn't look Megan's way again, but she felt her there like a dark, menacing shadow. A wave of weariness overcame her. Something was compelling her to look at Derek again, but she resisted the urge with her last ounce of strength.

"Is there anything else you need?" her father was asking one of the officers.

"Not right away."

"I just want to go home," Shanna implored quietly.

Half an hour later, after Alicia's needs had been attended to and Shanna had assured herself that no harm had fallen on her, she did just that. Her small, two-story house near the University of Waterloo looked as if she'd never been away. However, the somber nature of the homecoming was far different than what she had anticipated with such excitement that morning.

Only much later did it occur to her that Derek Morgan had indeed kept his promise to her, and that all the gratitude in the world could never repay him for returning her precious child to her safely.

DEREK WAS SPRAWLED on his black leather couch that night, his companions a glass of scotch and a thick binder of revised tariff regulations. But his mind had wandered to something his ex-lover Rachel had said during their last fight, although their parting discussion could hardly be called a fight. It had been too calm, rational and controlled, confirming what he'd suspected but never admitted about their relationship. At some indeterminate point it had burned itself out, grown stale and predictable. The prospect of marrying thirty-two-year-old Rachel had been inconceivable to him, no matter how sound her arguments had been and how unexpected her ultimatum.

When she'd realized, to her own obvious surprise, that he didn't see marriage as the next logical step in their seemingly compatible affair, she'd resorted to a new argument. Although she had never been interested in starting a family, being perfectly content in her executive position at an insurance company, she would consider "going through with it" if that was what Derek secretly wanted, although he had never seemed the fatherly type to her.

"Besides," she'd told him, "bright, affluent couples like ourselves probably have a responsibility to contribute at least two bright, advantaged children to the world. For the betterment of society."

He had never comprehended why exactly people chose to give up their sanity and freedom to raise children, and Rachel's reasoning hadn't brought him any closer to the truth. "I didn't say that's what I wanted."

"Of course, there's no hurry," she'd hastened to add with relief. "I'd like a few more solid years of management experience under my belt and a promotion or two before I'd consider any interruptions."

"Rachel, marrying or not marrying you has nothing to do with kids. I care for you a great deal, but I just can't marry you."

"I know we never discussed it in so many words, but I always assumed...everything has gone so smoothly for almost two years...."

He'd just shaken his head sadly. "Maybe that's our problem. Everything is too smooth, too scheduled, too perfect."

She'd stared at him in disbelief. "Maybe that's *your* problem. I always gave you the benefit of the doubt, but you really are a cold person, Derek," she'd said, her composure breaking more than she'd ever allowed it to in front of him.

He'd been glad she'd rushed away before they could hurt each other any more. She'd said she wouldn't be back unless he changed his mind and he'd believed her.

He'd also known it wasn't a question of making up his mind, but of finally facing the inevitable.

Now, two months later, he still missed what she'd added to his life. The occasional female companionship—they'd kept separate apartments and had usually seen each other only Saturday nights and Sunday mornings, except for a couple of trips south together. The sex, of course, although even their passion had lost something indefinable. And the comfort. He had been able to unwind with her over weekly drinks, dinners and breakfasts, and he needed that.

He could always start over, with someone else. He'd done that before. But what bothered him was the fact that he would face the same situation again, and next time a split would probably happen more quickly. Because he knew Rachel had been dead-on about one thing. He was a cold person. He must be. He'd never really loved anyone. Not in the way others had described to him—completely, their lives meshed without each feeling stifled.

Surely if he were capable of such noble emotions he would have felt something akin to them in his thirty-six years. He'd felt infatuation, but it had always worn away once he attained the object of his obsession. He'd tried variety, celibacy and monogamy at various points in his life, and he was still no farther ahead, still as unsettled as ever.

He genuinely liked women, although sometimes they were like a mysterious species to him. As a rule, he got along fine with them as long as he kept certain things to himself. He and Rachel had never discussed his business life in detail, for example. He needed his times of solitude as much as he'd needed his time with her, and he'd never felt he was missing anything—at least not until her comment about his coldness had finally struck a raw nerve.

His emotional life had been on hold since she'd broken off with him. The last two days with Megan and Shanna, however, had shaken him out of his slump. He kept reliving his encounters with them, wondering how he could have handled the situation more effectively. And should he do anything now to remedy the aftershocks of the experience for either of them? After all, he had introduced them. Then again, a part of him wished he could forget the whole mess.

As happened sometimes when he was stressed out, he seemed stuck on one thought. He kept remembering the look of sheer joy on Shanna's face as she welcomed back her baby, and the way she had lashed out instinctively at Megan and the crowd at the hospital, like an animal defending her young. Shanna Rhodes was not a cold person. No, she was full of warmth—even her pain and anger had passion, the fire of a strong integrity and pride.

But he wouldn't invent excuses to get in touch with her. If he couldn't commit himself to a beautiful, intelligent and self-sufficient woman like Rachel, what on earth could he offer a recent widow with a new baby? Surely her emotional needs and expectations would be far greater than he could ever hope to fulfill. Why he was even entertaining such thoughts was a mystery to him. Maybe it *was* time he put himself back into the singles circuit, although if the crisis with Megan had taught him anything, it would be to exercise more care with a woman's mind, more caution with her body.

Mustering up extreme self-discipline, he returned to his tariff regulations. But haunting eyes, as green and vivid as sun-warmed meadows, kept interfering with his concentration....

CHAPTER FOUR

As SHANNA PUSHED the carriage down the tree-lined sidewalk, she couldn't believe that six weeks had passed since she'd been home with the baby. With the occasional catnap, she was sleeping enough to feel strong again, almost like her old self—except that certain poignant memories of Michael kept tearing at her heart. Recently his parents had visited her and Alicia from Vancouver. While the reunion had been joyous in many ways, it had also been painful because of Michael's absence.

Suddenly a man stepped out in front of her from behind a high shrub. She drew in her breath and tightened her grip on the carriage. He nodded at her, then proceeded to walk his black Labrador in the opposite direction.

It was broad daylight on a sunny Saturday morning in May, the street was bustling with activity, and she was paranoid! At odd moments like that one, she recognized that the kidnapping episode haunted her still. She hoped she could learn to live with her fears. Still, nothing would make her give up her precious daily walk through her neighborhood. Not only was the fresh air good for the baby, but Shanna needed the change of scenery for herself. Today, Alicia was awake, her pudgy sleeper-clad legs protesting against the restraint of a light blanket as she stared intently up at her mother.

At the next street corner a homemade cardboard sign pointed to a garage sale a few houses away. Always on the lookout for baby paraphernalia, Shanna turned, excited at the thought of bargain-hunting. She'd come by it honestly enough. Her mother had always loved "garaging," as she'd called it. Every birthday or special occasion, Shanna had received an assortment of knickknacks, some useful, others that were soon discreetly packed away, all of which her mother had picked up "for a song."

To Shanna's delight, several homes had joined forces and an ample selection of infant clothing and toys was for sale. Soon a safety gate was propped against Alicia's stroller, over which hung a few new-looking outfits. Shanna was riffling through some children's books, debating whether to go for the Beatrix Potter or Dr. Seuss series, unaware that a sleek black car had slowed and that the driver was staring at her. The driver parked the car and sat, both hands on the wheel, for a few seconds before finally getting out.

But the confident voice that greeted Shanna showed none of that hesitation. "Hello, Shanna. I see you're getting ready to teach your star pupil to read."

Shanna jumped as if a firecracker had gone off at her feet. She looked up into blue eyes brighter than the sky. "Oh, hi, Derek. You...startled me." The forced calmness of her voice masked the huge understatement. "What are you doing here?"

"Just taking a shortcut. My CD's on the blink." He started flipping though a stack of faded album jackets, marked at fifty cents apiece. "Maybe I should haul out my old turntable, though, and check out some of these oldies, but, ah, goodies." He pulled out two. "Jim Nabors. The Monkees. Now there's an unbeatable deal for a buck.''

At his diversion, Shanna began to relax. She took in Derek's casual appearance, his white cotton shorts and T-shirt and his canvas loafers, his wonderfully shaped muscular legs with their very masculine sprinkling of dark hair. A light wind was ruffling the black hair on his head, giving him a raffish look. For her part, she seemed destined to always run into him without any makeup or flattering clothes. The first time she'd met him she'd been in a bathrobe, and today she wore a shorts set in a pastel pink, yellow and green that probably did nothing for her against her pale, untanned skin.

After pretending to be in a great dilemma about whether to buy the albums, Derek finally returned them to the table. Shanna watched, then decided to voice something she'd been thinking about for a while. "I want to thank you for finding Alicia." She drew a long breath. "I wasn't as appreciative after the kidnapping as I should have been. In fact, as I recall, I was downright rude."

His eyes held hers. "Apology accepted. You were under a lot of strain. How is she, anyway?" he asked, his voice softening as he glanced at Alicia, who was eyeing him with equal interest.

"Fine." Almost reflexively, Shanna grinned at her daughter and tickled her chin. Alicia broke into a quick, open-mouthed smile in return, or Shanna could swear it was a smile.

"And you?" His voice seemed to carry that same trace of softness she'd detected a moment ago.

"I'm okay, too. Except I probably won't let Alicia out of my sight for at least sixteen years."

"Well, if you ever need a bodyguard for her..."

"Sure." She took another deep breath. "How's Megan?" she asked as casually as she could manage, determined to deal with the unwanted specter.

"I think she's finally realizing the seriousness of the kidnapping. If she's convicted, she could face a long prison term."

"What she did could have had serious consequences," Shanna said quietly.

Derek's gaze didn't waver as he replied, "But she needs psychiatric care, not more punishment for her temporary lapse, for lack of a better term."

While Shanna still harbored troubled feelings about the ordeal, her anger had faded. "Did she have to go to jail or anything?" she asked.

"You sure you want to hear all this?" Shanna merely nodded and he went on, weighing his words carefully. "Well, Megan was taken from the hospital to a police station for questioning. Because of the unusual circumstances, she was released without bail having to be posted. She's had two brief court appearances, but the judge adjourned the case until what's called a predisposition report could be prepared. By a social worker."

Shanna nodded again. "Must be the same woman who contacted me. I didn't ask her anything about the case, but I'm meeting with her next week, in fact, to give her some kind of victim impact statement." She smiled wryly. "Sounds mighty ominous and official. I hope my feelings fit into the right categories."

"What you say will probably greatly influence the judge at the sentence hearing," Derek said slowly.

"Don't worry. I'm not out for revenge. I'll stick to the facts, but Megan *is* guilty of taking my child," she added as a remnant of her old anger flared.

"No one's disputing that. In fact, George recommended that Megan plead guilty, but he's—"

"George?"

"George Shrier. A friend of mine. He also happens to be a certified specialist in criminal law."

Shanna studied him closely. "You're being very accommodating toward Megan...."

"Someone has to," he retorted sharply. "Until Terry gets back."

Shanna realized that Derek had been responsible for securing Megan one of the best defense lawyers in the Kitchener-Waterloo region. But he obviously wasn't eager to dwell on the reasons for his involvement. He continued, "George is confident that he can get a hearing fairly quickly, especially since he knows the Crown attorney prosecuting Megan. He believes that he can win Megan a conditional discharge from the offence, based on the circumstances. Megan's lack of any previous criminal convictions. The trauma of losing her own baby. Extreme postpartum depression. Also, no harm came to the victim, and she believed at the time that Alicia was hers."

Shanna shuddered as she remembered the sight of her baby being held possessively by Megan. Her knuckles turned white as they clutched the carriage handle.

"I'm sorry." Derek touched her arm with a gentleness that took her off guard. "I thought you wanted to know."

The strength and warmth of his hand on her cooler flesh had more than a comforting effect. Especially when his fingers lingered there briefly, exerting the faintest pressure, almost like a caress on the delicate skin of her inner arm. Her whole body grew warmer, more sensitive, as her eyes met his, embarrassed by the heated awareness. His fingers drew away with an exquisite slowness, and his eyes flickered mysteriously.

She stared at him, her insides churning, searching for words that would aid her out of this awkward impasse, but none came.

"Well?" he finally asked on a daring note, reaching out to touch her again, this time cupping her chin between his thumb and forefinger, then brushing her lips with a purpose and a question.

She turned away, refusing to meet the challenge. His hand dropped, and she didn't have to look at his eyes to know they were accusing her of cowardice. She didn't care.

"I better pay for all this stuff," she said in a voice an octave higher than usual, carelessly tossing a handful of books into the basket of the carriage. She picked up the gate and made her way to the cash table. Derek followed determinedly, and for once she didn't even try to bargain.

"Do you need a lift home or anything?"

"No, I'm fine." She heaved the gate under her arm, trying not to wince as the hinges dug into her. In the same polite tone she'd used with the woman at the counter, she said breezily, "Bye now," then hurried down the street.

She looked back once to find him still watching her. And she knew that ignoring the unwanted sexual currents between them left her feeling just as unsettled as acknowledging them would have.

When she arrived home, a record ten minutes later, her father was pulling weeds out of the front lawn. She'd asked him to baby-sit while she gave her first tutoring lesson to Kim, but he was an hour early. She sighed. It wasn't that she didn't appreciate his help or enjoy his

company, but Ned happened to drop by *daily*. His outside interests were minimal since his early retirement.

"Hi, Dad." She wondered if she looked as flushed as
she felt after the brush with Derek Morgan. But her father didn't seem to notice her at all. In his endearingly
doting fashion, he bent over the carriage to peek at Alicia, who'd fallen asleep during Shanna's pell-mell race
home.

"Hi. I see you wore out my little girl. Where've you
been?"

"Just out garaging." He smiled stiffly at the near-
forgotten term, then bent to examine the gate she'd just
set down. Although Shanna often caught her father with
that sad, faraway look that meant he was missing her
mother, he still could not speak freely of her. At least he
didn't spend as much time sitting in his favorite chair at
home, feeling sorry for himself. He'd practically moved
into Shanna's house instead.

"Hmm—this looks as if it's kept a few hellions at
bay." He pointed to the nicks in the wood.

"What do you want for five dollars?"

"I'll touch it up for you." He straightened. "Anything else you need doing outside here? It's such a nice
day. I had some time to spare, so I thought I'd come early
to give you a hand."

"Dad, I hope your own place isn't falling apart.
You've been devoting so much of your valuable time to
mine lately that—"

"Not to worry. The woman from Polly Maids was in
yesterday to give mine a once-over, not that it's that dirty
with just one fellow around, but I haven't the heart to
cancel the service. And it frees me up for when you need
me."

Shanna sighed in resignation. "Have you had lunch?" she asked, although she knew the answer.

"I was going to ask if you wanted me to pick up some burgers and fries."

"We had that the day before yesterday, didn't we? Come on, I'll make us some sandwiches."

"If it's no trouble . . ."

"As easy for two as one," she replied with what was becoming a standard line. He never seemed to notice the repetition, though, or perhaps he pretended to be oblivious because he hated eating alone so much.

One of these days, she would have to sit down and have a good talk with her father about his future plans. His growing dependence on her had to end sometime. But today wasn't the day. Shanna had to feed the two of them, then Alicia, and get presentable for her first tutoring session with Kim. As promised, they'd kept in touch, and both were looking forward to their lesson together, their first semiprofessional venture away from exclusive baby care.

One and a half hours later, despite a crying bout from Alicia that made Ned less than confident to see her leave, Shanna found herself at Kim's apartment door, close to Kitchener's main shopping mall, Fairview Park.

Kim greeted her with quiet enthusiasm. "Hello. Come in. Teddy is sleeping. So is Roger, so is good time for us, I hope."

"It's definitely more peaceful here than it was at my place before I left."

Kim smiled knowingly as she led her into a fairly small living area where every inch of space had been put to maximum use. Along with the regular furniture, there was also a piano and exercise bike, as well as a baby's change table, swing and play mat. The couple's eastern and western cultural blend was evidenced in the room's decorations. Two lovely watercolors with colorful birds and flowers, painted in the delicate Oriental fashion, graced the wall above the sturdy, tweed-covered couch, while a soapstone Eskimo carving sat on a black-lacquer table.

After gathering some books, Kim crossed her legs and sat on the floor by that low table. Shanna followed suit, her back against the couch, folding her legs comfortably to one side. Pulling her own materials from her briefcase, she remarked, "Those are beautiful pictures. Did you bring them from Korea?"

"My mother painted them. She sent to Roger and me for a wedding gift."

"So that's where you get your artistic talent."

"But my fingers only know how to play piano, not to paint."

Shanna had learned that Kim had a music degree from South Korea and that she intended to return to university here in order to teach music in Canada, eventually. But to qualify for the new school system, she first had to pass the rigorous TOEFL examination, or Test of English as a Foreign Language.

"I see you were able to buy the book I mentioned to you on the phone." Shanna pointed to the thick workbook designed to prepare students of all backgrounds for the advanced English proficiency test.

Kim nodded and flipped through it, shaking her dark head. "So much to learn. I am afraid never will we finish it all."

"First lesson," Shanna said brightly, slipping easily into her familiar teaching role. "Whenever you have such negative thoughts, you must tell yourself that you know more today than you did yesterday, that you are constantly learning and that you *will* succeed. But more importantly, you have to believe it.''

Kim still looked dubious, but she gave a gallant smile. ''That is why you come here, too. To make me work. I am busy with Teddy and Roger. And tired. It will be very hard, I know.''

''I will be cracking the whip—'' At Kim's puzzled look, Shanna explained, ''Motivating you, giving you assignments.'' Kim nodded in understanding. Shanna went on, careful to speak slowly and clearly and to pause often. ''But you have to motivate yourself, too, Kim. You must study not just once or twice a week in our structured lessons, but every day, no matter how briefly. The records that come with the workbook contain drills for you to practice. You have a stereo, don't you?''

''Yes. But already Roger is not happy I play my Chopin or Mozart records. He like very different music—rock and roll, blues.'' She made a face as if she'd just tasted something sour.

''I'm sure Roger won't mind cooperating in this case.''

''Who am I supposed to cooperate with?'' Roger asked, emerging from the bedroom. Unshaven, he wore a gray flannel tracksuit. His short hair managed to stick out at perpendicular angles to his scalp.

''Mozart may have to take a back seat to mini-dialogues and question sessions that develop Kim's listening comprehension,'' Shanna told him.

''I'm all for that,'' he said with a quick grin, unsuccessfully stifling a yawn. ''Sorry. I worked late last night.''

''Again,'' Kim added pointedly.

''We can use the overtime money,'' he countered sharply, then explained in a more subdued tone, ''Things were humming after one of our trucks jackknifed on the highway. When the stuff finally came in, everything had to be reloaded and checked for damage. Plenty. Needless to say, both the shipper and consignee won't be happy.'' From the adjacent kitchen he poured himself some orange juice. "All the bosses were around. Even Derek Morgan was there, dressed in greased-up overalls! He looked just like the rest of us flunkies.''

"Take away the fancy clothes and he probably *is* just like the rest of you,'' Shanna remarked.

Kim shot Roger a look of warning. "Remember, Mr. Morgan found Shanna's baby,'' she said softly.

"I'm not saying he's not a decent guy. But there's no denying that some guys have it easy from day one—and others, well, we have to fight for every break we get. Or put up with every raw deal we can't do anything about.'' Roger's face had suddenly taken on an intensely hard cast. As he cupped his fingers to light his cigarette, his hands were shaking, and Shanna sensed the bitterness she saw was only the tip of the iceberg.

"Roger—'' Kim looked from him to Shanna, then down at her hands.

He inhaled deeply, and by the time he had exhaled the smoke from his cigarette he seemed to have a grip on himself once again. He didn't look at either of them as he made himself a cup of coffee, the clanging of the spoon against the cup reverberating in the tense silence that had fallen.

From the second bedroom came a baby cry that made Shanna jump to attention, until she remembered that Alicia was miles away. Kim's reflexes were just as quick, but Roger told her, "Stay put. I might as well put my afternoon off to good use.'' He swiftly heated some milk formula in the microwave, carried the bottle into the bedroom along with his own mug, and soon the crying stopped. They could hear him talking in a low murmur to the baby.

"Roger very angry inside sometimes," Kim confessed sadly, her voice just above a whisper. "I tell him he must talk to me about it, but he says no. He's happy now, for first time in his life, and that is all that matters, he say."

"It does seem as if he'd do anything for you," Shanna said, a tad wistfully. "You are very lucky in that respect. Maybe in time he'll open up."

"I know he loves me. That is not problem." Her eyes were shining fondly. "But I wish he would not work so hard. He tells me the money is good and he wants us to have nice things. To buy a house some day. Have more children. Is very important to him."

"Does he come from a large family himself?"

"He will not speak of his family. I do not know where they live. Nothing. Roger said they are good people, but he does not want to see them. Maybe he had fight with them or he is ashamed of me. I don't understand." Her eyes filled as she glanced warily at the bedroom door, expecting it to open at any moment. "But we are here to study," she said firmly, sitting up straighter, swiping at her eyes. "No more problems."

"We can talk today. Conversational practice is good, too," Shanna said, reluctant to end the discussion.

"Then let us talk about happy things. How is your little girl?"

"Growing out of many of her newborn outfits already."

"Teddy is same. He likes to drink his bottle. Roger say he has big appletite, like his father."

"Appetite."

With Shanna occasionally correcting Kim's vocabulary or pronunciation, they proceeded to share anecdotes about their plunge into motherhood. To her horror, Kim had mistakenly splashed some rubbing alcohol in Teddy's eyes while treating his drying umbilical cord, which resulted in a visit to the hospital emergency ward. Shanna didn't have a story to rival that, but she did confess to frequent nocturnal visits to ensure her child was still breathing—that is, until exhaustion finally prompted her to abandon them.

Shanna learned how Kim had met her husband. The South Korean woman had been visiting her brother, a doctor who'd immigrated to Canada several years ago. During the annual Oktoberfest festivities, he'd taken her with some of his colleagues to one of the *Festhallen* to enjoy the traditional Bavarian entertainment and cuisine. As the evening progressed and the beer flowed, Kim had been overwhelmed by the boisterousness, despite the spirit of good fun. Somehow she'd started talking to a quiet man at the next table—Roger. They'd taken a pleasant walk outside together, and had fallen in love instantly, Kim insisted. They were married within a few weeks and Kim had never returned home, as planned. Her belongings had been shipped to Kitchener.

During the last hour of the three-hour lesson, Shanna familiarized her pupil with the format of the workbook, as well as the terminology used. She gave her a grammatical exercise to prepare for next week, plus some new vocabulary to study.

Shanna left their session with the familiar satisfaction teaching always brought her, intensified this time because of the close contact with her pupil. She looked forward to their next lesson, on an evening midweek, having assured Kim she didn't mind if Teddy was awake, since Roger's schedule was always unpredictable. Shanna wanted to help the struggling couple, and she'd almost been tempted to refuse the token fee she'd previously agreed to charge, but she feared that would have offended them, especially Roger. Whatever the cause of Roger Hartly's bitterness, she knew he was a proud man and that his pride had been severely trampled upon.

As she drove home, the car window rolled down, the warm spring breeze blowing her hair around sassily, she felt more carefree than she had in a long time. Alicia was never far from her mind, but Shanna loved caring for her daughter and didn't consider her a burden. Her father's overdependence, however, was a more complicated matter she intended to deal with shortly.

Suddenly she recalled her encounter with Derek that morning. In retrospect, she was relieved she'd run away from his advances. The two of them were at vastly different points in their lives. Plus, she suspected such come-ons were almost reflexive for him. But alone in her car, it was harmless, really, to relive some of their lighthearted banter and the unexpected sparks between them. Maybe it was her upbeat mood, the pleasant weather or delayed spring fever, but she let herself savor her thoughts of him—and the way he made her feel attractive again.

He'd appeared briefly in her life when she'd needed a diversion from all the serious changes. She supposed that reading a funny book would have accomplished the same thing, but chatting with Derek Morgan had been a lot more enjoyable.

CHAPTER FIVE

SHANNA HAD JUST PUT Alicia down for the night, or at least for a six-hour stretch. She was contemplating going to bed early herself, flipping through reruns on the TV or picking up her long-abandoned Atwood novel when the telephone rang.

Ned had just left, so he likely wasn't calling. Expecting either Talia or Kim, Shanna reached for the phone in her living room and was surprised to hear a male voice.

"Shanna?"

"Yes?" she asked, although she had no doubts about the identity of the caller.

"It's Derek Morgan."

"Oh, hi." She sat up straighter, gulping. It had been almost three weeks since she had seen him at the garage sale.

"I hope it's not too late to call."

"No. Actually Alicia just went to sleep."

"I won't keep you long." He cleared his throat. "I have a favor to ask."

He sounded brisk, businesslike. Her initial apprehension about the purpose of the call faded. She kept her voice as formal as his. "And what's that?"

"Megan would like to meet with you. To apologize for what she put you through."

Shanna's anxiety rose again. "I don't think that's such a good idea."

"I can understand your feelings. Just let me explain. Have you heard the outcome of her sentence hearing?"

"Yes. I gave my statement to the woman who came here a couple of weeks ago, and I think I was...fair, but I—I just want to put it all behind me. She said I wouldn't have to testify or meet Megan again or—" She stopped, then released her building indignation. "How can you even ask that of me?"

"Megan wanted me to," he said quietly. "I really think it would help her, and I was hoping you—"

"She's still under psychiatric care, isn't she, as part of her conditional discharge? Why not let the professionals deal with her?"

"Megan needs something more personal. She *appears* to be coping better, but...I don't know. Shanna, I know how hard it must be for you, and I wouldn't ask if I didn't feel it was important. Not only for her, but maybe for you, too."

It wasn't only the pleading in his voice that weakened her. It was the genuine caring she detected behind it. She felt something soften and melt inside. She looked around the familiar room, weighing her choices. "You don't expect me to meet her here, with Alicia, do you?" she asked at last.

"Of course not. I'm not *that* insensitive," he said on a breath of relief, reverting to his half-joking manner. "Besides," he added more somberly, "Megan's not allowed to be around any children, at least not any unsupervised ones for a year, so I don't think now would be the time to rub it in."

Shanna swallowed and felt herself sympathizing with Megan more than she wanted to. She thought of the joy she derived from Alicia and other children now, too, in a ripple effect, and she could not imagine that being taken from her. "Where shall we meet, then?"

"Would you mind going to Megan's? I don't think a public place would be appropriate, do you?"

"No, but I don't want to be alone with her," she said emphatically.

"I'll be there, if you like."

"Okay." Actually she'd assumed that from the start, but she didn't want to admit it. And she wouldn't be going through with this if she hadn't sensed Derek's complete confidence that it was the right thing to do. "I only want a brief meeting, nothing too prolonged or chatty."

"You got it. The time and day is up to you, too."

A slow-building tension was twisting her stomach as they matter-of-factly arranged the meeting for next Tuesday evening at Megan's apartment. She started to say goodbye, when Derek interrupted.

"Shanna?" The rolling murmur of his deep voice repeating her name made her catch her breath. "Thank you." An expectant silence fell. Then Derek added, "The best part of all this will be seeing you again." Again he waited. "Bye," he said after a while.

"Bye."

A few moments later, Shanna recognized why a small smile was tugging at her mouth. His last words had caused it. Yet she hadn't been able to say the words he'd been trying to coax from her, that she was looking forward to seeing him, as well. But she knew the words had been on her lips, ready, and he probably knew it, too....

SHANNA HAD BEEN STANDING at the torn screen door leading down to Megan's basement apartment for several minutes. Surrounded by a small patch of yard that was a mixture of dirt, gravel and weeds, the old house was in a state of disrepair. Two skinny cats, one calico, one black and white, eyed her suspiciously. Finally, gathering her nerve, she knocked loudly.

Thankfully Derek appeared, his warm smile as welcoming as it was reassuring. Her memory hadn't done justice to the startling blue of his eyes. "Come in," he said evenly, perfectly in control. "Did you have any trouble finding your way here?"

"No, your directions were fine. I'm a little late because I ended up with most of Alicia's last feeding on my other outfit. She likes to assert herself at the most inopportune times."

"I could say her feminine wiles are budding at an early age...." Shanna looked mildly disapproving, as he'd expected. "But instead I'll say that you look lovely in *this* outfit." And he took full advantage of the chance to eye not only her loosely belted, lemon-colored sundress, but her lightly browned shoulders, arms and legs. The heat and humidity of the late June day had lingered into the windless evening, so Shanna's prime concern had been to stay as cool as possible.

"Thank you," she said nonchalantly, telling herself the compliment was Derek's standard charm at work. He looked as urbane as ever in his dark walking shorts and cream-and-navy-striped polo shirt, the sleeves pushed up jauntily, and his deck shoes, worn without socks. However, the sheen along his brow, the damp waves of his hair and the day's-end shading along the strong line of his jaw all combined to give him an earthiness all the more striking when juxtaposed with the casual sophistication of his apparel.

He stepped back to let her descend the narrow stairway first. Her eyes were growing accustomed to the change of light, so her first glimpse of Megan below was of a shadowlike figure. The younger woman stepped forward, and Shanna saw instantly that she was nervous, too. They nodded hello to each other, then turned to Derek.

"Well, ladies," he drawled, on cue. "Here we are."

"How are you, Megan?" Shanna asked, determined to be civil.

"*Coping* much better, as they say, which sounds so stuffy. I prefer to say I'm just doing okay. You can interpret that any way you want, which is really what people will do anyway, isn't it?" Megan talked rapidly, breathlessly. She smiled politely then, slipping into the role of the charming hostess. "Would you like something cold to drink? I've just made some lemonade."

"That would be great." Shanna sat down hard on the sofa.

While Megan busied herself in the adjacent kitchen, Shanna glanced around. Although the small apartment was dim, with only one tiny window for natural light, Megan kept the place clean and comfortable. An eclectic blend of prints stared out, including a haunting black-and-white silhouette of a woman perched on a window ledge, one leg dangling as if to climb out, and another of a mass of hands, stage-level at a rock concert, against a backdrop of dazzling blue-and-red lights. The sofa and chair in white wicker with thick gray-and-pink floral cushions constituted the only seemingly new pieces of furniture in the room.

Tucked into a corner, beside an antique hat rack, was another wicker item—an infant bassinet, similar to the one Shanna owned. Newspapers, magazines and an umbrella filled it. Shanna turned away and saw that Megan was watching her.

She took a glass of lemonade from her and sipped quickly from it. Megan sat on the chair at right angles to her, her jean-clad legs tucked under her, while Derek leaned against the doorjamb.

"I hate small talk, so let's jump right into it," Megan began quickly, staring past Shanna. "I know I can't undo what happened at the hospital. I still don't know why exactly I did it, only I thought…at the time…that I could make everything right, for me, at least." She focused on Shanna then, her eyes troubled. "But I just screwed it up more, for both of us, didn't I? All I can do now is to say I'm sorry. I really am."

Her words hung in the air, like gray clouds heavy with rain. Nothing the other woman could ever say could erase the horror Shanna had felt when her child had disappeared mysteriously. But facing Megan now, so young and so sad-looking, almost a victim herself, Shanna made a huge effort to bury those awful memories forever. "I accept your apology," she said quietly.

Megan's face broke into a tentative smile. "They said I won't have a criminal record because of the discharge, but what matters to me is hearing you say that."

Shanna smiled back, just as faintly. "Well, in that case, I'm glad I can be of some help." She sipped from her drink. "How is your counseling going?"

"It's going," Megan said, standing abruptly and reaching for the pitcher of lemonade on a wobbly side table. "More?"

"No thanks."

"I'll have some," Derek said, and both women started, having completely forgotten his presence.

As Megan refilled his tumbler, she said to Shanna with sudden bitterness, "Did you know I can't be alone with any kids for a while?"

"I heard," Shanna answered, glancing at Derek.

"They're treating me as if I'm some sort of menace to society, like a rapist or a child abuser. I'm not like that," she added petulantly, almost tearfully.

"We know that," Derek intervened smoothly. "But just try to count yourself lucky that a harsher sentence wasn't imposed on you. Some judges are less fair than others."

Megan shrugged, the contriteness she'd displayed earlier with Shanna no longer apparent.

"We could debate crime and punishment all night," Derek continued, "but didn't some Russian already write a *long* book on that subject?"

"Dostoyevski," Shanna supplied, smiling inwardly.

"And I believe Shanna has some other plans. How does that ditty go, teach? Places to go, people to see, miles to walk . . . ?"

Shanna just shook her head and pretended to shudder. "Misquoting Frost is one thing, but calling one of his finest poems a *ditty* . . . !"

Derek looked suitably chastised as Megan eyed their private exchange with interest. "Are you a teacher?" she asked Shanna, looking from her to Derek again.

"Yes. I teach English as a Second Language."

"Oh." She sat on the floor, crossed her legs, pulled her baggy T-shirt over her knees. "My mom always wanted to be a teacher, she said, but she quit school to have me. She ended up a switchboard operator. I told her the world needs switchboard operators as much as it needed teachers, but she never seemed to agree, you know?"

No one spoke. Finally Shanna queried gently, "How are you and your mother getting along?"

Megan laughed, a shrill sound that seemed to bounce off the walls of the small room. "She's too much, she really is. She said she was embarrassed by the whole thing. I'm falling apart—or I was," she corrected swiftly, "and she's embarrassed by my immaturity, as she called it." She darted a look at both of them, trying to read their guarded expressions. "I tried with her. I really did. Somehow I doubt, though, that we'll ever have one of those nifty, pally relationships, like you see on TV. Maybe in my next life. But with my luck, I'll be born a spider or something."

A resounding knock sounded, and Megan rushed up the stairs as if reaching for a life buoy. "Act two, scene three. Mystery guest appears," she called out, then flung open the door. "Hi, Terry," she said with the same forced boisterousness.

Shanna had barely kept pace with Megan's erratic behavior before, and she wondered what was in store now. She watched the infamous Terry with undisguised curiosity as he came down the stairs. Strangely, Megan didn't seem surprised to see him.

His sun-bleached blond hair was cut short around his face, but was long and wavy in the back. Although he didn't share Derek's coloring, and he was slightly taller on a lighter frame, he had the same impish grin and bright blue eyes. Dressed in immaculate white cotton pants and an oversized shirt, he also appeared to possess the same relaxed fashion style as Derek.

"I came by to see if you wanted to catch a movie tonight," Terry was saying to Megan, but his eyes were travelling inquisitively from Shanna to Derek. "I didn't know you were busy."

"Terry, this is Shanna Rhodes," Derek interjected. "From the hospital. The . . . baby's mother."

"Really?"

"Megan wanted to talk to her. To apologize. Face-to-face."

"Oh." Terry shot Derek a look as if to say, "Oh, boy, what's next?" Megan's head was down, so she didn't see it. When Terry's and Megan's eyes met, Terry wore an expression of polite interest and Megan's face had set into willfulness.

"Shanna used to go to our high school," Derek went on to explain.

"Yeah? Small world and all that . . ."

Terry couldn't stay still. He radiated a restless energy that contrasted with Derek's aura of calm assurance. Terry Morgan seemed to live on the edge of life, Derek in a more comfortable middle terrain, Shanna thought. "I understand you were recently in France, Terry," she could not resist commenting. "When did you return home?"

"I don't know—a couple of weeks ago," he said vaguely.

"Terry just showed up out of the blue one day, like a wounded soldier home from the war." Megan didn't even try to hide the accusation from her voice.

Terry tried to move, pace, but it was impossible in the small room. Instead, he brushed at some dirt he'd spotted on his shirt. "I lost a big match there and I wasn't in the greatest shape. Since I've been back, though, Megan's been a good listener when I needed to talk. A real friend."

Shanna wasn't fooled for one second. But she knew Terry needed to believe he was making it up to Megan somehow by letting her think she was important to him. He seemed to feel more guilt than anything toward the girl who'd lost their baby.

Megan began gathering glasses, even though they were still half-filled. "Terry quit tennis. For good," the younger woman told Shanna, making a big clatter when she deposited the tray onto the kitchen counter. "We've got a lot in common now. We're both unemployed," she added, trying to make light of it, but disappointment edged her voice. Clearly she was less than impressed with her former idol.

"Could be the start of something bigger and better for both of you," Derek said with his customary heartiness, crossing his arms. "You have to think positive."

"Easy for *you* to say."

"True enough," Derek said lightly, ignoring the hostility in Megan's tone, and the potentially uncomfortable moment was glossed over.

Terry was as determined as his brother to alleviate the tense undercurrents in the room. "So, how 'bout that movie, Megan? I'm in the mood for a good thriller, and I need someone to hold my hand."

No spark lit Megan's eyes as she accepted, although she managed to inject enthusiasm into her voice. "Sure. I'm game. But what about you guys—"

"Oh, no. I have to be getting home," Shanna said quickly.

"Not tonight . . ." Derek began at the same time.

Jumping to her feet, Shanna was truly anxious to be on her way. "It was nice meeting you, Terry. And Megan—" She stopped. "I hope—"

"You hope never to see me again?"

"I hope everything works out for you. I know it will."

"Another positive thinker. You and Derek must get along famously." She eyed the two of them with a narrowed gleam that could have been either jealousy or curiosity.

"Shanna knew me when I was but a sweet innocent schoolboy," Derek murmured, smiling angelically.

"What? At six years old?" Terry sputtered.

Derek took a smiling Shanna firmly by the elbow and led her out. "Bye, Ter. Talk to you, Megan."

When they were walking outside, the day's heat cocooned in the still air, Derek's hand continued to rest lightly in the hollow of Shanna's back. Because he was so natural about touching her, she let herself enjoy the near-forgotten warmth of a man's guiding hand.

"So that wasn't so bad now, was it?" he asked.

"Well, I'm just glad it's over."

"So am I."

"Do you think it'll really help Megan?"

"Yes, I do. Why do you ask?"

Shanna stopped and his hand fell from her. She stared off, trying to find words for the niggling unease tugging at her. "The whole thing seemed like some sort of charade she was playing out. I get the impression she's more overwhelmed than she lets on. She's so...skittish."

Derek didn't look quite as worried. "Megan tells me the psychiatrist thinks she's making progress. And since I've known her, she's always had a high voltage kind of personality. She just needs to channel it in the right direction. Or maybe it's her version of the typical teenage mania."

Shanna shrugged. "I don't know. Maybe it's just me. I can't help seeing her as some sort of time bomb, ready to explode."

"At least she's more realistic about Terry. I mean, I like my kid brother, but he's not perfect by any means. Myself, on the other hand—"

"Unfortunately I won't be able to listen to the fascinating list of your virtues tonight." She matched his teasing gleam as she reached in her purse for her keys, having noticed that they were approaching her car.

"I'd like to take you out for a drink," he said swiftly, putting his hand over hers and the keys. "What I'd really like to hear about is you. Not me."

His imploring tone compelled her eyes to meet his, and at the impact she felt the strangest buoyancy in the zone between her stomach and head. "My dad's with Alicia. I shouldn't—"

"Call them. I'm sure they're fine."

She moved her hands away. "You're a very persistent man."

"You can take part of the credit for that," he said wryly. "You're not making it very easy for me."

"I have my reasons."

"Good. They'll give us something to talk about." Shanna's resistance was faltering against his determination, and she really did need a break. He saw her wavering and acted. "It's a perfect night to sit at an outdoor patio-bar. One of my favorites is on Frederick. We'll take my car and pick up yours later."

"I'll take mine, thanks."

Twenty minutes later, Shanna found herself sitting opposite Derek at a tiny wrought-iron table, their knees touching. She'd called Ned, who'd assured her that all was running smoothly and he'd practically commanded her to have a pleasant time. That wasn't too difficult with her companion, who was making a great show of treating her royally.

In a mock-conspiratorial aside to their young waiter, Derek had confessed, "Carlos, it's taken me almost twenty years to get this woman out for a date and I don't want to spoil my big chance. I want everything to be impeccable." Carlos had winked knowingly.

Sure enough, Shanna's wine spritzer came accompanied by a deep red rose. A sunken candle appeared on their table, as well as a tray of smoked salmon, cream cheese and tiny crackers—compliments of the chef. Hanging baskets of ferns and flowers gave the tiny courtyard a lush, romantic ambience.

Nibbling one of the appetizers, Shanna remarked, "I'm trying to decide whether A, you have a company account here, B, Carlos knows you tip well because you bring all your female friends here, or C, he really does have a sentimental nature."

"Ye of little faith," Derek said, declining to answer, looking at her in a way that really did make her feel special and suddenly even warmer in the sultry night air.

"How's work going, anyway?" Shanna asked in an effort to get a straight answer from him.

He sipped from his Scotch. "We've had a problem with some missing shipments lately. That's becoming a pain in our corporate backside, shall we say. But I promised we wouldn't talk about my life."

"Would you rather hear about a great treatment for diaper rash or the amazing fact that there's always traffic on the street at the 4:00 a.m. feeding?"

"Some other time, perhaps. I'd rather hear how Alicia's mother is doing."

"She's content, tired, in awe at seeing her child growing in different ways, every day."

He studied her, and for once he didn't have a quick reply. She moved the conversation to more common ground. "I'm also doing some tutoring... with Roger Hartly's Korean wife. He said he works for you."

He nodded at her, then at Carlos, holding up his fingers for two more drinks. "In shipping and receiving. So how'd you meet up with them?"

"At the hospital. His wife had a baby at the same time."

Derek stirred the ice in his drink absentmindedly. "Actually I saw Roger there, but I was playing detective at the time, so I wasn't exactly at my congenial best. I remember, though, that when I gave him the usual congrats at work about his son, his face lit up like a Christmas tree. He's not the friendliest guy around. Does his job and does it well, but he doesn't mix much with the rest of the gang. I guess you'd say he's basically a loner."

"I know what you mean, just from the few times I've seen him, but the odd thing is he's a real family man, too," Shanna said reflectively. "He thinks the world of his wife, and he's great with Teddy... although Kim did say he's estranged from his own family or something." She stopped, guiltily. "Maybe that wasn't supposed to be public knowledge. Please don't say anything."

Derek held up both hands. "You have my word, and I'm a man of honor, in certain matters, at least." He smiled wickedly. "Aren't you going to ask when I'm not?"

"No."

"Ah, woman, you infuriate me."

"Is that why you asked me out tonight?" she asked, smiling back at him just as daringly. "Because you know I'm not into dating these days and your male ego won't admit defeat?"

"What if I said I wanted to be with you as much as I didn't," he answered slowly, almost reluctantly, "and that the real challenge is in defying myself and figuring out why I'm so schizoid?"

She stared at him, taken aback, knowing he was being honest with her. "Are you currently involved with someone else? Is that it?" she asked carefully, her curiosity vying with her reticence about prying into his personal life.

Their second round of drinks arrived, so Derek didn't answer right away. "No, I'm not currently involved with anyone," he said at last, avoiding her eyes.

"But you *were?*"

"I was."

"And?"

He looked up at her, then around. "Persistence must be in the air tonight."

"Must be." She peered at him encouragingly, relentlessly, as she took a slow sip from her glass.

"I kept company, as they say, with a smashing gal called Rachel," he replied, needing to escape into frivolity. "But apparently we had different ideas about our...dalliance and came to a parting of the ways a few months ago."

Shanna looked interested, but said nothing, wanting him to keep talking, hoping that inadvertently he would reveal more of what lay under his slick exterior.

"It's just as well it ended when it did," he went on in a rush. "It was inevitable, really. I don't seem to be willing or programmed or whatever you want to call it to stay with anyone, although," he added on a note of forced optimism, "I did break new ground with Rachel in one respect. We lasted a record eighteen months."

"So you think your problem is one of tenacity?" Shanna murmured.

"I didn't say it's a problem. Just a fact of being." At Shanna's skeptical expression he elaborated, "Actually I'm a very tenacious person, in every *other* area of my life. I grew up listening to my dad drill into us, 'Without stick-to-itiveness you'll never have anything to show for yourself. You are what you have and what you prove to the world.' I guess more of that rubbed off than I realized. Except I like to stick to the kinds of things that *I* can control, things that can be measured in concrete terms." He leaned back, smiling lazily, well-satisfied with his self-analysis.

Shanna felt compelled to nudge him off the safety of his perch. "So, talking in numbers then, don't you miss the things that Rachel added to your life?"

His eyes narrowed barely perceptibly. "Such...matters can be added or subtracted and *I'm* still intact. I don't understand why people allow themselves to be divided up when they part ways with someone, and I've certainly never felt compelled to multiply myself with offspring," he added, slipping into word play, but his grin died when he saw her expression. "I'm sorry. That's just my perspective. I know you've just lost your husband—"

"Have you never loved anyone?" she asked quietly.

He blinked. "No. I don't think I have."

She continued to look at him, feeling as if she were adrift in those troubled deep blue eyes, and for the life of her she couldn't believe he was incapable of love. "That's a shame..."

"I was quite attached to a terrier I had once—Peppy. Mind you, she preferred the mutt down the street." He shifted in the patio chair, the spreading lines of his smile incongruous with the clouded expression that lingered in his gaze a fraction of a moment longer. "I wasn't supposed to be on the hot seat tonight. Tell me more about Michael," he commanded suddenly.

Her heart thudded in her chest. "What would you like to know?" she asked with deceptive calmness.

"I've always heard that to make a marriage last, you have to *work* at it. I've never understood that. Really. I can see that you have to be able to compromise, to be decent about sharing the dishes and laundry, and you have to remember anniversaries. But how do you work at something in a good way, without taking all the—the spark out of it? How did you and Michael do it?''

Talking about her marriage was easier than talking about Michael's death. But Shanna was still unused to talking in the past tense. No soft glow surrounded Michael's memory, only the starkness and shock of his untimely demise. "That's a tough question," she finally admitted. "In our case, there was a lot of work, the drudgery kind you mentioned, but there were moments, fine moments, sometimes spaced far apart, unfortunately. They made the rest all worth it, though," she added wistfully.

"Would Michael have answered the same?"

She glanced at him sharply. "I think so...." And the wistfulness remained, despite the defensiveness in her tone. "It's just that...before his death, Michael had been so preoccupied with work, his cases. He took them all so seriously. I told myself it was just another of the valleys—between us—that come and go, but I'll never be sure." She looked away. "It seems as if twin ghosts are haunting me—the hazy, lost memories of the early years, the best years, and these...these later unresolved ones, and I'll never get a second chance to make everything right...."

She was determined not to cry in front of him, but her throat turned as dry as a desert with the effort. With trembling hands, she reached into her purse for a tissue, more for something to do than anything. "I must have used the last one when Alicia spit up," she muttered. She looked up at him, shaking her head. "See, that's why I probably shouldn't be here tonight. No one wants to hear about ghosts and memories and—and wet burps."

Derek's fingers cupped her upturned chin and he murmured, "Hey, I do. Call me weird, but—"

Tiny crinkles appeared on his face, then his eyes were laughing and she started laughing, too, although a lone tear had broken free. Some of the laughter seemed to trickle into the wounded place she'd opened for him, and she felt lighter all of a sudden, deep within. Then his face was coming closer and his lips brushed hers before settling into a firm friendly kiss. As they slowly pulled away, they stared at each other's mouths, then eyes, in surprise.

Neither mentioned the unexpected kiss as they finished their drinks and retreated into small talk, trading news about some of their former classmates. But the memory of the contact hovered between them like a fickle butterfly. Eventually Derek paid the bill and escorted her out.

With nightfall a light wind had arisen, cooling the balmy air. Silently Derek walked Shanna to the small deserted parking lot behind the restaurant. When they reached her car, she turned to thank him and found his arms ready to hold her, and it was as if the earlier kiss had never ended. His eager lips met hers again, parting them with his tongue, taking his sweet time to explore the warm moist recesses, inviting her to join him. She did, instinctively, pleasurably. As their bodies pressed closer, Shanna could feel the steady beat of his heart, or maybe it was hers pounding so vigorously. His hands were moving slowly, carefully, following her contours with a restrained intensity. Her own hands remained still, wrapped around his waist, but she became intimate with the hard lines and angles that defined him. The kiss deepened for one furious moment longer, then he drew back, his breathing shallow.

Their first kiss had happened spontaneously, but this one had been planned, anticipated. Shanna also recognized that she had enjoyed the second even more and that it had tapped a well of buried sensations. However, a dark, blinding confusion was building inside her, instead of any satisfaction at the physical release. She dug into her bag, found her keys, opened the car door.

"Shanna? Shanna...that was good, wasn't it? Wasn't it?" Derek repeated, his voice low, staccato. He clutched her by the arms.

"You're the first man to kiss me since—" As she looked at him, her eyes were huge, bright, imploring him to understand. "Only Michael ever made me feel like that . . . he's still here somehow, but he's not, and part of me is in that other place with him and it's not fair to you or me or—"

"Shanna!"

She jumped at the loud urgency of his tone. Then to her amazement he smiled softly, in a friendly, almost brotherly way, one arm encircling her as he gave her a gentle nudge into the car. Her legs folded beneath her and she sank gratefully into the seat, then she rolled down the window, her eyes suspicious.

"Go home," he told her. "Tuck your daughter in, soak in a nice hot bath, do as you normally would every other night. Don't even think of me or anything remotely connected to me. Pretend I don't exist, that we repulse each other or that the kiss never happened, whichever you prefer. Just carry on with your life, okay? And I'll see you later." He crouched down and, with one elbow resting on the window frame, tapped his forehead against hers. "Because *I* know a good thing when it hits me between the eyes." He tugged at her hair, then stood slowly. His knee creaked unmistakably. "Us old guys gotta make our moves before it's too late. Now git going."

Slowly Shanna drove away and stole a glance back at him. He was hobbling to his own car, then he leaped forward, flipped into a wild somersault, then landed miraculously on his two feet. Amidst the cloud of dust he waved at her. Her lips were twitching as she gave a single wave back.

CHAPTER SIX

DEREK AND RAY had to stand because there were more
bodies than chairs in the office. The curtains were drawn
across the glassed panel overlooking the desks of the
clerical staff, giving the meeting an air of conspiracy. The
group encircled Leo Morgan, a white-haired command-
ing figure at the head of a solid oak desk.

Janet Bowes, the personnel manager of Morgan's, occupied one of the black leather swivel chairs. A thin,
plain-looking woman with pinkish skin, mousy brown
hair and an unfortunate prominent jaw, she wore an
expression of the utmost seriousness, as if she herself
were partly responsible for the matter to be discussed.

The other chair was filled by the bulk of Jack Jalsevac, his prominent belly above his low-belted jeans made
more pronounced by his sitting position. Currently pos-
ing as a relief driver, he was the only suitless man in the
room. Perspiration lined his balding brow, most likely
due to the heat in the room. He didn't look like the kind
of man who would be intimidated because Leo had just
introduced him as the industrial security consultant he'd
recently hired and all eyes were upon him for an update.

"So what do you have for us, Jalsevac?" Leo asked
with the curt toughness that had built a trucking empire.
"You've been snooping around the dock for two weeks
now, at all hours. Surely you've come up with something." Derek knew Leo had paid top dollar for the

professional's services and he expected a return on his buck as soon as possible.

Jalsevac didn't hide his annoyance with his employer's impatience. "You know that tracking down criminals *properly* usually takes time. Most of 'em, professional or otherwise, aren't stupid enough to hit the same place all that frequently. Your own records and audits will attest to that. The missing shipments have appeared so sporadically over the last year that you didn't even think there was a problem at your end until the shortage on those aircraft parts was big enough to get everybody all fired up."

"On the small stuff, we took the rap for what we thought were merely customer accounting errors," Ray cut in. "We didn't think an investigation was worth jeopardizing good relations with our shippers—"

Leo froze him with a glance. "Just let Jalsevac get to the point."

The consultant, who'd kept a straight face until that point, let slip a suggestion of a self-satisfied smile. "Like I said, a couple weeks is hardly long enough for a problem of this nature, but I have a suspect for you. Nothing firm, but a good suspect." He waited for a curious gleam to light Leo's face, but none came.

"Go on," Derek said, indulging him, knowing his father rarely showed emotion.

"I've been keeping a close eye on your dock workers, because this kind of thing is usually an inside job. Office staff are too conspicuous in the warehouse. I was soon certain that one of your men, Roger Hartly, had served time."

"What made you so sure about that?" Derek asked sharply.

Jalsevac leaned forward, predatory-like. "I used to work as a prison guard at Kingston. To someone else, the signs might not be so obvious, but to me they were plain as day."

Derek continued to drill him. "Such as?"

"Oh, the way he cupped his cigarette, almost secretly in his hand, or the nervous way he kept looking around, even during coffee break. He was full of fear, mistrust. And that bitter look in his eye... I knew he'd spent a good few years behind the walls of a prison. Those places do strange things to a man. Even me. That's why I got out." He saw Derek's skeptical look. "Just to be sure, though, I did a routine check on him. Sure enough, he's served almost five years on three convictions—two were petty, but the last one, a gas station holdup, involved a gun."

He glanced around. For the first time, Leo's expression betrayed a glimmer of interest. Jalsevac went on, excited, gloating. "He's been out for about two years. He served the minimum for good behavior, but he's still on parole for another year. Whether he's responsible for stealing and double-crossing you, I can't say yet, but he *is* a prime suspect. I also confirmed he was working the night the three boxes disappeared, amidst all that chaos with the jackknifed trailer."

Silence fell in the room as he sat back. Janet Bowes reacted first, tugging at the sleeves of her navy business suit in agitation. "Well, I must admit that that news comes as a shock. I had a hand in hiring Roger myself, and not once did he mention any criminal record, verbally or on his application form, and it specifically asks—"

"Ex-cons rarely do," Jalsevac told her matter-of-factly. "Would you?"

"I—"

"I say we fire him right away," Leo interrupted abruptly. "It's clear he lied and I won't stand for that. If he's guilty of lying, who knows what else he's guilty of?"

Janet had worked with Leo for twenty years, and she knew when he tolerated gutsiness and when to bite her tongue. It was an acceptable time to rally back now; such an important decision could have sweeping consequences. "I agree that we have to deal with the lie, Leo. But let's be careful not to jump to conclusions about Roger's guilt. During his eighteen months here, he's been a reliable and steady employee."

"You're just protecting one of your brood, as you always do," Ray said, his blue eyes cool, ignoring her quick intake of breath. Looking to Leo for approval, he added, "I'm all for canning the guy, too. We have the legal right, don't we, because he lied on his application?"

Janet nodded, reluctantly murmuring, "Willful misconduct."

No love had ever been lost between those two, Derek knew. While Janet begrudgingly put up with Leo's tyranny because she admired his business acumen, she had no respect for the way Ray wielded authority in matters that didn't concern him, simply because he was the boss's son. For his part, Ray found Janet humorless. Plus, he secretly resented her unwavering dedication to her job—she had never married and rarely dated. No one, with the exception of Leo himself, put in so many hours. Ray feared her spotless record downgraded him in Leo's eyes whenever he needed time off for family-related emergencies.

"Also," Ray added, on a roll of self-aggrandizement, "Hartly's breached the basic trust needed between employer and employee. Luckily we're not unionized, so we don't have to go through a whole rigmarole. We can simply boot the guy."

"No."

From across the room, Ray shot Derek a dark, surprised look for his outburst. "Why not?"

Derek tapped his pen on the window ledge as he gathered his thoughts. "If we fire Hartly, even on legal grounds, a message is going to go out to the rest of the staff. No one will ever come forward for help, if it's needed, or reveal any weaknesses or mistakes. How are we going to deal with such problems if we're always two steps behind in discovering them?"

"That's a counterproductive attitude if I ever heard one," Ray said, shaking his dark-haired head.

"People aren't products," Derek countered hotly. "We've got the lowest turnover rate around because we treat our staff fairly. We're tough, but fair. Everyone will agree with that."

"Aren't you forgetting why we're here?" Leo studied Derek with characteristic shrewdness. "Someone is stealing from us and costing us a bundle, not to mention a lot of wasted time in figuring out what's going on behind our backs."

"I still haven't heard one bit of proof of Hartly's guilt. You got anything else?" Derek asked Jalsevac.

"No, but given time..."

"What makes you so sure he's innocent?" Leo was still staring at his second oldest son. "That *is* what you're saying, isn't it?"

"I have a gut feeling. That's all. I'm giving the guy the benefit of the doubt, if anything."

"So it's your gut feeling against ours," Leo said.

"Maybe, but everyone stands to lose if you're wrong." Derek saw the faintest crack of indecisiveness in Leo's demeanor and leaped on it. "Let me talk to Roger's parole officer. That'll give Jalsevac a chance to dig up something more concrete."

"Next, you'll be giving the guy a raise," Ray mumbled. "We gotta take a hard-line approach in these matters."

"No skeletons in your closet, Ray?" Janet asked coyly, effectively silencing him. His office indiscretions were common knowledge. "I'm with Derek, Leo. I think a degree of restraint is in order."

Strong disapproval creased Leo's brow. But to Derek's relief he ended the meeting with nothing more than a threat. "If you're wrong about this, Derek, and we waste more time and money..."

"Trust me, Dad," he said with the kind of powerfully persuasive smile that a television evangelist might use to reap millions.

In Leo's case, it only brought Derek a small reprieve. "One week."

"One week," Derek echoed, giving a thumbs-up signal to Jalsevac, who'd won another week of employment.

"No one say anything to Hartly," Jalsevac warned.

But as Derek left the room, ignoring the curious stares of the clerical staff and the dispatcher, he was thinking that wisely or not he intended to call Shanna and find out as much as he could about Roger Hartly. *If* Roger was indeed guilty, which Derek's instincts told him was not the case, at least he himself would save some face by helping to *prove* that. Maybe, through her association with Roger's wife, Shanna would know if Hartly had happened to come into any money recently or she would be able to give him another clue he could follow up. At least he finally had an excuse to call her.

His sudden luscious thoughts of her were decidedly inappropriate for the office, though. He decided to wait until he was in the privacy of his own home before he talked to her. He'd already waited a week—a long week for him, but strategically necessary, he figured, to let her defences drop again.

How and when the green-eyed widow had gotten under his skin, he wasn't sure. But she was there, all right, maddeningly so, despite his qualms and her reticence, which he was confident he could overcome—and determined to. He wanted her—with a blood-boiling excitement he hadn't felt in years. But then he was always best at beginnings, spurred on by the thrill of the chase, the challenge of obstacles, the lure of the unknown. Endings, however, were another story.

His relationship with Rachel had ended by coming to a slow, jerking halt. He sensed that with Shanna it would end in a sudden painful crash. But he was already well onto the course, and there was no going back....

MEGAN SLOWLY SKIRTED the playground at Victoria Park, watching the gaiety. Two young boys climbed the wooden tiers, then squirmed through tires and cascaded down tubes with ceaseless energy. Tripping in the sand, they ran from swing to slide and back. Their mothers, keeping an eye on them, laughed and chatted as one rocked a carriage.

Megan turned. She walked past the park pavilion and wandered along the path beside the winding waterway. She stopped on a bridge. Below, a platoon of ducks fought the currents of a man-made fountain until finally they were forced back the way they'd come. Gulls screeched overhead in a protest of their own.

Trees, gardens, lampposts, passersby, houses, seemed to merge and blur as Megan suddenly hastened her steps homeward. She hadn't been able to escape the claustrophobia of her basement apartment, after all, because that horrible boxed-in suffocating feeling was really within herself.

She'd told her psychiatrist once, several weeks ago, about that feeling. He'd said it was perfectly normal after what she'd been through. He'd said she should scream or cry any time she wanted to release her pent-up emotions. She'd thanked him for the permission, then never mentioned it again. She'd even managed to convince him the feeling was gone, or maybe he was just waiting her out. She didn't like or trust him; that much was for sure.

Today had started like every other day lately. She'd woken up, feeling completely and utterly alone. There was nothing to get up for. She'd lain there until she'd realized that today could be different, today could change everything. She could solve her money and job problems. She would never have to see Terry again and be reminded of the foolish girl she'd once been. She would never have to worry about the humiliation of love or its absence. She could make her mother sorry for betraying her.

She'd slowly packed up her belongings and tidied up. She'd taken the walk through the familiar park as a sort of goodbye ritual. But she hadn't felt nostalgia, only detachment.

She returned to her apartment. Impulsively she picked up the phone and dialed Derek Morgan's home number. She hardly knew him, but he'd been like a friend to her. His machine answered. The irony of it struck her as incredibly funny. She was going to hang up, then the beep sounded and she was talking. . . .

When she hung up, she looked at her watch. Seven o'clock. Maybe he was with Shanna. Anyone could see the desire in his eyes when he looked at Shanna. He'd never looked at her that way. Then again, Shanna had a healthy child to fascinate him, to stir his paternal instincts, to love.

The doctor had just renewed her prescription for sleeping pills, and without a second thought Megan swallowed the whole bottle, smiling because she knew she would be reunited with her own baby. . . .

THE GREEN LIGHT was blinking twice on Derek's answering machine when he came home. He almost ignored it, fearing that another of the problems that had bogged him down all day at Morgan's had cropped up and he was being summoned back. It was ten o'clock and he was dog-tired.

He loosened his tie and tossed his jacket over a chair, then curiosity won out. He hit the message button. The alterations on his new suit were completed; he could pick it up anytime. He breathed a sigh of relief, while crumpling a personally addressed envelope announcing he was eligible for a fifty million dollar sweepstake, again.

At first he barely recognized Megan's voice or what sounded like her muffled laughter. "Sorry, Derek. I never know what to say to these things. It's me, Megan. I just wanted to thank you for everything and to—to tell you I thought about this. And to wish you happiness. Do I have more time on this?" The line crackled as she paused, sniffed. "Looks like it. Anyway, why don't you give my teddy bear to Shanna's baby? It's not that I'm not grateful. Oh, what am I saying? Bye."

Something in her voice alarmed him more than the scrambled message. He called her back, but there was no answer. Grabbing his coat, he rushed out the door.

CHAPTER SEVEN

"WHAT DO YOU MEAN you quit the course already?" Shanna said with dismay into the telephone. "You hardly gave it a chance."

"I stuck it out for two classes. Any more and you wouldn't get a refund," her father replied in his unruffled fashion. "It just wasn't my bag."

"You did say you should learn to cook properly some day, didn't you?"

"Only in passing."

"And you love to eat *good* food, don't you?"

"Well, yes—"

"You are on a budget?"

"Of sorts."

"So a gourmet cooking class for the budget-minded would have been perfect," Shanna concluded, exasperated.

"You forgot to mention one thing when you so kindly enrolled me in it, without consulting me, I might add. That it was for the fifties-plus age group."

"What difference does that make?" Shanna asked as she rocked Alicia's recliner seat with her foot and shook a soft clown rattle at her.

"Let's just say the majority were well into their pluses. By a decade or two. I'm only fifty-six, Shanna."

Her foot stilled as she started to understand. "What's wrong with feeling younger than the rest? I could use that kind of tonic once in a while."

He went on blithely, without answering her question. "The other problem was that I happened to be the only man in the class. Among about twenty sweet little old ladies. I heard the life story of almost every one of them—whose husbands had passed away and how, where they were buried, whose mates had arthritis, heart problems, even constipation, I swear. It was downright depressing. And then there was the hounding."

He sounded so forlorn and hard-done-by that she suppressed a giggle. "Hounding?" she asked as nonchalantly as she could manage.

"Yes, hounding. My financial status seemed to be a popular topic of interest, among the widows especially. Although *that* I could dodge. It was the other suggestions that really threw me. Are modern women all that . . . forthright?"

This time Shanna couldn't resist a smile. "Weren't you even a tiny bit flattered, Dad? Was there no one there the least bit . . . interesting?"

"Was this whole scheme an unsubtle attempt on your part to do some matchmaking, Shanna? Because, if so—"

"Of course not," she said swiftly, knowing how very much alive her mother was in his heart and understanding his loyalty completely. "But you are going to have to deal with these kinds of things. You're a well-versed, handsome man. You're bound to meet lots of new people, male and female, and there's nothing wrong with cultivating friends."

"Friendship isn't the issue here," he said dryly.

Holding the receiver tightly, she spoke carefully, realizing she had to be more direct with him, but afraid of hurting his feelings. "Dad, I may have been wrong, but I thought the classes would have at least given you a night out, a change of scenery, some new faces. Maybe some other course—"

"I'm perfectly happy with the familiar scenery and faces, thank you. I've had enough changes lately. I—" He stopped, then began again in a quieter strained voice. "Are you sick of seeing me so much? Is that it, Shanna? I know it's a tough time for you, and I thought I'd help out a bit, but—"

"Oh, Dad, both Alicia and I love you and—and appreciate your help. It's just, well, I decided to take the initiative with the classes. You know how you always mean to get around to new stuff, but never do. Then once you were there, I'd hoped you would start to enjoy yourself...."

"I can look after my own life," he told her firmly.

She was up against his pride now. He was her father, after all, and he did so much for her. How could she be so ungrateful as to tell him he was infringing on her privacy, her space?

"So much for some of those gourmet feasts I was looking forward to," Shanna said, sighing in resignation. "Goodbye fettuccine Alfredo. So long baked Alaska."

"Oh, I meant to tell you," he said excitedly. "I found a little deli not far from here that makes the best lasagna. I'll bring a tray over tomorrow for dinner. I can never finish one myself."

"Okay, Dad..."

Later, as she was giving Alicia her overdue bottle—she still nursed her in the morning and late-evening, but planned to wean her fully soon—Shanna was contemplating her next strategy with her father. She hadn't given up on him by any means. She wanted him to be more self-sufficient, not only to give herself a break occasionally, but for his own sake, too. As much as he protested otherwise, she knew he wasn't as happy as he'd been when her mother had been alive. For one thing, he'd visited the doctor more in the last year or two for every ache, pain or digestion problem than he probably had in his whole adult life. She knew his biggest ailment was the hidden stress of grieving and all the adjustments he'd had to make in his life-style, not that he'd ever admit it. Shanna was familiar with such stresses, but at least she had Alicia. Ned needed some other activity, some all-absorbing outside interest or interests to take his wife's place. Getting him to try something new, though, was harder than moving a stubborn mule.

Maybe the problem was she had no idea how to reverse the roles she'd lived with for her thirty-five years. Although she and Ned were both mature adults, he was still her father and she wasn't used to bossing him around. He wasn't ill or senile, after all—just uncooperative in matters of change. She had no ready solutions as she set a dozing Alicia into her crib.

Suddenly the doorbell rang. At midday it could only be a salesperson or a neighbor. She was wrong. Derek Morgan stared at her through the screen. His exhausted appearance shocked her as she unlocked the door.

"Hi...come in. What's the matter?"

"Could I have some cold water, please?" he said in a strange flat voice. "I've been driving around and I'm parched."

His white shirt and charcoal gray suit pants were wrinkled, as if he'd slept in them; his dark hair was un-

combed, bushy; his shoulders slumped under a great in
visible weight; but his eyes, completely lusterless, worried
Shanna the most. She led him into the living room and he
sat on the sofa, robotlike. When he finished his tumbler
of water, a few moments later, he reached for the second
one in her hand, not noticing it had been intended for
herself.

"Megan died last night," he said, his hoarse words
shattering the silence like glass hitting a hard surface.
"She took her own life—an overdose of sleeping pills."

Stunned, Shanna could only stare at him.

"It's all of our faults and no one's fault but her own.
I spent most of the night coming to that double-edged
conclusion. And maybe it's as simple as a chemical im-
balance or as complex as all the experiences and influ-
ences that make up a life." He ran his fingers through his
hair as he'd probably done countless times. "I've talked
to a lot of official-type people, explaining what I found
at her apartment after I got her message on my machine,
doing what had to be done. I really can't talk about it
anymore, not yet, okay?"

"Okay..." Shanna found her voice, sank to the car-
peted floor, leaned against the plush navy-and-peach-
colored couch near him.

Derek seemed barely aware of his surroundings. Absently he picked up the colorful clown. "Where is Alicia, anyway?"

"Sleeping."

"That's next on my agenda," he said, making the effort to smile, looking at her for the first time. "I had to
see you first."

"Why?"

"I don't know." His eyes searched hers with needle-
like precision, flamelike heat. "Yes, I do know. I like

being with you. You're beautiful and different and intriguing. I think you're good for me, too. We *are* going to be a greater part of each other's lives, aren't we?''

The emotion he'd stirred in her from the moment he'd walked through the door, in need, his barriers down, sifted into her voice as she was compelled to answer simply, "Yes."

"Good."

In one smooth motion, he pushed himself down beside her, stretching out his legs. His arm had landed on her shoulders where it stayed, carelessly intimate, as natural as if they sat side by side every night, perhaps watching television or reading the paper. Shanna's vivid awareness of his presence, though, transformed the ordinariness of their position, penetrating beneath her clothing and skin to the places where pulses hammered and nerves tingled. Derek, however, became more distant and preoccupied the longer they sat there.

"You know, I was only seven when my mom died, and I felt like this, too," he finally said, and his voice sounded so normal he could have been talking about the weather.

Shanna wasn't fooled. "How?"

His jaw was sawing back and forth, barely perceptibly, but no emotion showed on his face as he considered his answer. "She had an aneurysm one day, and we came home from school and she was just . . . gone. I remember I never cried. All I felt was a—a great blank. How do you describe a big horrible nothing? Is that how it was when you lost your own mother? Or Michael?"

"No . . ." She drew out the word. "I hurt each time. It was like icy daggers were piercing me." But she didn't want to talk about that today. "Who looked after you?" she asked softly, drawing him back.

He snickered as a host of boyhood memories flooded him. "Oh, we had a string of housekeepers. I guess you'd call them nannies now. They never lasted long, though. Ray and I competed at bullying them, I'm afraid. Terry was only a baby, at first, but he soon caught on."

"And your dad?"

"Dad? I suppose he did his best to keep us in line. He certainly didn't believe in sparing the rod, whenever we saw him, which wasn't too often. He started Morgan's up, from barely nothing, and gave it one-hundred-and-ten percent for quite a few years. Now he's cut back to about ninety-nine percent," he added wryly, his fingers drumming her shoulders and running through the soft strands of her hair, almost unconsciously.

Shanna's mental image of the hard-driving, unaffectionate Leo Morgan was completely opposite to her own lenient and doting—albeit overprotective—father. Derek had not been deprived in any material sense, she gathered, but he had certainly been shortchanged when it came to receiving any constant loving warmth after his mother's death.

He stood abruptly and walked to the window, his restlessness barely contained. "You know, most of us just take our life for granted. We work and feel important at whatever we do, we make money so that we can own more and more, we get married, maybe divorced, we have children and custody battles or neither, if we've managed to avoid all that—" he shot her a guilty look "—but we all hope to retire some day and look back on it all with some degree of satisfaction...." He stopped, his neck flushed. "Megan's death is as senseless as my mother's was, but just as inevitable. It could be me tomorrow or next year, and what would I have? A nice gold plate on my office door with some impressive title? A lot of GICs that haven't matured? A few women who'd say the same about me? It's all so ludicrous," he finished wearily.

Shanna realized that Megan's sudden death had released something in Derek, like a spring on a tightly coiled trap. Although his eyes were dry, he was crying inside. He couldn't answer his own questions and she understood such helplessness. His special lightness had slowly eased her pain since she'd known him, and now she moved toward him, wanting only to ease his.

Her arms slipped around his neck, turning him from the window. She paused, but not out of hesitation. Gently one finger traced the outline of his lips, committing their perfect shape to memory, preparing them for the bountiful softness that was to follow. Her head tilted, yet the meeting of lip upon lip was in perfect alignment. Their mouths moved together, the melting warmth suffusing upward, downward, within, to Shanna's very bones. As Derek relaxed, the kiss, intended to be one of comfort, swiftly grew into more. Yet Shanna no longer felt threatened, perhaps because she'd taken the initiative.

In those intense moments she also realized just how much she had missed her old self. Since Michael's death, her sexuality had been locked away, frozen, in a place she'd dared not visit. But Derek Morgan was leading her back there, thawing her, renewing her. What's more, she finally acknowledged, after the birth of Alicia her womanhood had ripened into a deep hungry need, different from what she remembered, as frightening as it was strong.

When Derek's lips eased away and trailed with tantalizing slowness along the column of her throat, her head arched backward. At the same time, her fingers curled deeper into the thick mat of his hair. Just as their lips had aligned moments ago, their hips pressed together in perfect comfort. Derek's male firmness had the opposite effect on her, making her feel pliant and weak.

Shanna's light blue blouse and wraparound skirt offered no protection from the heat, shocking in its fury, that was spreading along her flesh, like a fire gone out of control. Their lips joined again. Despite the melding moistness, flames continued to spread.

Although Derek had not touched her breasts directly, he'd brushed against them with his chest and they were aching with a sweet torment. Either he sensed his omission or he was following a natural order of sensuous exploration. His hand, in confident Derek Morgan fashion, slipped beneath her shirt then and stroked her through the soft fabric of her nursing bra. The circles grew smaller until he centered on her hardened nipple, sending an arrow of pleasure through her.

His hand stilled. Slowly his lips left hers. He was looking at her in surprise and she suddenly understood. Shifting mental gears, she proceeded to enlighten him why her breasts were leaking, even though she had started to wean Alicia....

Derek listened to her shy explanation, his hand reluctantly dropping away from the fullness of her breast. He murmured, in a low uneven voice, "I'm sorry. I didn't think—"

"It doesn't bother me, if it doesn't bother you," she murmured back, her breath sweet and warm as it fanned his cheek.

Bother him! The knowledge was sending erotic signals to nerve endings already overcharged by the driving need in his loins. Shanna's natural earthy quality had always attracted him, and now, with this new awareness, her womanhood took on a powerfully intimate dimension.

"No, I don't mind at all. In fact, I'm quite fascinated by everything about you. You're driving me wild," he said, grinning as he pulled her by the hand toward the couch, guiding her down lengthways, leaning over her, half-sitting, half-lying.

"What are you doing?" The wild tumble of her hair about her face, the passionate lights in her eyes and the sexy laugh that caught on her lips made a mockery of the innocent question.

"I haven't slept all night. Doesn't a guy have the right to lie down?" As he stretched beside her, she was forced to turn sideways. Their legs playfully entwined until all four found a comfortable place.

"Aren't the quarters rather cramped?"

"Just the way I like them...."

He couldn't take his eyes away from the green splendor of hers, having watched the longing in them become incredibly vibrant, as if a thick veil had been lifted. For the first time, he realized, she'd opened herself to him in a deeply intimate sense and he couldn't bear being shut out again. She'd also managed to ward off the demons that had plagued him, transforming his cynicism into a swelling joy to be alive because he was with her. His lips didn't have far to go to kiss her again, with a surprising tenderness.

He proceeded to prove to her just how inventive he could be within a limited space. His kiss was no less thorough; his hands were easily able to rove the silky smooth curves of her back, sliding an amazing distance down her bare legs, then becoming even more familiar with her breasts, which he managed to behold for the first time after a few deft maneuvers of buttons and fastenings. She was lovelier than he'd imagined, lush, womanly in a way that increased his desire for her almost more than he could stand.

He wanted to make love to her more than he had wanted anything in his life. But he also knew that he should wait—even if that waiting would be the worst torment he'd ever had to endure—not only for Shanna's sake, but for his own, too, for reasons he couldn't define. So he tried not to lose control, concentrating instead on the physical closeness he needed today almost as much as physical completion. He savored the sweetness of discovery, the wonderful scent, taste, feel of her. Yet he was incapable of moving away from her, of deciding which sensuous moment would be the last.

When she sat up abruptly, or more accurately wiggled to a semiupright position, he felt almost as much relief as disappointment because his good intentions were being put to the supreme test and eroding fast....

Her face wore an unexpected expression—a mix of shock, pain and puzzlement. She was craning her neck as she pulled at her clothes. "Alicia..."

Distractedly, he heard the distant cry, too. His legs dropped to the floor as he swiveled around, letting her pass by him. "That's okay. I'm familiar with time-outs, at least in other sports. Sometimes they are good strategy," he added on a long intake of breath. His arm held her back before she bolted away, and he planted one final lingering kiss on her warmed lips. "To be continued?"

She didn't answer, staring at him with a half-lost, half-languorous look. Suddenly he knew she was remembering her husband, maybe comparing the two of them, or worse, using him to exorcise the other man's ghost. His chest constricted tightly. Nothing in his confident smile,

though, showed the unsettling sharp turn his thoughts
had taken....

SHANNA CARRIED DEREK'S self-assured gaze with her as
she ran up the stairs to Alicia's room. Guilt flooded
through her as if she'd neglected her child longer than the
few moments she'd been crying. Shanna recognized that
she needed a life of her own, but whether that life involved Derek Morgan was the big question; whether she
was ready yet was an even bigger one.

As much as she'd tried to block out thoughts of Michael, he'd returned to haunt her—strangely as soon as
she'd begun to lose herself in the pleasurable world Derek
offered. Maybe a part of her had willed Michael back,
but why? Fear of starting over? Fear of Derek Morgan?
Fear of the mysterious new depths in herself?

It took longer than usual to calm Alicia. As she started
to undress her for changing, she hummed along with the
Brahms lullaby on Alicia's animal mobile, her usual
practice, but today she needed the soothing, too. Alicia
chortled back, kicking her feet joyfully. Shanna wished
that she herself could be as carefree and that her mind
could feel as rejuvenated as her body undoubtedly did.

A sound came from the doorway. She wondered how
long he'd been watching her. After his eyes had brazenly
reminded her of their interrupted activity, Derek surveyed the nursery, from the bright border of balloons and
clowns, her father's wallpapering handiwork, to the zoo
of stuffed animals that toppled over each other on every
available surface.

"Quite the place," he said, looking disoriented.

"No lack of stimulation here."

He came up behind her, his arms slipping around her,
warmly, familiarly. "I'll second that motion."

His closeness was exciting, disturbing with Alicia awake. "How would you like the enriching experience of changing a diaper?" she suddenly asked, hoping to throw him off balance until she could get back on track herself.

Without missing a beat he replied, "I'm game, as long as you're the teacher."

His fingers moved in slow circles on her waist. Her own hands topped his before gently easing them away and facing him, eyes dancing. "Okay, lesson one. Tidy removal of Exhibit A, otherwise known as the dirty diaper. Then, the tools of the trade." While Alicia stared curiously at the two of them, Shanna proceeded to explain the order and purpose of the various powders, creams and cloths she used.

"Got it," he said with utmost seriousness when she'd finished. "I didn't realize it was such a complicated affair."

"Next, the physics of the diaper itself. Tabs go this way. Like so." She positioned the clean diaper under Alicia. "She's all yours. Aim for a tight but comfortable fit."

With bumbling fingers and a brow creased with the deepest concentration, he set to work. No sooner did he join tab to band in perfect alignment when one of the ends broke free. "Very funny. You've given me a defective one," he said indignantly.

Shanna laughed. "You must have brushed the sticky part with some Vaseline."

Shaking his head in self-disgust, he tossed the diaper away. "Give me another one. I'll get this right yet." And very slowly, as if mastering a scientific feat for a Nobel prize, he repeated the steps he'd been shown, then cried out in glee, "Presto! You're ready to conquer the world now, kiddo.'' Alicia grunted at him, and he smiled back, clearly pleased with his accomplishment.

"Don't be so hasty." Shanna pretended to look stern. "The final lesson is efficient tidy up." She rolled up the old diaper for him and tossed it into the pail, then reorganized the cleaning aids.

"A piece of cake," he drawled.

As Shanna searched through Alicia's drawer for a new outfit, she saw Derek carefully pick up her daughter, who looked so tiny in his large masculine arms and a little bemused by the awkward grasp.

Gaining confidence, he adjusted his hold until Alicia was peering over his shoulder. Gently, timidly, he patted her back. Alicia appeared quite comfortable.

"I've never held a baby before," he admitted. "It's kind of neat. They smell nice, at least."

"That's all the baby powder you dumped on her," Shanna said dryly, feigning mild interest in the sleeper she held up, hiding her rush of emotion as suddenly she was reminded that Michael would never hold his own child.

Derek roamed around the room, giving Alicia and himself a well-animated tour of the contents. To Shanna he remarked, "Activity blanket, activity elephant, activity books—even her socks are psychedelic—when does this child ever rest?"

But Shanna's attention was caught by the reddening of Alicia's face and her familiar noises. "I think Alicia needs a new diaper." Derek looked at her disbelievingly, then groaned. When he went to hand her back, Shanna shook her head. "This time, from scratch, without any professional consultation."

With great exaggerated gestures, and no shortage of complaints, he set out once more to prove he'd mastered the fine art of diapering.

Derek continued in his playful mood during the few hours that Alicia was awake. Shanna watched him in surprise because he really was quite good with her. Perhaps it was the novelty, she told herself. Whatever the reason, his efforts to amuse or quiet Alicia were sometimes bumbling, but always sincere. Endearingly sincere. Shanna didn't comment on his attentiveness, though, for fear of making him self-conscious about it.

He didn't mention Megan again, nor did Shanna bring up the subject, knowing he needed psychological distance from the disturbing events of the previous night. Alicia went back to sleep at four o'clock, after Derek had been there a surprising three hours. Needing to fill the conversational lull after she returned from the nursery, Shanna finally asked him why he didn't seem in any hurry to get back to his job.

"I called to let my secretary know why I wouldn't be in today. I thought I'd be sleeping, but here I am. I must be on my sixth or seventh wind by now."

"Would you like a coffee?" she asked belatedly.

"That would be great."

While she was preparing it, Derek stood in the doorway of the airy kitchen, looking more gorgeous than any man had a right to, Shanna thought. His dark tousled hair, the cocky tilt to his head, his lazy blue eyes and well-proportioned all-male body were bad enough. But today he'd displayed a vulnerability beneath his usual unflappable veneer that had made her less resistant to exposing her own vulnerability. Shedding that layer of self-protection scared her. If she wasn't careful Derek Morgan could hurt her—badly. She hadn't had a chance to toughen up yet, as she knew she would have to should she begin to play the dating game in earnest.

He was studying her relentlessly. When she heard him mention someone else, Roger Hartly, she felt a keen relief. "What was that?" she asked, unplugging the whistling kettle.

"I was wondering how Roger and Kim—that's his wife's name, isn't it—are getting along?"

"Why?" She glanced at him sharply.

He shrugged, outwardly nonchalant, but she hadn't missed the shrewdness that had glimmered in his eyes as quickly as the flicker of a firefly.

"I don't know . . . he seemed particularly edgy at work lately. Enough to make his foreman mention it to me. But don't say anything to Roger or Kim, in case it doesn't amount to anything," he added hastily.

"Well, everything seemed fine between them, last week, at least. Of course, money's always a problem, but who doesn't worry about that these days?" She handed him the steaming mug, reluctant to discuss the Hartlys any further.

"Does Roger seem like an honest sort of fellow to you?"

"What kind of question is that? Sure, he's honest. Hard-working, devoted to Kim and Teddy. But you already know that."

"Did Kim ever say what Roger was doing before she met him? They've only been married a short while, haven't they?"

Shanna nodded. "She didn't say much."

She went to move past him, but his hand shot out to stop her. "But she did say something?"

Shanna succeeded in getting by him, so she wouldn't have to look at him as she thought how to evade the question. Kim had confided in her, friend to friend, about Roger's bitterness about his past, and Shanna would never violate such trust. "Roger's a very private person. Kim respects that, as we all should." Despite her curiosity, Shanna refused to probe into Derek's motives for asking about Roger, knowing he'd only try to bait her further.

He assessed her, saw her reticence was unshakable, then switched tracks. "Perhaps some of us could learn from Roger then," he said, softly blowing on his hot coffee. "If indeed he is successful at putting his past behind him and starting over, on a clean slate...."

"I *am* trying, if that's what you're getting at," she retorted, tired of talking in circles.

"I know you are. And I've elected myself to be your aide."

Aide. An apt choice of words, Shanna thought, because of its military connotations. Derek's persistence was a kind of force, his charm and sexiness weapons he knew how to use to advantage. He was determined to help her deprogram her heart and brain from all that marriage to Michael had meant to her and from the lingering pain of his death. But if he succeeded at the task he'd set for himself—seducing her—what then? She couldn't help but think that Derek would only act as a bandage to her wounds, but that the invisible scars would never heal.

"What do *you* hope to gain from a relationship with me?" she asked point-blank, her eyes holding his.

He set his coffee down on a table and moved closer. "The same thing you stand to gain. Many delightful hours together." His hands took hers and set them around his waist, leaning into her. Then placing his own arms on her shoulders, he glanced down at her with provocative eyes.

"I don't think you really understand, Derek," she said slowly, unable to move away from his solid warmth, conscious of the needs he wrenched open inside her with butcherlike carelessness. "My *life* fell apart, everything I held dear, and you talk so—so flippantly, as if mere hours will make it all right again."

His expression sombered instantly and he pulled her close enough to feel the steady rhythm of his heartbeat. "I don't mean to be...flippant, Shanna." He stopped, began again in a muffled voice, his cheek buried in her hair. "I've come to a crossroads of sorts, too. I need more than what I've had with other women, but I don't know how much. I'll take whatever you want to give. It's crazy, but that's the way it is."

Shanna had lost contact with his eyes, her usual telescope to the truths behind his outer facade, but his words were as genuine as gold.

He pulled back, far enough to meet her gaze. Blue fused with green as he murmured, "I can't leave without kissing you again." His lips sought hers with a powerful language all their own, a sweet, tender vocabulary, familiar and new at the same time.

Their bodies swayed, then regrounded as Shanna's hand slipped beneath his bunched-up shirt to rest in the heated hollow of his torso and his fingertips slid under her curtain of hair to apply wonderfully firm pressure points between her neck and shoulders. A slow fire started burning in Shanna again, crackling, then spreading with lightening speed.

"Hmm...I was wrong about the hours," he said huskily, close to her ear. "A few minutes like that can keep a lonely guy going a long time."

She grimaced at his boyish, extremely hard-done-by tone.

"See, you need me around to keep you smiling. Admit it."

"True enough, although Alicia does her share in that department, too." Softly she added what had to be said, "I can't just think of myself anymore, you know, my needs. Alicia's part of my life—and my choices, too."

Shanna wasn't sure if he stiffened or if she'd just imagined it, so subtly did his body shift position. But her doubts were dispelled with his next words. "Shanna, I have to tell you...I think your daughter is very neat...but if you're looking for a substitute father, I'm sorry, I'm not the one. We can share everything else. I—"

"How dare you presume—" She wrenched away from him, almost tripping as she stepped back. Loyalty to Michael, protectiveness toward Alicia, whom Derek had just dismissed so carelessly, and the need to protect herself, all arose within her as she faced him, green eyes blazing.

"Alicia is everything to me right now. She is my miracle, my gift, all that is possible on earth," she said, her voice clear, low. "You have no idea what I want for her or for the two of us. I don't even know. And you're a part of that giant, terrifying unknown."

He reached to touch her, but she shook him away, refusing to brush away the tears of indignation welling up in her eyes. "I think you should go now."

"I'm sorry to have offended you," he began, but his apology was ineffective against her outrage. "I want to be honest with you. I'm used to being on my own. I know my limitations and my strengths. I'm not ready for such a responsibility. I can't let you think I'm someone I'm not."

"Please go...."

This time he listened to her. Shanna didn't remember what civilities they exchanged as they parted. She only knew that everything good that had happened between them had been sullied with his words. And that her disappointment in him—irrational as it might be—was as strong as her anger. He'd been right, though. She shouldn't hope he was someone different.

CHAPTER EIGHT

AFTER MEGAN'S DEATH, Derek was more determined than ever to help Roger Hartly out of his own difficulties. As soon as he returned to work, he set out to find Roger's parole officer. Numerous phone calls later, even more than he'd expected when dealing with any government branch, he finally tracked down Kevin Ford. He was off sick.

The following day, Derek attended Megan's small funeral service with Terry, which rekindled all his dark emotions about her death. But his younger brother had taken the shocking turn of events even harder; he was uncharacteristically silent. Derek had to extend the awkward condolences to her family, arrange for flowers, drive from church to cemetery and keep up the appearance of normalcy.

After the service, as they were walking along a quiet side street toward their cars, he asked if Terry was interested in grabbing a quick lunch.

"Sorry, but I'm not really hungry. I think I'll just go home. I have to see the superintendent."

"Leaky faucet?" Derek asked dryly, frustrated by his unsuccessful attempts to draw Terry out about Megan.

"No. Actually I'd like to sublet my apartment or break my lease, if necessary. I'm moving to Toronto as soon as I can. I'll be staying with some buddies until I get my own place."

Derek stopped. "This is rather sudden, isn't it?"

"Not sudden enough. I need a change. Badly."

Terry was still moving, so Derek had to hurry to catch up to him. "Ter, I know you're feeling guilty about Megan. We all do, but don't be overly hard on yourself—"

"Let me feel guilty, okay? I *need* to feel guilty." His raised hand punctuated his words as he faced his brother with tormented eyes. "I was incredibly thoughtless toward Megan and I've got a lot of belated thoughts now, believe me. I *know* I had a lot to do with her death, so let me deal with that, okay. Don't gloss over it. I did that to myself long enough before all this happened." Terry turned away quickly and in a few long strides had reached his car where he fumbled with his keys.

"So what are you going to do in Toronto?" Derek asked in a quiet voice, close behind him.

"Find a job."

"Where?"

"I only know where I *don't* want to work. Anywhere related to tennis—I've finally outgrown that part of my life. Or in an office. I can't sit still long enough." The two men shared a brief smile of acknowledgment.

"Well, in a city that size there has to be some place you can fit in."

"I have this—this idea of finding a job that will suit *me*, my energy and drive, instead of molding myself to fit a job, but we'll see. Most of all, I'd like to learn to laugh again. The old ways of having fun don't work anymore, haven't for a long time. I can only play tennis with friends if we rally. No scoring." He hesitated, began again. "And since I've been back from France, I haven't gone to bed with a woman or even *wanted* to. After what happened with Megan, I'm still afraid—afraid, do you believe it?—

to try again with someone else." He looked away self-consciously. "This is strictly confidential, okay?"

"Of course. But there's nothing wrong with giving a new relationship time to develop, either," Derek added, thinking of his own slow-growing and confusing involvement with Shanna.

Something in his tone caused Terry to focus on him. "You haven't slept with Shanna yet, have you?" he asked carefully, disbelievingly.

Their eyes met and held. "No, I haven't."

"It looks like all the Morgans are losing the old touch," Terry said with a spark of his familiar light-heartedness. "Or are you just figuring out new touches?"

Derek smirked. "Just keep it to yourself, okay?"

"Okay."

"And Terry—don't be a stranger." He knocked spiritedly on the hood of the car as Terry finally eased himself into the driver's seat.

After turning on the ignition, Terry inserted a tape into his elaborate stereo system. The rumble of the engine was immediately drowned out by the blast of sound from the speakers. "I like to *feel* my music. See you," he shouted at Derek through the open window as he pulled away.

While driving his own car back to Morgan's, Derek deliberately didn't turn on the radio, needing the comfort of silence rather than the distraction of noise. He thought of Shanna. He hadn't spoken to her since his visit two days earlier simply because he'd been too preoccupied with other matters, and that very fact caused him to wonder if he *was* indeed the wrong person to be pursuing her, as she'd implied the last time they'd been together. But the thought of anyone else with her was just...unthinkable. The fight about Alicia ate at him, too, but he couldn't change the way he felt. All he could hope for was that once Shanna's mourning for her deceased husband ended and she became involved even more intimately with himself, the fatherhood issue would slip into the background for the duration of their time together. He couldn't explain his strong notion that they needed each other now, despite their differences.

More pressing at the moment, though, was his determination, bordering on obsession, to save Roger from an unjust dismissal. Kevin Ford was his only link between the ex-con's past and present. Immediately after returning to his office, he telephoned Ford again and to his relief he was in. Derek explained the reason for his call. He instantly sized up the parole officer as relatively young and idealistic, not seasoned enough yet to hide his extreme distress at the suspicions surrounding Roger because of his past.

"He told me he'd been straight with you about his record," Ford said in his own defense right away. "But you gotta see things from his point of view, man. The chances of something like this happening are ten times higher than if he had no black marks against him."

Derek's secretary, Joan, appeared at his door, but he waved her away. When she'd gone he replied, "That may be true, but there's still a lot of heat around here to solve the problem—and it's a big one. Thousands of dollars worth of freight are missing, and Roger, unfortunately, is the obvious suspect."

"I'm telling you, not only would Roger be devastated if he lost his job, so would his wife. They've got a young kid now. It would affect all their lives." Ford spoke quickly, hotly, arguing strenuously in Roger's defense, as if for himself. "A secure job is one of the most important factors in keeping an ex-con out of trouble. Hasn't he been a good employee?"

"Excellent. That's one of the reasons I have my doubts about his guilt."

"I know Roger and I can't see him blowing everything he's worked so hard to build up again. He's been real cooperative with me since his release, about a year and a half ago, I think. Yeah," he confirmed after rustling some papers. "The first six months after getting out are the big high-risk period, and Roger got through them, no problem. He met his wife and that stability made all the difference. Sometimes I can't believe he's the same guy who got himself into such a mess, but he's one of the lucky ones who benefited from rehabilitation. He made a few mistakes, but he paid for them and he deserves a second chance."

Derek was convinced that to Kevin Ford, Roger wasn't just another case. The parole officer believed in his innocence at Morgan's and was fiercely protective of him. Wearily Derek ran his fingers through his hair. "I agree with you, and I'll do my best to persuade the others around here. But you can't ignore the fact that he lied to us. I'm afraid we'll have to confront him about his record."

"Just inform Roger it became known during a general investigation, but," Kevin added earnestly, "assure him his job isn't in jeopardy. He'll probably be incredibly relieved to have the truth out in the open, and I bet he'll become an even more loyal worker. He's not stupid. He'll realize you could have treated him a lot more severely."

Again Joan appeared at Derek's window, waving a paper urgently for a signature, scrunching her face up as if to say, "Please?" He nodded at her, holding up his finger for her to wait a little longer. "I have to go now, but I've heard what you're saying. I'll call a meeting soon to inform everyone of your advice. I hope they'll listen to reason, which, believe me, isn't always the case."

"If there's anything else I can do to help, just call me any time. Here's my home number."

Derek jotted it down. "Roger's a lucky man to have you rooting for him."

"And you, too."

Derek hung up the phone and Joan was immediately at his side, sidetracking him with other business matters....

"OKAY, KIM, I'll read the statement aloud once only, so listen carefully. Then you read the four sentences in your book, choose which is closest in meaning to the one you just heard, and mark it on your answer sheet. Ready?"

"R-ready," Kim said loudly, enunciating the *r* with far more vigor than she had been capable of weeks ago.

Later Shanna would work with her on toning down her pronunciation, but for now she was pleased with her improvement. "Statement number one," she began. "Susan ordinarily meets her husband for lunch. But today he's out of town on business."

Shanna waited the fifteen seconds allowed for this testing segment of the TOEFL model exam. Kim weighed whether Susan was out of town; she ate without her husband today; she and her husband ate lunch in town today; or she usually eats alone. Shanna realized for the umpteenth time in her many years of teaching how difficult the vocabulary, syntax and subtleties of the English language could be to someone of another tongue, even a student as quick-minded and eager to learn as Kim.

With bravado Kim answered promptly, "The answer is B. Susan ate without her husband today."

"Good!"

"Easy as pie," Kim told her with satisfaction, repeating a favorite expression she'd picked up recently.

Last Friday, a week ago, Shanna had attempted to test Kim on longer dialogues and prose passages, but Kim had scored so poorly and felt so discouraged afterward that Shanna had decided to keep this lesson more manageable in order to restore her self-confidence. "We only have nineteen more statements to go. We'll check the answers at the end this time, okay?"

"Okay. I think I'm on a r-roll."

Shanna smiled as they got down to business again. She was thoroughly enjoying the one-on-one contact of her tutoring sessions, but she knew she was being spoiled for when she had to return to her teaching post in September. Class sizes had been steadily increasing since she'd completed her teacher's degree and certified ESL courses almost fifteen years ago.

Suddenly behind them the apartment door opened and slammed so hard they both jumped. Roger stormed in, his churlish expression sending a stab of fear through Shanna. Her eyes flew to the closed bedroom door where Teddy slept, but thankfully the noise hadn't awakened him.

"What is wrong?" In contrast to Roger's reddened face, color had drained from Kim's. She stood, reached to touch him, but instead her hand caught the grease-stained overalls he was flinging to the floor.

"Leo Morgan just fired me," he ground out, his voice deadly calm.

Kim just stared at him, speechless, aghast. Shanna had been debating whether to leave discreetly, but all such thoughts fled as she blurted out, "Why on earth?"

"He was angry as hell. Another missing order—a huge one—showed up on the invoices today." His hands were shaking as he sat and pulled off his safety boots, then lit a cigarette, staring back at them, not only in defiance but with a pained, beaten look that tore at Shanna's heart.

"Why did he fire *you*?" Kim asked slowly, her back straight, her eyes deeply concerned as she looked at her husband, who had crumpled in his chair like an old scarecrow without his stuffing.

Roger used his cigarette to draw a deep steadying breath, then seemed to exhale endlessly. "I spent a few years in prison, a lifetime ago, or that's the way it feels now," he finally said coldly, lifelessly. "I never told anyone at Morgan's. It was none of their damn business and they probably wouldn't have hired me if they'd known, even though I wasn't bonded or anything. Ex-cons are branded; we might as well wear a sign across our foreheads—Don't Trust Me. Morgan said he was firing me for lying about my record. I know better. He thinks I'm his thief. I'm not."

For the first time he looked at Kim to gauge her reaction, his small eyes weary, his anger dissolving into helplessness.

"I believe you," she said firmly. "But how could you keep your secret from me—your wife?" Her expression was as hurt as Roger's; they'd both been betrayed.

Shanna was afraid to interrupt the fragile communication. The couple appeared to have forgotten her presence.

Roger finally answered with a dark, chilling bitterness. "I wanted to put it all behind me. To start over with you. I thought I had. Now I wonder if there was any point in going straight."

Kim, whose limbs had been immobile as her brain had tried to make sense of his words, moved toward him then and sank to the floor beside his chair. She took his hand, stroking it with the same force that was in her voice. "No! No! No! You must not say that."

"I'll probably lose you, too," he continued in self-pity, staring at his hands.

"Of course not, but you must not lie to me again."

"I never lied. But I was afraid of the truth. In case you wouldn't want me. And I needed you so badly." His voice finally broke, but his arms lay rigid at his sides.

Without any hesitation, Kim rose to her knees and wrapped her arms around her husband. "I would have known, who you were before, you are no more," she murmured as he buried his face in her hair.

Shanna saw how shaken the two were at the grossly unfair turn of events. She remembered Derek's mysterious probing about Roger. Anger welled up in her. Surely he'd known this was going to happen and surely he had the power to correct the wrong done.

She stood abruptly, suddenly aware of the cramping in her legs. "I'm calling Derek Morgan," she announced quietly, and they both jumped at the unexpected sound of her voice. Lost in their shattered world, neither bothered to object.

The phone was on the kitchen wall, and Shanna turned her back to give them a semblance of privacy. After reaching the operator, she dialed Morgan's, counting to ten to control her rising anger. She was told Derek was in a meeting. She insisted on waiting for him, stressing the urgency of her call.

"You'll have to get in line," his secretary told her dryly. "Mr. Morgan is a busy man."

"I'll wait," Shanna repeated. Her impatience building, she wrapped and unwrapped the phone cord around her fingers. Although Kim and Roger spoke in low tones, their voices still carried to Shanna in the confines of the apartment.

"I think is time you tell me what happened...before," Kim was saying softly, encouragingly, without any condemnation.

Keeping her back turned, Shanna could hear the springs of the chair as Roger shifted uncomfortably. "I don't know where to start."

"Does your family know?"

"Oh, yes," he said with a renewed harsh bitterness that made Shanna feel as if she'd been stung. "They knew, all right. They never want to see or hear from me again. I was their only child, and they said they preferred to be childless after I disgraced them."

There was a shocked silence. "But what did you do and why?" Kim finally asked.

"I was never good enough for them, anyway," Roger said, evading the question or perhaps answering it in his own way. "I never did well in school, hated it as a matter of fact. Dad was a doctor, a heart specialist, and Mom was a philosophy professor at the University of Toronto. They didn't hide their disappointment in me very well. Finally, in high school, they switched me to a technical course, hoping I'd get a degree, even if it was *only* in the trades. I dropped out."

"Why?"

"I don't know. I guess I was used to failure by then. I started hanging out with guys who at least accepted me the way I was. Mom called them 'shiftless.'" He laughed stonily at the memory. "We got into some trouble. My folks bailed me out the first time, kicked me out the second. My buddies and I needed money, so we pulled a few holdups. Small stuff, really, just to get a start. At what, I don't know, but something. We got careless...and caught."

"You are different now. You have found your place. You were punished for breaking the law and you have a new life, a good job—"

"Had," Roger reminded her.

Shanna stole a glance at Roger over her shoulder as he reached for one last drag on the cigarette that had burned down in the ashtray. She saw a victim of child abuse, not physical abuse, but psychological. Roger's parents had committed a form of violence against their son by making him feel inadequate, suppressing his emerging sense of self-esteem and lighting a fuse of rebellion that had exploded years later when he'd turned to crime. Roger, though, seemed to have survived the prison ordeal, his sense of decency rebuilt, intact. Until now...

Roger stared back at her and realized why she was still holding the receiver. "Just give up."

"No," she told him. "No."

"THE GUY WAS IN PRISON for five years, Dad. Five years. He already paid his debt to society or whoever the hell makes the rules, whoever helped make him the way he was."

Derek faced his father, more furious than he'd ever been. He'd just learned of Leo's rash firing of Roger Hartly without any more evidence or before Derek had had a chance to call his meeting. But Derek could tell immediately from his father's impassive expression that his anger would get him nowhere.

Leo had always encouraged his sons to stand up for what they believed, with one exception. They didn't get too far when they crossed swords with him. Derek dared not accuse his parent of taking out his anger at the recent thefts on the most convenient scapegoat, Roger Hartly. Leo would shut him out completely. He tried another tack instead.

"By firing Hartly the way you did," he pointed out in a more rational tone, "what you're really saying is, he's only paid the interest on his past misdeeds, but not the debt. That's a case of loansharking on your part, as far as I'm concerned. And *that* is against the law."

"An interesting argument," Leo replied, in an infuriatingly calm voice, "but I made up my mind long before you stormed through that door, Derek. Hartly lied, and we don't need people like that around. Nor do we need to take a chance on more costly shenanigans, hassles with customers or insurance companies. At the very least, Hartly's firing might scare off the real crooks."

"So you concede it's highly likely he's innocent," Derek said sharply.

"We seem to differ on the degree of probability. I still don't understand why you care so much. He's just one employee out of two hundred or so. We can easily replace him."

Derek didn't answer right away. The old Derek would have agreed with his father, letting the Roger Hartlys of the world go their way while he remained safe on his own comfortable perch. He would have been more concerned with the tough battle of winning his father's approval. But he'd changed, ever since he'd walked unwittingly into Megan's and Shanna's lives. He saw right and wrong more clearly now, without the shadow of what he stood to gain obscuring his vision. And he wanted to do everything in his power so that Roger wouldn't be pushed to his limits, as Megan had been.

"The fact is I *do* care," he said quietly at last, the steely determination in his voice making his words strong-hearted, not soft. "I know you won't change your mind, and unfortunately I don't have the authority to overrule your decision. But I'd like to ask for one concession."

"What's that?"

"Don't dismiss Jalsevac right away."

"Why not? Our chief suspect is out of the picture."

Derek held his father's blue-eyed gaze, so like his own, but watery with age. Leo's face was well-lined, and Derek felt as if he were staring into a mirror of his future. It tore at him because, for the first time, he recognized a deep unhappiness in his father and the hollowness of his fight. He wondered how long Leo had been like that. He feared he was already heading there himself. In that crystal-clear moment Derek swore he would be different, somehow.

"I think you owe me that much," Derek said evenly. "You didn't hold up your end of the bargain. My allotted week wasn't up. You never heard the outcome of my call to Roger's parole officer, which I admit was delayed, due to other unavoidable factors." He didn't mention Megan's death because he knew Leo didn't want to hear any more about it. He kept out of his sons' personal lives. "Do you want to hear it now?"

"It's too late."

Derek's eyes narrowed. "So do we keep Jalsevac until *I'm* satisfied he's no longer needed?"

After several long seconds, Leo silently nodded, tipping the precarious balance between the two strong-willed men. Only when Derek left the room, did Leo's mouth curve into a satisfied smile, as a teacher might acknowledge a pupil's progress. Something else lingered in that smile, as well—a startled pride because the pupil had outwitted the teacher.

Derek's office phone had three separate extensions and all were blinking when he returned. Even though two of the waiting calls were long distance, according to Joan, he took Shanna's first. "Shanna? Are you still there?"

"I'm here all right. I'm over at the Hartlys, and I have to talk to you about Roger."

An icy fear ran down his spine. "Is he okay?"

"Reasonably. But how could you let this happen? You *can't* let it happen—"

"Just stay put. I'll be right over. I want to talk to Roger, too. Where does he live?" Shanna told him. "Just stay there."

He hung up, handled the other two calls just as expediently, speed-read a few memos before initialing them, placated Joan while on the run, then found himself at Roger's apartment in record time.

Roger answered the door, blocking his path, his large burly body more than a match for Derek's solid but shorter frame. "Why are you here?" he asked bluntly.

In that instant Derek saw the disillusionment in Roger's eyes, and if he'd harbored an iota of doubt about Roger's innocence, it vanished. "I think my father was wrong in firing you. I want to help you and to get to the bottom of this."

Roger stared hard at him, then dropped his arm. "Come in," he said gruffly.

The small, crowded quarters were reminiscent of Megan's apartment, and Derek's resolve to amend matters strengthened even more. Roger sat beside his wife, who was holding the plump baby, clad only in a diaper, while Derek perched on the edge of a kitchen chair near Shanna. He'd tried not to look at her browned shapely legs, crossed demurely beneath her short denim skirt, nor at the powder-blue tank top that left little to his imagination, but his resolve lasted about two seconds. He could almost believe she was still the teenager he'd barely known in high school, for there was an innocent quality, a serious idealism, about her. But there was a toughness, too, the kind that came from having survived pain and loss.

He drank in the sight of her, her beautiful green eyes, her long russet hair, the proud angle to her chin, her soft curves, and his heart turned over. He'd missed her. More than he'd realized.

"So how do you propose to help Roger?" Shanna asked, folding her arms, as if in self-defense.

He forced his gaze away from her and focused on Roger. "I've convinced my father to keep on the security guard we secretly hired. Indefinitely. Sooner or later, we'll nab the real thief or thieves."

"So he's the one who found out about me. Leo wouldn't say. Who is he, anyway?" Roger studied Derek suspiciously, challengingly.

"Jalsevac. The new driver."

Roger's eyes narrowed. He recognized that Derek had trusted him enough to breach the confidentiality of such information. "It may be a hot case to all of you, but I'm still out of a job and I'm still an ex-con."

"I'm going to do everything in my power to get your job back," Derek vowed. "You're an ex-con who's gone clean. I know that. The others will know it soon, too."

Teddy started crying, despite Kim's soft, soothing sounds and attempts to keep his pacifier in his mouth. Roger picked up his son and supported him so that he could face forward. When Teddy had quieted, Roger asked, "Why are you doing this for me?"

"I have to. I want to," Derek said, shaking his head, not quite sure why himself. "Can you think of anything that might help me—anything, however irrelevant it might seem?''

The two men discussed various operating procedures, trying to figure out how such discrepancies between goods shipped and goods received could occur, after numerous signatures of various personnel along the way. Derek asked about each of Roger's fellow workers, but dug up nothing unusual. Finally he said, "Look, call me if you think of anything. I have to get back to work. Why don't you all go out for a drive, a walk or a swim on such a warm summer's day?'' Undaunted by the lack of enthusiasm that faced him, he added, "Believe me, if I wasn't so swamped this weekend, I'd be heading north to some pretty lake where I could just float on my back and meditate on the clouds or something equally taxing."

"Maybe this is nothing," Roger suddenly said slowly, his gleaming eyes disputing the words, "but a long time ago, after one of my night shifts, I forgot my thermos on the dock—Kimmie's always after me for that—and I went back for it. A guy I didn't know was hanging around, just waiting for Burns to get off, he said, so they could drive up north for the weekend. It was Friday night, his car was there, all loaded up with cottage gear, so I didn't pay much attention. Except I noticed a packing box like the ones we'd just unloaded in with their stuff. There's always extra empty boxes lying around, so I thought I was mistaken. Maybe it was nothing."

Derek shrugged. "I'll tell Jalsevac to keep an eye on Burns, anyway. Call me if anything else comes to mind, okay?''

Before Derek and Shanna left, Roger extended his hand to Derek. "Thank you. I'll buy you a beer some time, even if it's with my unemployment check."

"Scotches on me, when you're back at Morgan's."

Derek wished to hell Roger wasn't looking at him as if he were full of empty promises.

"I WANT YOU TO KNOW I admire your support of Roger," Shanna said when they'd exited the crowded elevator and were walking through the lobby. "I gather you won't be popular at Morgan's for taking such a stand."

"That doesn't bother me," Derek said as he opened the rear door for her and they stepped into the sunlight. The midday heat was of a desertlike intensity, reflecting off the asphalt of the parking lot.

"I think you're becoming a more genuine person," she said daringly, trying to meet his eyes, but he was squinting against the sun's glare and looking around for his car.

"What was I before? A fake person?"

"No, just different."

"What you see is what you get." Bending his knees, he flexed his muscles to perform a brief body builder's pose.

She refused to laugh at his habitual escape into humor when she tried to get close to him.

He saw she wasn't laughing. "I missed you," he suddenly admitted. The sentiment seemed to come out like a stubborn tooth that had to be pulled.

Hers followed just as unwillingly. "I missed you, too."

One long uninhibited look, and the familiar tension, taut and crackling, escalated between them, heating Shanna's skin more than the sun that blazed down. Slowly he drew nearer. His lips gave hers a mere brush of a kiss, with the promise of passion.

"I missed that, too," he murmured, his voice quiet, deep.

Whenever he touched her, long-hushed desire stirred in Shanna, stronger each time, as if he were approaching its center, layer by layer. But she remembered the restrictions he'd placed on their relationship—he wanted her, not Alicia, and she had serious doubts about continuing to see him under those circumstances.

"I intend to wait until you're ready...." His breath fanned her cheek as he hovered within kissing distance.

The assumption that some day she would be ready hung in the air, too, as did the question of when. She felt neither pressure nor impatience from him, but a tightly controlled obsession with her that frightened her. Perhaps she felt so vulnerable because she was still in limbo herself. She'd traded the one she'd inhabited since Michael's death with another, shared not only with Derek, but Michael's memory and her wish to do what was best for her daughter.

"I can't be certain of anything, Derek. I may never be ready...and even if I do reach that point, what if it's a mistake for both of us?"

Undeterred, his lips sought hers. "Being with you will never be a mistake. But I want you to come to me freely, without anyone or anything between us."

"What if that's not possible?"

"You worry too much."

He pulled back to look at her with eyes bluer than blue, sparkling, fun-loving. She remembered a line she'd heard in a movie once about choosing to go through life on a merry-go-round or on a roller coaster. He made the latter so very appealing.

"By the way, I'm free tomorrow night," he murmured from somewhere deep in his throat, and her stomach plunged as if she'd ridden over the edge of that roller coaster and was heading down. "I haven't gone out on the town in a long while."

"Really? If it's excitement you're after, you'd love the pinball arcade at SportsWorld. I hear it comes alive on a

Saturday night. Then there's always a rousing game of miniature golf to top off the evening.''

"Not exactly what I had in mind..."

"Or...you could come over for a quiet dinner with Alicia and me."

"Hmm, sounds tempting." His voice betrayed only the faintest hesitation, as he realized she'd invited him to her home so that her daughter would be included. Slowly he nodded, then drawled, "Well, thank you for the invitation, ma'am. Mighty thoughtful of you to take pity on a poor lonely dude such as myself."

And once more she left him with a smile on her lips and the sweet aftertaste of one of his kisses....

CHAPTER NINE

SHANNA POURED the rosemary mustard sauce over the lamb chops. Since the meat should have been marinating all day and it was after four, she was definitely behind schedule. She glanced out the kitchen window to see Talia wandering in the backyard. Her friend must have splashed her flushed cheeks with the hose, since her short ash-blond curls were as wet as her face. Only the effervescent Talia, wearing tight black spandex shorts and a tank top knotted at the waist, would be out biking in the intense July heat.

"I'm in here," Shanna called out.

Talia entered noisily by the back door. She looked in surprise at the upheaval in the kitchen. "How did you know I was dateless tonight and planning to hang around for supper?"

"I didn't. I'm having company."

Talia spotted Alicia playing on her blanket. "Hi, sweets. My goodness, look at you holding your head up. Who're you having?" she asked Shanna, feigning nonchalance as she reached for a plump strawberry from the draining bowl.

"A friend."

"Not your father, at least. That's good. Male or female?"

"Male."

"You have obviously been holding out on me. This is not a burgers 'n franks kind of buddy-buddy dinner. Asparagus . . . homemade salad dressing and pie crust, even."

"It's just a simple barbecue. Help yourself to some lemonade in the fridge."

Talia eyed Shanna suspiciously as she poured herself a drink, then sat down at the kitchen table. "Wine is chilling, too, I see."

"Oh, I thought it should get used up. It's been around since my pre-pregnancy days."

"Shanna!"

"Okay, Derek Morgan is coming to dinner. It's no big deal."

"Wait a minute. Did you say Derek Morgan as in high school Derek Morgan, dream-boat, king of jocks, son of Morgan Cartage? Things are getting stranger. Am I in a time warp here?"

Needing to sort out her own mixed feelings first, Shanna hadn't discussed Derek with Talia. She'd even avoided mentioning his name when she'd alluded to the kidnapping and Megan's subsequent suicide. But she couldn't avoid the facts any longer. Briefly, while slicing strawberries, she informed her friend of Terry Morgan's connection to Megan, her own meeting with Derek in the hospital and her continued involvement with him through Megan and Roger.

When she'd finished, Talia stared at her, aghast. "So you two have a hot date tonight?"

Shanna laughed self-consciously, trying to ignore the fluttery anticipation she'd felt all day. "Frankly I don't know what we have."

"Is he fat or balding or suffering from any kind of substance abuse?" Smiling, Shanna shook her head. "No ex-wife, current wife or girlfriend in the wings?"

"Not that I know of...."

"Then go for it, kiddo." Alicia was starting to fuss, so Talia picked her up, her large brown eyes and wide smile captivating the child. "Do you know what a rare gem you've found? Look, if you want an expert's appraisal, I'll stick around and check him out myself."

"That won't be necessary."

"So what's the problem? Even if he's only half as good-looking or funny as he used to be, he's probably twice as well-off...."

Shanna turned around and slowly dried her hands on a dish towel. "Come on, Talia. You of all people should know those kinds of superficial things wear off pretty quickly. He's also self-centered and probably just out for who knows what? He's thirty-six and never married. Doesn't that tell you something?"

"Yeah. He's been smart enough to avoid divorce."

"I honestly don't think I'm ready to date yet. I had a deep intimate commitment—marriage. How do you forget all that and start from scratch again, worrying about sweaty palms, pretending it doesn't matter if he never calls again or—or wondering what he's thinking. With Michael, I just knew. It was so comfortable. We fought, sure, but even with that, I knew what to expect. And Michael's so ingrained in me, I still feel like his wife, like I'm being unfaithful when Derek..." She looked away.

"So you *are* attracted to Derek?"

"Well, yes, but that's what complicates all this so much."

Talia smiled knowingly. "My dear girl, that's what makes all this worthwhile. What else? Why are you still

looking perturbed?" She made faces at Alicia until she
coaxed a big wet grin out of her.

"I don't know . . . he's as much as told me he won't be
around forever."

"That's what they all say at the beginning."

"But I don't want Alicia exposed to a series of her
mommy's boyfriends, even at this age, especially if I
know Derek's not Mr. Right. How can I even say that?
I'm not even *looking* for Mr. Right."

"How can you be so sure he's not?"

"I'm not sure of much these days." She began rinsing
romaine lettuce under the tap. "He makes me laugh and
feel sexy and he fills the gap left by Michael, and it's all
very flattering, but, but, but. He's not husband or father material. He was very clear about that. And I have
to think of all that now, for Alicia's sake."

"Why not just consider him a stepping-stone to your
future?"

"More like a big immovable rock. Somehow he wan-
gled an invitation out of me for tonight. Part of me is
excited, the rest is plain full of doubts." She reached for
her salad spinner and started rotating it with a ven-
geance.

"Try to enjoy yourself and don't try to make the relationship into something it isn't. Do you know how long
it took me to learn such a simple lesson? And
Shanna—"

"Hmm?"

"Shouldn't you, ah, put the lettuce in there first? Do
you need some help?"

Shanna gave herself a little shake. "No, no. Your just
keeping Alicia happy is great. I'm probably beyond
hope."

"Anybody home?" Ned Bennett, looking sporty in his powder-blue shirt and trousers, entered by the back door, carrying a six-quart basket of strawberries. "Fresh-picked this morning," he said proudly, nodding at Talia, beaming at Alicia. "Oh, I see you have a few already. We can freeze some of these later tonight, if you want. I've got some time."

Shanna and Talia exchanged glances.

"Did you two have some other plans?"

Talia had less difficulty blurting out the truth than Shanna. "Shanna's got a big date tonight."

"With who, honey?"

"It's nothing, really. Just Derek Morgan. The guy who found Alicia when Megan took her."

"I'd love to see him again. Maybe I'll just stick around." He winked at Talia. "Have to make sure he's reputable enough for my two girls."

"Dad, I'm not sixteen," Shanna said sharply, then added on a softer note, "Not tonight, please. Things are testy enough."

He sat down slowly beside Talia, then put his arms out to hold Alicia, whose eyes had lit up when she'd spotted his familiar face. "The problem is, I can't really go home. I've been getting...harassed on the phone."

"As in obscene calls?" Talia asked, leaning forward, her interest mildly piqued.

"No, no. Someone I know, actually."

"Then don't answer the phone."

"What if it's an emergency? Shanna calling or something?"

"Work out a code. Or get an answering machine. They are the greatest invention since—"

"Who's bugging you, Dad?" Shanna interrupted.

"Her name's Helen. I met her in that cooking class," he said pointedly. "She's one of the widows, and I swear her husband must have leaped into the grave to get some peace and quiet. She's certainly exhausted me the few times I've been trapped with her."

Carefully avoiding Talia's eyes, Shanna pretended to be absorbed in breaking the lettuce into pieces. "You mean you've seen her...since the course?"

He nodded miserably. "She got my number somehow and kindly volunteered to give me private cooking lessons at home. I refused, but before I knew it, she was at my door, with some excuse or another, armed with cookbooks and crazy gadgets—she must have bought every de-pitter in the hardware store!"

Shanna was glad of a chance to break into an acceptable smile. "So how was the lesson?"

"A lesson in listening," he answered, shaking his finely combed head darkly. "We made some fruit tarts—she ate half of them...did I mention Helen isn't a petite woman? And I heard about the general health, sexual preference and various idiosyncrasies of every member of her family tree, including a few juicy tidbits from other neighboring trees."

"Have these...lessons continued?" Talia asked with a perfectly straight face.

"I avoided my own home like the plague for a week." Shanna *had* noticed she'd seen more of her father than ever lately. "But it seems she's in cahoots with one of my neighbors who knows exactly when a lone light is shining or a car slips into the garage. Finally I told her no more lessons."

"And?" Talia and Shanna queried simultaneously.

He sighed. "She's really a phone-aholic, anyway. And it saves her from taking the bus. She never seems to notice the conversation is all one-sided, or maybe she does and loves the sound of her own voice. I can't take it anymore.''

"Dad, you can't keep escaping from her. You have to be blunt with her—as kindly as possible."

"She outtalks me! If I say I'm sick, she's got some old family remedy. I've already made it plain I have no wish in becoming...amorous with anyone, but she sees herself as a one-woman Help-Lonely-Spouses-Recover campaign. Apparently she's caught more than one of us in her web. So you see, it's not so simple. I can't go home or she'll sense I'm there, I know it."

"Mr. Bennett—Ned," Talia began, standing, her eyes sparkling. "Would you do me the honor of escorting me to a movie or dancing this evening?" At his taken-aback look, she added, "Solely for the purposes of giving Helen of Troy something to share with her cronies. Think what fun they'll have discussing your foibles with a woman young enough to be your daughter. Maybe she'll even enjoy talking *about* you more than talking *to* you."

He assessed her a few seconds before replying. "That sounds like a wonderful idea. How be we freeze the berries tomorrow and I meet your fellow another time, Shanna?"

"Fine by me," Shanna said, sharing a relieved look with the friend who'd seen her through most major—and minor—crises in her life. She knew Talia's last-minute scheme was only a temporary remedy to Ned's dilemma, but she wasn't in a position to be picky.

"We'll let Shanna get ready," Talia was saying to him. "You should get home and get ready yourself. Look dressed up. Splash yourself with a little cologne. Don't answer your phone for anything, and I'll drive over 'bout six-thirty. Don't look so dazed. Lots of women pick up their dates for convenience these days. Plus, we want to be seen while there's plenty of light. This should be fun...."

"I HOPE YOU DIDN'T go to too much trouble tonight," Derek murmured as they sat side by side on matching yellow lawn chairs. Their empty coffee cups were abandoned on the picnic table that took up half of Shanna's small backyard patio.

"Not too much."

"I want you to know that the way to this man's heart is *not* through his stomach, although the occasional strawberry custard pie does help pave the way."

Shanna laughed, languorous after two glasses of wine and a large meal. She gave what she hoped was a surreptitious tug to the upper region of her sleeveless, black cotton dress. It felt even snugger than when she'd put it on several hours ago. If she hadn't felt so unexpectedly comfortable all night with her relaxed and entertaining companion, if he hadn't been so delightfully goofy with Alicia before she went to sleep, and if a bright half-moon wasn't in her full view over the treetops, she would never have asked the question he was undoubtedly setting her up for. "So what *is* the way to your heart, Derek Morgan?"

Her skin tingled because she knew he was bound to kiss her then, but to her amazement, he didn't move. "I don't know," he said instead, so seriously that she was afraid to glance over at him. "No one, least of all me, has figured that out yet. Maybe you should try," he added, staring straight ahead, too.

The suggestion was caught in the balmy night wind and blown away, without a ready answer.

"You know, it's still strange to me, meeting you again after all these years," he said after a time.

"Why is it strange?"

He leaned back, stretching his legs, which made his white shorts rise a few inches higher, revealing his thick, muscular thighs. His face was illuminated by the small outdoor light. "Well, now that we aging baby boomers are drifting into the 1990s, nostalgia is so popular—I mean, all the old songs are being resurrected to sell everything from butter to beer. That spirit of nostalgia seems to be hitting me, too. I feel as if I've missed something, but that I have to look in the present for what really went missing in the past. So maybe what I'm looking for is not here, or everything's changed so much that I wouldn't recognize it, anyway. Does that make any sense?"

She'd turned to watch his profile as he'd spoken—the earnestness of his moving brows, their troubled pull toward the center, the way his lips settled into a straight, dissatisfied line. "It makes some sense. But how do I fit into this search for your new improved nostalgia?"

"I don't know," he replied swiftly. "You just do. But I like that phrase. What was it? My new improved nostalgia."

"Good ad copy for something."

"No, just another example of how you make me see my life more clearly. I like the ways we reflect off each other, Shanna, making everything seem brighter, sharper."

She faced him and said immediately, "I like that, too." And his soul-piercing look was suddenly frightening in its intensity because it had the power of abolishing everything, everyone else, from her mind, if she let it.

Her eyes moved toward the dark corners of the yard as she leaned away from him, concentrating on twirling her hair around her fingers, a habit she'd developed years ago while anxiously cramming for exams.

For a few moments neither spoke. "Do you have any games?" he asked suddenly.

She was getting used to Derek's quick changes, and for once she appreciated his attempt to lighten the atmosphere. "As in checkers or Scrabble?"

"Anything but Scrabble. I want to win, teach."

"Let me see. I used to enjoy a word game called Boggle—" She stopped, made herself say it. "With Michael. He tended to beat me, *but* they were close games. And I don't intend to lose with a new hotshot of an opponent."

"You're on. But what's the prize?"

"Why do we need a prize? What about the challenge of the game itself?"

"Come on, we need goals, stakes, rewards...."

She laughed because he really meant it. "Just try it my way, okay?"

"We'll see...." he said, unconvinced.

They moved to the kitchen table then and played intently for a good hour. Finally they tallied their individual scores. Derek had won by a margin, after he'd carefully, gravely, double-checked the figures.

Shanna heard Alicia stirring. She glanced at the clock, shocked to see it was after midnight. Oddly she wasn't tired. Derek heard Alicia, too, and took his cue to leave. He stood and gently pulled Shanna to her feet, too. With one hand holding her face, he planted a firm warm kiss upon her lips.

"Hey, you're claiming your prize, after all," she murmured, not entirely displeased.

"Actually, no. But if that's the way you want to think about it, then go ahead." He kissed her quickly again, then left so suddenly that she wondered if something was wrong.

His car stayed in her driveway, however, for at least another ten minutes. She realized that self-restraint was no easy matter for Derek Morgan, but to his credit he never reappeared at her door.

"DAD, IT'S FOR YOU." Annoyance laced Shanna's voice. "It's Helen. She introduced herself to me for five minutes, then spent another five querying my feelings on older men."

"Just tell her I've stepped out for a second."

"You tell her. How did she get my number?"

"She'd put the slyness of Columbo and the nose of a bloodhound to shame," he said, shuffling to the kitchen phone disgruntledly.

"Tell her to leave you alone. Or I will." In exasperation, Shanna flopped down on the spot he'd vacated beside Derek.

"Unwanted suitor?" Derek asked, tearing his eyes away from the Blue Jays ball game on the television.

"More or less. Derek, am I rotten daughter for wish-ing my father didn't hang around so much?"

"No... especially since I've spent the last two out of three of my visits with him, too. And if he's not here, Alicia's awake. All I can think of is what I'd like to do alone with you." He proceeded to demonstrate. "First, a little fun..." Playfully his lips nuzzled her neck. "Then a little savagery." His arms pinned her wrists down to the couch and he towered over her, leering, "Ah, my pretty," before capturing her lips in a hard swift kiss. "Now for the denouement.'' In one swift motion he swept her into his arms and stood.

Stunned, Shanna grabbed his collar for support as she kicked out, but his grip held her firm. ''Derek,'' she warned, laughing spiritedly. ''Now what are you going to do?''

''Drop you?''

''You wouldn't dare.''

''Rip your bodice, whisk you to your chamber and take you for mine?''

''You wouldn't dare.''

''Wouldn't I? I can't be a good little boy forever, you know,'' he said, his eyes suddenly losing their mischievous glint. ''And I don't think you like being celibate any more than I, do you?''

It was the first time he'd raised the issue since he'd taken to dropping over during the past few weeks. Pressed against his solid body, their eyes locked, his inviting lips inches away, her blood dancing to the sweet merry tune he always evoked in her, Shanna felt anything but celibate. ''I—''

''Oh, I'm sorry,'' Ned mumbled, hesitating in the doorway, then quickly recovering as he sat down again on the couch. ''Did the game start to get dull?''

Stepping back to give Ned room, Derek replied evenly, ''Not exactly. Shanna just seemed more interesting.''

''How's Helen?'' Shanna asked dryly.

''As ingenious as ever. I told her my daughter and my new *friend* take good care of me. I don't need her mothering. Maybe that'll keep her away.''

Suddenly Derek's eyes were riveted on the set and he let out a hearty whoop. ''Did you see that base-stealing? And the Jays were going to trade him.''

"He can sure run better than he's been hitting lately," Ned replied. "Look who they've got pinch-hitting now...."

"He's a good bunter."

"True enough. Ah, it's good to have a man around the house who knows his stuff." Ned looked up to flash Derek a smile. "The only Blue Jays that interested Michael, God bless him, were the kind that flew around."

"Michael must have done something right," Derek quipped back.

"Okay, King Kong, you can put me down now, please," Shanna finally interrupted, irritated not only at Derek's resentment of Michael, but at her father's unfair comparison between the two men. Michael had always fallen short in Ned's estimation because of his indifference to sports.

Derek released her, searching her eyes briefly, then sat down beside her father again, to bemoan the batter's strikeout.

It was clear that her father and Derek got along famously, sharing not only an interest in sports, but a fascination with long- and short-term investment strategies. Her father spoke from his years of banking experience, while Derek seemed to have more current hands-on knowledge and more disposable income, his "play money," as he called it. They even had some mutual business acquaintances, not to mention equally strong views about the government's wasteful spending.

Shanna slipped out of the room to check on Alicia, who'd fallen asleep in her carriage after her Sunday afternoon stroll. She presumed neither sports fan noticed, but when she glanced back, she caught Derek staring at her with a supremely ardent look. Ned said something to him, which he answered in apparent earnestness, then he winked at Shanna.

He was playing her father as strategically as he was biding his time with her. And neither of them stood a chance when he poured on the charm....

MOTH WINGS FLUTTERED aimlessly atop the old lamp on the deserted street. Only a few persistent stars peeked through the cloudy midnight sky as two heads, one taller, turned toward each other in a parked car.

"Can I ask you a small favor?" Shanna murmured, reluctant to leave, enjoying the cooling breeze through the open sun roof and the wonderful pressure of Derek's fingers on her neck, an art he'd perfected in the movie theater earlier.

"Hmm?"

"I have to tutor this Saturday morning at Kim's, and Dad's finally visiting some old friends in Kincardine, so I was wondering if maybe you could look after Alicia...just for a few hours...."

The night sounds of distant cars and hidden crickets filled the silence. "I'd love to, but if I don't have to work, there's a squash tournament at the club."

"Oh, that's okay then."

"Maybe another time. It's not as if I don't see enough of Alicia when I'm with you."

Her back stiffened involuntarily. "I can always ask Talia."

"You better do that."

She stifled her disappointment in him. What did she expect? He tolerated her daughter, but he'd never feel as responsible or as giving as a natural parent would. "Any news on the lead Roger passed along?" she asked, abruptly changing the subject.

"No, and no more cargo is missing," he answered without skipping a beat. "Even Jalsevac is getting impatient. And of course, my dad's convinced he was right in firing Roger. How *is* Roger, anyway?"

"You could have called him yourself."

"Not without anything concrete. Besides, I talked to his parole officer, who's keeping tabs on him."

"Well, Kim says he's filed for unemployment, but there's a waiting period to see if he's even eligible, under the circumstances. Apparently he applied for another job. He even told them about the mix-up at Morgan's, but they hired someone else. Needless to say, he was pretty upset about it. If only—never mind."

Derek exhaled slowly, releasing only a fraction of the pressure he was under. "I'm doing all I can. I can't be everywhere."

Shanna debated how honest to be with him because she knew he felt partly responsible for Roger's problems. "You should know that Roger is more down on himself than ever," she finally admitted. "In fact, Kim is petrified he might do something irrational. They're running out of money...."

Down the street, voices clamored boisterously as doors slammed. Two cars drove away with a squeal of tires. "I'll talk to him again," Derek said wearily, then they both fell silent.

To ease the tension, Shanna finally quipped, "So, could you please run by me the redeeming features of that so-called comedy we saw tonight? As I recall, I only laughed once—when it finally ended."

"Hey, we *could* have seen a rousing action-adventure instead."

"With lots of violence and ridiculous chase scenes where the good guys *always* get away. No thanks."

"And I refuse to spend my evening reading subtitles and being thrown off by lips and words that don't jive, making me feel I have a hearing problem."

"Even if the film won critical acclaim at the Cannes Film Festival?"

"Sorry..."

"So we compromised on a teenage farce and look where it got us."

Leaning toward her, he burrowed into her neck and began a series of tiny kisses leading to her lips. "Wasting time on a beautiful night. Ouch!" His hip had grazed the stick shift. "Like a pair of teenagers."

"Dad's in the house."

Frustrated, Derek sat back hard, despite the plushness of the bucket seat. "So we'll wait till he leaves."

"It's late," she murmured weakly.

"Maybe we need to spend some time away from here. Would you like to come with me to a family barbecue next Sunday?"

Shanna looked at him in surprise. "Where?"

"At my brother Ray's house. It's Dad's sixty-fifth birthday, so we'll try to celebrate, while he's ordering us to ignore the whole thing. Apparently Terry has the day off from his new job, so he's coming, too."

Curious to meet the rest of his family, Shanna accepted readily. "So where's Terry working?"

"At a Toronto bar. As a deejay, of all things." Derek looked unimpressed. "He's always been a music nut, but he must have done some fancy talking to convince his boss he knew what he was doing. Terry was always good at that. It all sounds a little flighty to me, but I hear from Ray that Terry's quite enthusiastic. I'll know better when I talk to him myself at the party. With Terry working nights, we keep missing each other."

Suddenly Shanna thought to mention, "As far as the party goes, first I have to make sure I can get a sitter."

"Right." He drummed his fingers on the steering wheel. "Don't you miss not being able to do what you want, whenever you want?" he asked slowly.

"Sometimes," she answered truthfully. "But I'm Alicia's mother. Looking out for her is like second nature. I guess you never understand that until you have your own." He said nothing. She gave him a quick kiss and pushed open the door. "'Night. I had fun, even though Siskel and Ebert we're not."

"Good night," he called after her. He went to start the car, then jumped out and caught up with her, grabbing her hand. "Let me at least give you a proper... or perhaps improper, farewell."

His eyes were busy on her face, the pulse at her neck, the swell of her breasts beneath her white cotton shirt. One hand fell to the waist of her navy walking shorts, the other cupped her face. His thumb stroked her chin, brushed her cheekbone, sailed over her brows, with feather-light pressure.

"I have to touch you, Shanna, hold you closer. Sometimes that's all I can think of." His arm tightened around her.

It felt so good to be treasured by words and looks and delicate touches. Her lips parted. The soft daring warmth of his tongue slipped into her mouth. Slowly he penetrated to taste deep inside, and she let herself sink into the engulfing sensuality. Fragmented impressions assaulted her, the threading of his fingers through her hair, her nipples erect against his chest, her quickening breath indistinct from his, the cool, damp grass at her feet, the shadows cast by the tall maple overhead. He pulled her closer, and their hips started moving, pressing, creating an ancient friction.

Shanna's body seemed to be funneling to a single receptor—the knowledge of his maleness seeking, needing, transforming the depths of her femininity.

"Shanna, please invite me in tonight," he pleaded huskily, with a raw, single-minded urgency that matched hers. "Not for coffee. For you, me, us."

She pulled back and their eyes met. A lock of his dark hair had fallen onto his forehead, and if she were to say later what swayed her decision at that moment she'd have to say that errant lock of hair, making him appear young and decadent and carefree, and making her feel the same. She nodded, then stepped toward the house, severing the fragile bond.

Minutes later, they were making light conversation with Ned, joking about the bad movie, asking about Alicia's night. Whether her father noticed the tremor in her hand or the distracted look in Derek's eyes, she couldn't be sure. It seemed to take him forever to leave, then Shanna was alone with the man who stirred such turmoil in her body and soul.

"I have to check on Alicia." Nothing in her voice betrayed the gut-deep somersaulting inside that had accompanied her decision a few moments ago. Slowly she climbed the stairs and stepped into the nursery. He stood in the doorway as she covered the child, whose tiny mouth was sucking rhythmically on her soother. Shanna stroked her warm head with one finger, then turned away quickly.

Derek took her hand as he led her to her own bed. A small lamp cast a faint light into the room. His eyes upon her, he eased her down and lay beside her. As if savoring the quiet moments of anticipation, he merely held her close.

All too soon, his hands and mouth began their sensuous exploration, pulling at clothing, and Shanna felt the familiar quickening of her heartbeat, the warm spirals of pleasure within.

Their pressed bodies only occupied a small strip on the edge of the queen-sized bed, and for Derek that seemed too confining. He rolled with her playfully toward the center, so that she ended up on top of him briefly, then he was straddling her, bending to rain kisses along the hollow of her throat. His eyes were dreamy, passion-glazed, confident. Suddenly she was reminded of Talia's words about using Derek as a stepping-stone.

"You like to roll," she stated in a voice unlike her own, disoriented, touching but not feeling him.

"That's not all..." And with practiced ease he dropped beside her to unbutton her shirt, then to knead her breasts, his mouth never losing contact with her neck, lips, ears....

Shanna's eyes stayed open and she became distinctly aware of her surroundings, the familiar mahogany furniture, the cobweb on the ceiling, the three layers of worn clothing draped over the chair, which used to drive Michael crazy. She shivered and Derek growled in satisfaction, thinking he had caused the eruption of goose bumps along her exposed flesh. Blinking hard, she turned her head. No picture of Michael remained in this room, where such reminders had been too painful, but a large framed photo of Alicia stared back at her from the dresser.

Derek continued to touch her intimately, his own arousal plainly building, and with growing detachment she finally acknowledged the difference between having sex and making love.

"Derek, I can't...."

He froze and stared at her disbelievingly. "W-what?"

"I can't. I'm sorry. I thought I wanted to...part of me does...but I can't. I'm not all here, it's not right...."

"Just relax," he murmured soothingly and his lips resumed a gentler teasing dance over hers.

But even her lips became lifeless. He fell onto his back, knowing it was over, and his angry look showed no understanding. "Do you want to talk about it?" he asked, drawing a deep breath, rubbing his eyes.

Talking wouldn't fill the great void of love crying out inside her, just as his body alone couldn't meet her deepest needs, nor replace what she'd lost.

"Shanna, you have to let go. He's not coming back."

"It's more than that. I loved him," she said softly. "With you, it's nice but different." She sat up, quickly, too quickly, making herself light-headed.

"I care for you, Shanna. I hope we care for each other, but we can't pretend love is there," he said from the other side of the bed, but the distance between them was greater.

"I know." She faced him, her hair a wild tumble, which she slowly pushed back. "So what are we going to do?"

Derek sat up, too, resting on his elbows. His brain was telling him to walk away. He didn't need this aggravation. He could have walked away from her numerous times already, but his compulsion to come back to her was proving as strong or stronger than his desire to flee. He was drawn to her tentative sensuality. He needed to explore its depths. He wanted to be the one to unfold the layers, the rich, ripe core of womanhood he'd barely touched. And he was starting to care for her more than he'd ever admit.

His arms crept around her from behind and she leaned back against his heart, the beat calmer than a few moments ago. "I'll pick you up next Sunday for the barbecue, okay?" he heard himself say.

"Okay."

He left quickly, his parting kiss tinged with longing and regret and feelings for which he had no name.

Later, as Shanna lay in the dark, she felt like the girl she'd once been who'd been disappointed to learn that the magician's tricks were only illusions. But that same girl had still been awestruck by the performance that created the illusions....

CHAPTER TEN

RAY MORGAN LIVED in a stately home in Upper Beech-wood, one of Waterloo's most prestigious districts. As soon as Shanna and Derek arrived, on a warm day that had threatened rain since dawn, Ray's wife Brenda took Shanna in tow. Shanna would rather have met the rest of the family who were gathered outside, but Brenda was determined to give her a guided tour in the air-conditioned comfort.

The classic Georgian-style house was certainly a showpiece, Shanna soon discovered, complete with cathedral ceilings, skylights, French doors, a magnificent oak staircase and an indoor sauna and Jacuzzi. Wallpaper and matching borders in bold jewel tones—sapphire, emerald, amethyst and turquoise—were perfectly coordinated with valences and balloon-style "window treatments," as Brenda referred to them. To complement each room's colors and textures, different abstract paintings had been chosen. Children's toys were restricted to the neatest playroom Shanna had ever seen.

Brenda herself was well-dressed, well-coiffed and well-spoken, put together with as much care as the interior decorating. But Shanna knew that problems existed within the house. During the drive over, Derek had told her that Brenda and Ray were having marital troubles. They'd been seeing a marriage counselor since Brenda had found out about Ray's affair with a young accounting clerk at the office who had since resigned.

When the women returned to the kitchen, they gazed out the sliding glass doors that overlooked a huge deck and the spacious backyard. Two men that Shanna presumed were Leo and Ray were talking to Derek on the lawn, their drinks in hand.

"So how did you become involved with one of the infamous Morgans?" the dark-brown-haired Brenda asked in her raspy voice. "Derek is never very...specific with us about his private life."

Shanna smiled, not surprised by that tidbit. "We attended the same high school, but as we said back then, we weren't on the same wavelength. I met him again at the hospital, just after I had my little girl. He told you about visiting Megan?"

Brenda nodded. "As well as about her...death. We all felt badly, especially Terry."

"Did you know that before all that—" Shanna drew an extra breath "—Megan kidnapped my daughter and—and that it was Derek who tracked them down?"

Brenda's brown eyes widened. "My heavens, you must have been beside yourself! No, Derek never said a word. All he told us was that he was seeing a widow with a young baby, and even that was surprising, considering his life-style—" She winced. "That was thoughtless. I'm sorry."

"Don't be," Shanna assured her. She hesitated, then decided to open up even more to Brenda, not only because of their common involvement with a Morgan brother, but because she desperately needed to talk to someone who knew Derek better than she did. "Sometimes even *I* wonder if I'm doing the right thing for both myself and my daughter . . . seeing a confirmed bachelor like Derek . . . in the long run.''

''There's always a trade-off, falling for a Morgan, as easy as that is,'' Brenda said quietly, wistfully, dispelling Shanna's hopes that Brenda might tell her she'd misjudged her brother-in-law. ''They're all bravado and brawn, little heart. Oh, they need us women in their own way, but they're used to living in a man's world, at home and work, and that's where they're at their best—happiest, perhaps.''

''How long have you been married?''

''Eleven years.'' Even Brenda's layers of makeup could not disguise the distress under her thin veneer of wellbeing. ''But I know what you mean about not just thinking of yourself, when you have a family to look out for. No matter what else he may be, my husband is a wonderful father. I want my boys to have security and constant love as long as possible. It's so important . . . as long as possible,'' she repeated, her voice trailing off sadly.

Suddenly the front door barreled open and two skinny youngsters tore in, followed closely by a frazzled-looking Terry, his long but well-styled blond hair as messy as the boys' dark heads.

''Mom, we caught four frogs at Laurel Creek, but Uncle Terry wouldn't let us bring them home in his car,'' the older boy immediately complained, stepping in.

''I should think not,'' Brenda said, recovering from her melancholy with amazing speed, smiling at Terry.

The smaller child had sat down and began pulling off his running shoes. ''Mom, how come Brandon's allowed in the house with his muddy shoes on?''

Brenda looked in horror. ''Sometimes I wonder who's ten and who's two years younger. Brandon, you take those off pronto and march up to your room and put on clean clothes. And wash your hands. You, too, Geoffrey. We have company.''

Round-eyed, they both spotted Shanna. ''Are you Uncle Derek's new girlfriend?'' Geoffrey piped up.

Tough question, but she opted for a simple answer. ''Yes.''

''You're pretty, too.''

''Thank you.''

''Move,'' Brenda ordered. When they'd disappeared, after tripping over each other while racing up the stairs, she added sheepishly, ''Kids...''

''Hi, Shanna,'' Terry said, removing his own ankle-high running shoes. He slipped on a pair of sandals he'd left by the door.

''Hi.''

Brenda studied them. ''I gather you two have already met?''

''Through Megan,'' he said shortly, then poured himself a glass of water from the purifier tank on the sleek white countertop.

''How are you?'' Shanna asked, and the concern in her voice made the question more than a cliché.

''Other than parched, dirty and worn out by those tireless whippersnappers, fine. I'm living in Toronto now.''

''So Derek mentioned. Still not playing any tennis?''

''No. Well, not competitively at least.'' He concentrated on emptying his glass in one long swallow.

''Do you miss it?''

His expression grew serious, his tone defensive. ''No. I was ready to retire long before I did anything about it. Except to take out my discontent on the wrong people. I honestly don't see myself as a quitter, but as someone who got swept along in the wrong direction and finally stopped fighting the current."

As he talked, Shanna watched him closely. He did seem different, calmer somehow, almost as if he no longer needed to hover on life's precipices, but had stepped back a pace or two. "Derek says you like your new job a lot better."

"Wrong. I *love* my new job. Some people might say I'm *only* a deejay, but I don't care. I'm a damn good one. I've always loved music, but I can't play a decent note. So I appreciate those who can, have some fun in the process and encourage others to have a good time, too. Maybe they'll even forget some of their problems for a while."

"Think you'll stick with it?" Brenda asked.

"Don't know. Maybe. Probably. It sure feels right for now."

His blue eyes glimmered with enthusiasm and the familiar Morgan devilishness as he added, "Besides, the only records I have to break are the vinyl kind, and even those are growing obsolete now."

"Don't forget that other record you've been working on," Brenda said with a teasing glint.

"What's that?"

"When I asked if you wanted to bring a guest today, you informed me you haven't dated in months. I didn't know whether condolences or congratulations were in order."

He seemed to take her teasing in stride. "Hey, I've got a reputation to uphold here. For Shanna's sake, I should add that my...sabbatical is by choice and that I have been extremely busy with my new job." He poured himself another drink. "Actually I've made some new female friends, which is another switch for me. But I'm thinking of asking one of them out soon."

Brenda shook her head knowingly but fondly at him. "Some new leaf you've turned . . ."

"Hey, I'm going to go *real* slow next time around, as in turtle-snail slow. And it'll work both ways. The lady in question—a waitress at the bar—has had lots of time to know *me,* too, so there'll be no big surprises. She may even turn me down, knowing full well my bad track record with waitresses, but I'm preparing myself for that chance, too."

"Sounds good, Terry," Shanna said quietly.

He hesitated then said to her, "You know, I thought a lot about what happened with Megan, why she died. It's too late to change that, but I can make sure that I care enough about the people I have the power to hurt to prevent something like that from ever happening again." He looked away, perhaps aware of the telltale flush of color spreading above his collar.

One of the boys hollered from upstairs, followed by a loud thud. "I have to inspect my platoon," Brenda said, already running up the stairs. "You two join the party. Pour Shanna a drink, okay, Ter?"

"My pleasure. Madam?" He graciously offered his arm and led her outside to the minibar set up on the deck. At her request, he fixed her a simple soda water with lime.

Shanna was conscious of the stares of the other three men. She'd worn a softly pleated, apricot-colored skirt and a blouse in a lighter shade, unbuttoned enough to reveal her summer tan. She'd spent ages straightening her hair, then parting it off-center with a softly moussed bang. Because she kept having to toss back the shiny weight of it from her eyes, she was regretting the style change. She had no idea how alluring at least one of the men, perhaps all four, found the mysterious slant of her auburn waves.

"Well, I couldn't talk her into one of my unforgettable Fuzzy Navels," Terry said as they joined the others.

"Is that what you're learning at that *establishment* you work at?" Leo Morgan asked, eyeing his son with unmistakable disapproval. His face was all angles and planes, surrounded by coarse gray hair. The only softening came from his blue eyes, Shanna noticed, but they seemed to have lost some of the brilliant cast that made Derek's so captivating.

"I'm a deejay, not a bartender, Dad. And that 'establishment' happens to be a small but very popular bar on The Esplanade in Toronto. We're talking trendy with a capital T."

"It's a cop-out of a job, if you ask me, not that you bothered. You'll never get ahead there."

"By whose standards?" Terry returned swiftly. "At least I'm not always under the gun there. I can even relax for the first time in my life without any pressure—"

"That *drive* is what keeps the world moving, with the right people at the helm." As he spoke, Leo pointed his amber-colored glass at his son and it seemed to Shanna that this discussion was a small manifestation of some deeper, long-standing tension between the two men.

"Nice birthday party," Ray mumbled, throwing Terry a warning look.

"*Gentlemen,*" Derek said smoothly, firmly, "may I formally introduce Shanna Rhodes to you and perhaps inject a note of pleasant civility into these proceedings? Shanna, as you may have surmised, this is my father, Leo Morgan."

"Call me Leo, as long as you put more respect into it than these lads tend to." The elder Morgan shook her hand as vigorously as if they'd just sealed a business pact, then he excused himself to get another drink.

He was indeed as lionlike, as kingly, as the astrological associations of his name, but Shanna was less intimidated by him than she'd expected. He said what he felt, no matter how brutally frank, and she could deal with that kind of person far more easily than with the other kind, the deceivers. Shanna respected Leo Morgan for his honesty, but he also seemed so cold, aloof, unhappy.

"And this is my brother, Ray, the lord of this manor," Derek was saying. The black-haired Ray, a slightly heavier version of Derek with thicker jowls and a rounder middle, had also inherited the heart-stopping Morgan eyes.

"You have a beautiful home," Shanna said, appreciatively scanning the perfectly manicured lawn and gardens.

"And a great investment. The lot alone has practically doubled in the eight years we've been here. You can't go wrong with real estate. Do you own your own home?"

"Yes—"

"Good. I'm always telling Derek he should sink more into land, commercial or residential, it doesn't matter. But he never listens."

Derek smiled tolerantly. "That's what I pay my brokers and consultants for."

Ray nudged Shanna's arm. "Do you know this guy has more faith in German workmanship than in that of his fellow North Americans? He's a Porsche man. I ask you, what's wrong with a good solid Caddie?"

"I—"

Derek jumped back into the ring before she could say anything. "And that's from a guy who sports the finest from Switzerland on his wrist, Italy on his feet, and pictures from some other galaxy on his walls."

"That's art, pal. Have you shown her *your* collection of old baseball cards yet?"

"Not yet. Even though they are pricelessly close to my heart, some of 'em are also highly valuable originals." Not willing to be outdone, he winked at Shanna. "Ray secretly wishes he'd been born a Rockefeller."

"Why would I want to be a member of one of the richest families on the continent if I'd lose you for a brother?" Ray countered.

Bemused, Shanna just smiled, not willing to jump into the brothers' verbal rallying, knowing they were acting out a long-familiar scenario. There was a good-naturedness to it, but also a distinct competitive edge. Leo had rejoined the group, silently observing his sons.

"And then there's our Terry," Ray went on. "His collections are of the more private nature."

"Before he bores you anymore with my *past* escapades," Terry intervened, skillfully rerouting the conversation, "maybe you should let us know what *you* collect, Shanna."

"Homework assignments," Shanna answered drolly.

Both Derek and Terry grinned. Leo's expression was indifferent. Only Ray looked thrown off. After a second he said, "That's right. Derek said you were a teacher. Can't beat that. Lots of holidays for top salary all year round. Maybe I should get into teaching when I'm ready to slow down."

"It's certainly not a profession for slouches," Shanna stated hotly, resenting his implication. "In fact, it can be very demanding, with as much work in off-hours as you're willing to give. And most of us use our holidays to take extra courses or teach summer programs.''

"Whoa," Ray said, pretending to back away. "Just kidding..."

"There you have it, Ray ol' boy," Terry said, almost in glee. "Not only does the lady have class, she's got backbone, too. Now about those private lessons, ma'am..."

"Are you a landed immigrant, new Canadian or part of a cultural exchange program?" Shanna asked, continuing to feel a simmering unease as well as Derek's eyes upon her.

"I can be anything you want," he replied with well-practiced charm.

Derek's arm glided proprietorially around her. "Sorry, but I've got her all booked up. And I'm an extremely slow learner in certain...matters."

"With a reputation for being a dropout," Terry countered, slipping his hands into his pockets and rolling back on his heels.

Shanna's building annoyance compounded into anger again. It wasn't so much Terry's transparent but harmless flirting, or Derek's possessiveness that sent her over the edge, but the way she'd become an object to be tossed around in their ongoing competitive game. "Excuse me," she began, her voice louder than she'd expected. As they all stared at her in surprise, she drew a shallow breath, then counted as far as three, while weighing the wisdom of making a scene on her first meeting. But the balance was already tipped. "I'll make it easier for you to talk about me as if I'm not here. I'll be back in a few minutes." With that, she stepped across the lawn and up the deck in as dignified a manner as possible, knowing four pairs of eyes were watching her every move. She dodged

Brandon and Geoffrey, who'd bounded out the door like race horses at the starting gate.

"What was that all about?" Brenda asked, standing in the kitchen doorway.

"Oh, they ticked me off. I felt like an outsider in their inner sanctum... at best, their latest scoreboard."

"Welcome to the club," Brenda said sympathetically.

As Shanna freshened up in the elegant powder room, she reflected on Brenda's disillusionment with marriage to a man who had fallen short of true commitment. She thought of Derek. By observing him with his family, she better understood him. She realized how materialistic values could take on more importance than emotional ones for him. She wondered if he was capable of changing. Some of the vulnerable, tender moments she'd shared with him rose up to haunt her.

When she returned, she saw that Brenda was arranging appetizers on silver trays. She glanced outside. The men and boys were playing a vigorous game of volleyball at the far end of the lot.

"Need some help?" she asked Brenda distractedly.

"No..."

"In that case, I think I'll give my best shot at volleyball." Already she was taking off her sandals.

"Good luck!" Brenda's laugh of delight followed her out the door.

Shanna dropped her shoes as the group watched her approach. Momentarily taken aback, Derek and Terry finally recruited her to their team against Ray, Leo and the two boys. Although Shanna hadn't played many sports during her school days, she'd always enjoyed volleyball. No previous match, however, was taken as seriously as this supposedly friendly backyard game.

The men mapped out distinct in-out zones, and more than once heatedly questioned one another's calls. No error escaped razzing, whether the culprit was an opponent or teammate. To the Morgans' credit, praise for a well-executed play came just as freely, and there were many of those. Even Leo was in amazing shape for a man of his age. What energy he conserved, though, was exerted by Ray's two sons. Ray was surprisingly good with them, encouraging, teasing, disciplining by turns, and it was clear the youngsters thought the world of him.

Shanna soon discovered that the closer the score, the more the men enjoyed the game. She could not help but get caught up in the excitement, while trying to hold her own as much as possible. Her serve was her strength, and she happened to be serving when her team finally beat the tie and won.

"Good game," Derek said to her, wiping his brow with the back of his hand and staring at her in true admiration.

"Same to you, partner." He'd taken off his shirt and she could not help but be aware of the bronze sheen of sweat on his rippling torso. One of the best parts of the game, she secretly admitted, had been observing her well-muscled jock in action.

"Who wants a drink?" Ray asked. "Winners or losers, just to show I'm not a poor sport."

"I do! I do!" the boys chorused.

"Then bring out a few cold beers when you come back."

"No way!" They jumped onto his back, rolling over with him in a mock-wrestle.

Finally they all made their way to the deck where refreshments awaited. The game seemed to have loosened everyone up. Terry's rift with Leo slipped into the background, and the men's talk, predominantly of business, lost the former rough edges. Perhaps, Shanna was realizing, the brothers actually *enjoyed* the mental challenge of their sparring. Derek wasn't close to his family in a physical sense—she never saw him touching any of them, even in jest—but a bond nevertheless seemed to exist between them, a strong loyalty, despite their disagreements and competitiveness.

No sooner had they all nibbled on appetizers, than preparation for another feast began. Brenda kept bringing out cold gourmet salads, while Ray, wearing a "World's Greatest Chef" apron, barbecued enough steak to feed two entire volleyball teams. He continuously doused the meat with a spicy, red-wine-based marinade he'd concocted, deftly controlling the flare-ups. Shanna looked on in amazement.

"Ray, if you're ever contemplating a change in career," she began, braving a reminder of their prickly first conversation, "forget teaching. You are the most proficient grillmaster I've ever seen!"

"Thank you. Perhaps if I ever do a little moonlighting. At the moment, I have to keep my lovely wife in the manner to which she's accustomed." He exchanged a tender but wary look with Brenda. "Now for my next feat, I'll swallow my tongs."

As he pretended to demonstrate, Brandon rolled his eyes in mock-disgust and Geoffrey mumbled, "Dad..." But they were clearly amused, looking up at him with nothing short of adoration.

A fresh fire erupted on the coals and the next steak flipped was more charred than broiled. "Don't give up your day job yet," Derek advised, and they all laughed, including Leo.

Hastily Ray squirted water on the flames. "You're diluting your special high-potency sauce," Terry said drolly.

"Just as well." Brenda approached her husband as he reached for his assortment of jars again, but another minifire at the back of the grill needed his attention first.

"Maybe you should turn down the heat," Shanna suggested quietly.

Everyone stared at the gauge, set on high, then watched as Ray meekly adjusted it.

"See what a university degree gets you?" Derek's mouth curved into a wide smile as he looked from Ray to Shanna before winking at her.

They finally ate the meal, sinking into the plump red-and-white-striped cushions of two immaculate patio sets. Shanna still felt as if she were under scrutiny by the Morgans, but she sensed that Ray and Leo were beginning to accept her more.

None of the men moved after the main course was finished, so Shanna took pity on Brenda, who was scrambling to clear the tables. She helped her bring out coffee and an elaborate chocolate mocha birthday cake. A pile of envelopes appeared by Leo's plate; he said he'd open them later, but he couldn't postpone a wrinkled one offered him by an eager-faced Geoffrey.

"I picked it out myself," the boy said proudly. "See, there's books and papers and a stuffed duck. Dad said it's really a library, but we can pretend it's your office. 'Cause that's your favorite place, right?" Something fell out.

"What's that?" Leo asked.

"It's a Batman sticker. You can stick it on your car. I've got one on my bike."

"Thank you, Geoffrey," Leo said in his usual formal manner, but his voice had thickened, almost indetectably. His head was down as he put the card and decal back into the envelope with fingers that may have been fumbling.

"Happy sixty-fifth birthday, Dad," Derek said solemnly. "From all of us."

"Thank you." The rest of the group was looking at Leo expectantly, and for once he seemed at a loss for words. "No speeches," he finally declared gruffly. "It's no big deal. Now eat up."

They all obliged since it was Leo's only birthday wish, and the cake did look delicious. The boys downed their pieces in record time, then dashed off to kick a ball around in the yard, dragging a reluctant Terry with them. Shanna nudged Derek to help Brenda with some heavy trays, and he disappeared indoors. She was left alone with Leo and Ray, who were speaking in low tones about Morgan's at the next table. Her ears perked up when she caught the name Jalsevac and something about wasting time.

It took her a few minutes to get up her nerve to interrupt them, but she couldn't ignore the idea burning its way through her. "I understand Roger Hartly used to work for you, Leo," she began, not missing the sudden narrowing of his eyes. "I tutor his wife, and, well, I've had a chance to get to know Roger and—and to be familiar with his situation."

Ray and Leo looked at each other. Shanna continued hurriedly, "It may mean something coming from an outsider—I would swear by Roger's innocence. I think he deserves a second chance."

"Why do you think that?" Leo asked, his voice low, ominous.

"Most importantly, because he *is* innocent," she answered, refusing to be intimidated. Leo wasn't a machine or a god, she told herself. As much as he'd tried to hide it, he'd been moved by his grandson's birthday gift. He *did* have human emotions. "Derek tells me he was also a valuable employee, but the bottom line is really for—for Roger's sake. If he can't find another job right away, or if he wallows in self-pity collecting unemployment insurance, he may become desperate enough to do something foolish."

"That's Hartly's problem, not ours," Leo ground out, glancing accusingly up at Derek who had rejoined them, then at Terry who'd also ambled over.

Shanna leaned forward, anxious not to be dismissed before she'd made her point. The image of Roger's pinched and bitter face the last time she'd seen him was uppermost in her mind. "Think of this issue on a wider social scale, then. I'd say you actually have a *responsibility* to hire an ex-con like Roger Hartly. Do you know how many tax dollars it takes to keep a prisoner incarcerated and how overcrowded the jails are?"

Leo merely shrugged, and she saw she hadn't made any headway. "That's the way it is. Are you saying we should let crooks loose on the streets and threaten everyone's safety?"

"No, of course not. I realize it's a complex problem and there are no easy answers. I'm saying that in this case, you might be partly responsible—not wholly, I admit—for pushing a reformed yet forever vulnerable criminal back into an overburdened system needlessly. Do you want that on your conscience?"

"My conscience has taken more knocks than that." He scraped his chair back, looking around dismissively.

Frustration was starting to build in Shanna at his unbending attitude. To her further chagrin, Derek wasn't helping her out one bit. In fact, he was actually scowling at her.

As a last appeal, she remembered something she'd read, which had stuck with her because of her sympathy for Roger's plight. "Do you know that about ten percent of Canadians have a criminal record? That's about two million people."

Leo's face flushed with anger, then he lost his temper completely. "What the hell does that have to do with anything?"

"Shanna, that's enough," Derek warned.

Leo turned to Derek. "Now I know why you've been so hyped up about Roger Hartly," he lashed out. "Your high-browed lady friend set you up to it. Who knows how else she's got you wrapped around her finger?"

"That's not true—"

But Shanna saw him flinch. Obviously, Leo had struck a raw nerve. "Derek, just let me finish...." she began.

"Stay out of this, okay?" Derek railed at her.

"I'm trying to help—"

"You may be hindering. No one asked for your interference."

Shanna couldn't believe his attitude. Undaunted, too far involved to turn back, she turned to Leo. "Can you look me in the eye and tell me with absolute certainty that you don't have an ex-offender somewhere in your own family?"

"I certainly can," he said without hesitation.

"You're wrong, Dad."

Everyone but Leo stared at Terry behind his father's chair.

"What do you mean?" Leo asked slowly, his arms rigid at his sides.

"After the tennis tournament in France, I spent a few weeks in jail there. On an assault charge. Not that it's any excuse, but I was drunk and depressed one night. I picked a fight with a guy who recognized me and asked for my autograph, 'even if I was only a famous loser.' He was kidding, but I'd lost my sense of humor, too. I pleaded guilty to the charge because I was."

Stiffly Leo swiveled to face his youngest son. "Why didn't you tell me?"

"Because I didn't want you looking at me with that shame written all over your face. And I didn't want anyone springing for me, buying my ticket out. I thought it was time I took an accounting of myself."

A stunned silence followed.

"Did they treat you okay?" Derek finally asked his brother.

Terry's face darkened, although he was trying to be cavalier. "Let's just say I was mighty glad to be free. But I'll never really be free. It's something I'll have to live with for the rest of my life."

"Just like Roger," Shanna could not resist adding softly. Derek was still eyeing her with his former put-upon expression, though, and Leo's face was stony, unreadable. She'd had enough. "Thanks, Terry, for coming forward. I know how hard it must have been. And thank you Brenda and Ray for a superb meal. I have to leave now. I'll call a cab. Bye." She avoided Derek's eyes.

She was looking around the kitchen for the phone when Derek stepped through the glass doors and carefully slid them shut. "Don't be ridiculous, Shanna. I'll drive you home."

"That won't be necessary," she said coldly.

"Look, I appreciate what you were trying to do. But it's a delicate situation and I can handle my father better—"

"Why? Because you're a man? Do you know why you were upset back there?"

"I have a feeling you're going to tell me, regardless of what I say," he answered grimly.

"You were angry with me because, just like the rest of your family, you like to be in control, especially with women. Sure, it's fine to show us off, but once we step out of our allotted space, look out."

"You of all people ought to know about control," he burst out, finally wavering from his forced composure. "*You* have been controlling *me* for weeks now, by refusing to decide whether you really want to start over or whether you want to cling to your memories."

"What does that have to do with this?"

"Everything. I'm not the only heavy here. I'm tired of it all, Shanna. I'm here, now. Take me or leave me, but don't keep me dangling. I can't compete with your precious past."

"I'm surprised," she heard herself say, numb by now to the hurtful words, hers and his. "Your number one love in business *and* pleasure seems to be the thrill of competition."

"At least I know how to experience life, get ahead, go after what I want. I don't let myself stagnate."

"Maybe I'm going slowly with you, or *controlling* you as you see it," Shanna went on heatedly, "because I know that once you've profited by me, you'll want to dispose of me. Is that language you can relate to better?"

"I don't know—you're the language expert. I thought we *both* stood to gain something worthwhile, but you've conveniently forgotten that."

Their tempers had flared to the point of no return as they faced each other angrily. Shanna felt as if everything fragile between them had suddenly crumbled without hope of repair. "Let's just forget all this, okay?" she said flatly, wearily. "We're probably better off without each other."

She spotted the phone then and quickly called a cab. This time Derek didn't try to stop her. She waited on the street until the taxi came, a long ten minutes later.

CHAPTER ELEVEN

"SO HOW WAS IT, DAD?" Shanna asked casually.

No sooner had he joined her on the back patio than he'd started picking dried geraniums from the flower boxes he'd planted for her previously. He looked up. "How was what, dear?"

"The wine tour yesterday."

"Oh, it was okay."

"Okay!" She held her exasperation in check, concentrating on applying sun tan lotion to her legs as she stretched out on the lawn chair. "Okay, as in fun, educational, what?"

"Oh, I learned that foot-stamping grapes is passé—they've got this new Europress that gently *massages* juices out. And I learned how to smell wine and swirl it around like a mouthwash in order to reach *all* my taste buds, so don't get upset if I embarrass you next time we're in a restaurant."

"I won't," Shanna promised, studying his face. "So did you talk to anybody, meet anyone?"

He sighed. "I knew that was coming. Yes, if it'll make you feel any better, I tagged along with a nice couple from Germany who were here visiting their son and new granddaughter. I showed Alicia's pictures, they showed me theirs, that sort of thing. They return home this week, I believe."

Back to square one, Shanna thought. After her disastrous date with Derek two weeks ago, she'd thrown herself into her campaign to expand her father's horizons, despite his resistance. She'd taken great pains to gather information on all the local courses and groups. Finally she'd presented her father with a wide assortment of educational and social activities to choose from, gambling that *something* was bound to appeal. Halfheartedly, he'd selected the bus trip to a winery, saying he'd always wanted to try one.

"We had some time to explore some of the shops. I'd forgotten what a pretty town Niagara-on-the-Lake is."

"You didn't say you'd been there before."

"Your mother and I stayed at a quaint bed and breakfast once, when you were in college. We went to a play at the Shaw Festival. All very nice, different."

His voice had choked up and Shanna knew the visit had unexpectedly revived memories. At least they were pleasant ones.

"In such a cultured place, I couldn't help but pick Alicia up a few books," he went on with an effort, pointing to the bag he'd left on the picnic table earlier.

"Dad, you shouldn't—"

"I know, I know. Couldn't resist." Eagerly he eyed the netted carriage where Alicia slept, the light breeze keeping her comfortable in the early August heat spell. "In no time she'll be sitting on my lap, devouring knowledge, like you did."

"Right now, she would literally devour those pages," Shanna said dryly. "She loves chewing."

He grinned. "So what did you do this weekend?"

"Not much. Talia came over last night and we rented a Mel Gibson movie. We were both in the mood to eat our hearts out."

"Any word from Derek?"

"No, Dad."

"I can't believe he'd give up that easily. Over a little spat."

"It wasn't a spat, Dad. It was a major parting of the ways. He wants me on his terms, I want him on mine, and we can't seem to meet in the middle." But Derek Morgan was the last subject she wanted to discuss. She was finding it hard enough to forget him. "By the way, I picked up a few travel brochures yesterday. There's some excellent cruises with a minimal single supplement."

"I told you. I hate traveling alone."

"On a cruise everyone dines together, so it's an easy way to meet people." She thought it prudent not to mention that the ratio of men to women was definitely in his favor. And had it not been more than two years since her mother's death she wouldn't even have suggested such colossal travel plans.

"Besides, all the men on a cruise seem to wear white shoes, and I *refuse* to wear white shoes," Ned said petulantly. "And you seem to forget my income just dropped substantially. It's a far cry from the full pension I would have received had I stayed on at the bank longer. I just don't feel I'm in a position to splurge on such luxuries."

"But you own your own home, Dad, and you've always been one to save, not to mention that lump sum they gave you—"

"I hope to be around a long time, God willing. That money has to last me into the next century."

Plan B. "Well, how about a less extravagant trip—say, a week in the Bahamas?"

"Maybe next year."

Shanna smiled inwardly. The conversation was going exactly as she'd expected it to. Plan C. "Well, Talia did mention that a friend of hers is looking to hire some part-time help. At a garden nursery. It would be perfect for you."

"I don't know...."

"We took the liberty of arranging an interview for you, Monday morning."

"Shanna!"

"Come on, Dad. We went to a lot of trouble. There's no harm in just talking to the guy."

"All right, all right. If it'll get you off my back. But this is it, Shanna. From now on—"

"Fine. Whatever you want," she said breezily, glee-fully, because she was sure this opportunity was custom-made for him.

She was wrong again. Two days later, Ned informed her that he'd been offered the job, all right, but he could not possibly accept the salary, barely above minimum wage. He'd been a bank manager, after all. He had to salvage some pride....

For his birthday, Shanna went ahead and gave him a subscription to a new magazine for "retirement-minded Canadians," on the off-chance that he'd glean some insight she was missing. He did read about the health benefits of walking, so several times a week, he walked the four kilometers to her house in the cool morning hours, then rested up, usually staying for lunch and sometimes dinner, before she drove him home. Thank-fully his friend Helen had found new prey and called him less frequently, so he didn't mind spending the odd evening at his own place.

At her wit's end, Shanna turned to Talia once more during a late night phone call. "I don't know what to do anymore, Talia. I can't turn him away, and I don't want to hurt his feelings. He loves to spend time with Alicia so much."

"I know. She's all he talked about on our big night out. It's like she's become his security blanket. He's almost afraid of trying something new."

"I think he still misses my mom. A lot. He rarely talks about her, and he won't let me clean out her things for him."

"Hmm...bad signs. But each person goes through bereavement differently. You can't push."

"I know," Shanna said quietly, from her heart.

"You've certainly tried every approach with him— surprise, coercion, repetition. How about simply letting him be?"

"That won't solve anything."

"Listen, Shanna. How can your dad be independent if you're doing everything for him? Maybe he'll venture out in his own time, when he's ready, when there's no pressure."

Shanna stilled, staring at the lively beer commercial on the TV. "Well, it's worth a try. If I can wait him out. I need some time alone, Tal, for myself."

"I know you do," her friend said softly. Shanna had confided to her how much the rift with Derek had shaken her and confused her about steering her own life. "Why don't you take off with Alicia, anywhere? That would do both you—and your dad—good. And when you come back, I have this wonderful guy in mind for you. A real family man, big, bearlike, with grown children, but he's very young at heart—"

"No thanks." Talia had a network of friends for every purpose or fancy, but Shanna just wasn't in the right frame of mind for any further entanglements.

But Talia persisted. "He loves the outdoors, camping..."

"Good night," Shanna said sweetly. "Thanks for all your *other* advice."

As Shanna lay in bed, she recalled her conversation with her well-meaning friend, and suddenly she knew what she wanted to do. It was time to return to Maple Lake.

When she and Michael were newly married, they used to rent a cabin in Northern Ontario from an elderly widowed aunt of his, Vera Flanders. Vera refused to sell, for sentimental reasons—the land had been in her family for generations and her husband had built a one-room cottage on the lot. She rarely used the place herself anymore, and she'd been appreciative that Michael had inspected it occasionally. Apparently none of his other relatives was willing to rough it out. The gloriously lazy times that Michael and Shanna had shared there so long ago had far outweighed such minor inconveniences as insects, outhouse or lack of a dishwasher.

Shanna had not spoken to Vera since Michael's death. The eighty-year-old woman was delighted to hear from her. She sounded as robust as ever, and she promised to mail the key to Shanna promptly, refusing to take any money for the proposed visit.

"Just have a good rest, dear. You sound both tired and sad, and that's a tough combination. And don't be afraid to think of Michael there. When George died, the lake gave me more solace than city life ever could."

Five days later, on a sunny Thursday, Shanna was coasting along the highway for the four-hour drive from Kitchener. Thankfully her compact car was overpacked with provisions and paraphernalia for Alicia, or Ned would likely have jumped in. He wasn't pleased about being left behind, especially since he worried about her staying in the so-called wilderness alone and having to open up the cottage without assistance. She'd assured him a dozen times that she'd be fine.

The drive northward was relaxing, therapeutic. Alicia was well-fed and lulled to a deep sleep by the car's motion. Kim had canceled her lessons while Roger was out of work, so Shanna didn't feel as if she'd abandoned her. And with each mile she was putting both physical and psychological distance between herself and Derek Morgan. He'd opened up needs, vulnerabilities in her. She wanted to close them again and retreat exclusively into the rich, satisfying world that a growing Alicia offered her. It was enough....

The towering granite and limestone rocks of Muskoka on the edge of the Canadian Shield gradually blended into the rolling hills of the Haliburton Highlands. Shanna passed many roadside lakes on her journey; none compared to her first glimpse of the sparkling blue Maple Lake, nestled in a valley below the highway, surrounded by a verdant ridge—like sapphires and emeralds in a priceless setting.

She maneuvered her way along the bumpy private road, past a half dozen or so other cottages, to the farthest lot. Excitement rose in her as she saw it, almost hidden from view. The tiny cabin perched atop a rocky embankment, as if on giant stilts. Solidly built, it had survived storms and erosion, season after season, but on that tranquil summer's day, the only evidence of its hardships was a few broken branches strewing the overgrown path to its door.

Shanna had always loved best the magnificent trees that Vera and her husband had refused to cut down. Tall and slender silver birches, vying for light, bent toward the sky, their smooth ivory trunks all the brighter amidst the rough-hewn gray-taupe bases of the maples and the dark brown of the evergreens.

An offshore breeze fanned the late afternoon air, so Shanna put on Alicia's hat before she took her from the car. Dry scrub scratched her legs in her haste to climb to the deck that encircled the cottage. The view was as breathtaking as she remembered, more than compensating for the unwelcome look of the boarded-up building.

A crooked stand of cedars sheltered the front deck from the northwest winds and offered privacy from the adjoining cottage a few hundred yards away. To the easterly side, the rocky point dropped off sharply, so the thickly treed land had never been cleared nor inhabited. Far below, at the base of a rocky incline with natural but worn footholds, the lake shimmered and beckoned invitingly. Shanna hadn't realized how much she had missed coming here. Michael had been so busy and self-absorbed the past few years....

Michael. Her serious and intense husband was as much a part of this place as the white caps on the water or the jagged peaks on the horizon. Yes, she had come here to try to make her peace with him, at last. She'd never been able to do so during her visits to his burial site—a stark, foreign and daunting place to her.

During the next few days, she didn't consciously set out to think about Michael. She was too busy opening up the cabin, airing it out, figuring out how to turn on the water pump, cleaning, clearing pathways. She found time to swim and dry on the sun-warmed rocks, like a contented seal. A small strip of beach had been dug long ago. She let Alicia splash in the shallow waters and feel the soft powdery sand in her toes, revelling in her daughter's delight.

Shanna had just finished nursing Alicia at four months old, and she was surprised at her own renewed energy. She ate heartily, cooking frequently on her little hibachi. The fresh air and exercise invigorated both her and Alicia as much as it tired them at day's end. They slept long and well, Alicia in a small portable crib that Shanna had also used as a child, and Shanna on the soft mattress of the cottage's only bed.

She didn't talk to a soul. Occasionally she saw power boats and canoes glide by on the lake; she heard cars rumble by, dogs bark or voices call out from afar. Strangely she didn't miss more direct human contact. She drove once into the town of Haliburton for additional groceries and more paperbacks, having already read the few she'd brought with her. She stopped along the way to fill her jug with spring water, the most refreshing she'd ever tasted.

At odd moments certain memories of Michael caught her off guard—rubbing cream on his tender, sun-red shoulders, naming the constellations in a clear black sky together, discussing philosophy by the fire as they ate handfuls of jujubes; the candy was one of Michael's only frivolities. And for the first time, Shanna remembered a particular fireside night that she'd unconsciously blocked before. Michael had murmured that he wasn't afraid of death, only of life's incompletion. Later, he'd made love to her with an urgent desperation—perhaps because he'd sensed, uncannily, that he would die young.

The memories touched her gently, like a fine mist, but to her surprise they were not accompanied by the pain she'd once known. Why or when the pain had dissolved she didn't know. Perhaps it had left her as slowly as the ticking of time or as suddenly as the sun that burst through a cloud-draped sky.

However it had happened; she had finally found a place in her heart to lay her memories of Michael to rest—the good ones and the less-than-perfect ones, too.

The following dawn, before Alicia woke up, she went for a vigorous swim. Her naked body slashed through the still, mirrorlike lake, sending ever-widening rings outward. Treading water in the center of the ripples, she felt more alive, more in control, than she had in a long time. She had the kind of energy needed to travel the world or climb a mountain, but for now she was content to believe that happiness was within her reach and her power, as surely as the circles that radiated from her motion.

Her euphoria lasted for several more days. She went for long walks along the quiet back roads. Alicia loved to snuggle against her chest in her denim pouch or face outward if she wasn't sleepy. One elderly couple who stayed up at their own small cottage during the weekdays used to wave at them from their porch. Shanna made up her mind to chat with them the next chance she could, but then rain fell all day Friday, so she didn't venture out.

Confined indoors, she found the isolation started to get to her. She was finally ready for home and its comforts. She'd been away two weeks, and she wondered how her father was doing. Deliberately she hadn't called him. She decided she would leave first thing tomorrow.

By daybreak, the sun rose onto clear skies. Wrapped in a towel and wearing only her thongs, since she had never encountered anyone at such an early hour, she rushed outside for her last morning dip. She stopped to gaze out from the front deck. Because she knew she was leaving, she savored the rich woodsy scent of the wet earth and trees and the glistening sight of the wildflowers—the daisies, buttercups, devil's paintbrushes and starflowers that had become so familiar to her.

She rounded the corner of the deck and froze. A flash of black metal had caught her peripheral vision. A car. A car she recognized. Slowly she approached it. Stretched out on the reclining seat was Derek Morgan.

A twig crackled at her feet, or maybe he heard her heart pounding. He blinked and sat up abruptly on his elbow. He saw her, blinked again, then rolled down the window.

"Morning," he drawled, stretching, as if it were perfectly ordinary that he was there, hundreds of miles from home. He smiled, his blue eyes as roguish and heavenly as ever.

In those pure, obliterating seconds, Shanna felt only gladness to see him . . . and a renewed optimism that they could work everything out.

CHAPTER TWELVE

DEREK EMERGED from the car, straightened his jeans—jeans, and old jeans at that!—and kicked out the kinks in his cramped legs.

"Don't tell me you happened to be passing by?" Shanna asked giddily.

"No." He looked around curiously, pulling down his cranberry-red football shirt, but not before she'd glimpsed the mass of curling dark hair on his torso. He managed to act confident, despite his tousled hair, wrinkled clothing and above all, the possibility that she might be unwelcoming of his visit. "No, I drove through rainstorms and traffic snarl-ups, over hill and dale, not to mention several dark cottage roads—the wrong ones—just to see you. But in my wildest dreams," he added, his voice lowering huskily as his eyes came to rest upon her, "I never thought I'd see so much of you so soon."

Brazenly he stared at the low-cut band of her towel and the flash of pale thigh where the ends did not quite meet. Shanna restrained herself from tightening the knot. She could act as nonchalantly as he. "I like to start the day with a swim. It's invigorating."

"I can imagine...." And his boldly provocative look gave her a clue as to what he was imagining. "Come here, Shanna."

Before she could step forward, though, his arm had reached around her and he was kissing her deeply, tenderly. All that held up her towel was the pressure of his firm body as it molded itself against hers.

"Hmm . . . *good* morning," he repeated, pulling back, his hands interlocking about her waist, and it didn't matter that the towel had slipped lower. Their eyes were busy with amazement and questions.

"I couldn't stop thinking about you," he explained. "I ran miles on the track, I slammed balls on the squash court, I snapped at everyone at work, and I even saw Rachel again." Tension coiled within Shanna. "But even that didn't help, except that this time we parted more objectively. I grew frantic when I couldn't reach you. Finally I tracked your father down. He gave me vague directions and his blessing to check up on you. Even my own father banned me from the office until I showed up less miserable. I've done all I can for Roger right now, his parole officer is keeping a close eye on him . . . so here I am."

"I—I don't know what to say."

His lips breathed a hot trail from her forehead, past her ear, curving along her chin. "Can you put up with me for a day or two?"

"I can try," she murmured with no effort at all.

"I even dug out my old Boy Scout tent. For old time's sake. And I wasn't sure about the accommodation. . . ."

The morning wind suddenly picked up, rustling through the trees, filling the silence. "You're not afraid of bears?" she asked softly at last.

"No, only of why I'm here."

A hunger cry from Alicia rang out through the open window. "The day begins," Shanna said, green eyes meeting blue with a powerful force.

"No, it's already begun," he answered softly. "Are you still going for that swim?"

"No." She didn't tell him she no longer needed one. He'd already made her heart pump faster, her skin tingle, her brain grow alert. Nor did she tell him she'd intended to leave today.

She adjusted her towel and slowly stepped away from him. They headed toward the cabin, exchanging little smiles of disbelief and anticipation.

Not until later, after Shanna had cooked a hearty breakfast of ham, toast and eggs, and they were sitting on an old log by the lake, did she mention the harsh words exchanged at the barbecue. With Alicia sitting contentedly on her lap, the rustic cabin perched on the rocky cliff behind them like a watch guard, and the dappled sunshine working its warming magic, the dark forces that had pulled them apart seemed so remote. But they had to be faced.

"I think we should talk about what happened," Shanna began, reluctantly.

He gazed off at the play of shadows and light on the distant hills, a mosaic of dark forest green and bright emerald. "I know...I realized I shouldn't have let my father come between us."

"Your father wasn't the issue."

"What was the issue, Shanna?"

She, too, stared ahead, across the lake to the sharply serrated tree line against the blue summer sky. "I don't think we saw each other clearly enough. For *who* we really are," she answered carefully. "I can't profess to understand the world you live in, your man's world, and I was wrong to condemn you for it."

"And I can't fully understand yours," he admitted quietly.

"But nothing is going to change my world. I'm a mother and a widow, Derek. I can never think like a single person again. Not like you, perhaps. Alicia and my marriage are both a part of me. But that's *me*, and I want to do the best I can, with what I have left, now.''

As he listened, he looked sideways at her, from her long auburn waves to the faint freckles on her tanned legs that matched the ones dusting her nose. In her simple white beach robe, she was like beauty personified to him. Strangely he felt as close to her as to an old lover, yet they'd never crossed the threshold of deepest intimacy. The child propped placidly in the circle of her arm was a familiar sight, too. But something had changed in Shanna's voice, her eyes, her manner.

''You seem different here. Happier, somehow,'' he said.

Gentle waves curled over her toes as she buried them in the cool sand. ''I suppose I am. I've made my peace with Michael,'' she added, voicing for the first time her acceptance of his death.

''Just to see you like this—serene—has made my whole trip worthwhile.''

She faced him. With his baggy shirt, faded jeans and bare feet, with his hair uncombed and his face unshaven, he was a far cry from the man she'd first known, the sophisticated Derek Morgan who coveted money, material goods and victories more than love and intimacy. Yet without his glib talk and designer clothes, in this uncivilized setting, he seemed a different person, too. Or maybe she was just seeing another side of him, one that had never been revealed to her before. She still didn't fully know the man beneath the confident humorous facade, but she had learned that he was not as self-centered as she'd once thought. He'd been kind toward Megan and decent to Roger without thought of personal gain. And to herself... that was harder to define.

She sensed in him a deep reservoir of tenderness that had rarely—if ever—been tapped. Did he keep coming back to her because he needed her to help him find its source or were his motives predominantly sexual, more base? And would he choose to move on before she could decipher the truth, as he had with Rachel and the other faceless women before her?

As she thoughtfully studied him he was silent. Soon a familiar, slow, teasing smile began to curve his mouth. "Can't resist doing a little grading, can you, teach, even during off-hours?"

"Guess not."

"You know, you and I are like the English language. We don't follow all the rules. In fact, we are one big exception. Otherwise, what would a nice girl like you be doing in mosquito country—" he swatted one that had just alighted on his arm "—with a crazy guy like me?"

"Good question."

"Maybe we should figure out the answer together. I find that answers creep up when you least expect them to, so why don't we just plan a fun day, forget about questions or arguments about who's controlling whom, and see what happens?"

His sunny smile was absolutely engaging. "Okay..."

"I just happen to have brought along *the* luckiest fishing rod in the world with the friskiest frog lure to ever dip into this lake. All I'm missing is a five-hundred-horsepower boat to reel in my king-size prize in style."

"Would an inflatable rubber dinghy do?"

He shook his head in mock disappointment. "Guess I'll just have to stake out the best spot on the shoreline. I'd also like to squeeze in a little deep-water diving, barefoot skiing, hiking, tree climbing, wood chopping, then, this afternoon, all warmed-up, perhaps I'll take a go at a butterfly stroke across the lake, before I set out to challenge Vicki Keith's world records.''

"Be my guest. I think I'll just watch you in action, though.''

"Guaranteed thrills, spills and chills.'' But he didn't seem inclined to move, and they passed the morning just sitting lazily by the shore, continuing to banter light-heartedly.

Finally, while Shanna was giving Alicia her midday bottle, Derek gathered his shiny, expensive-looking rod and a box full of fancy gear. He took off his shirt and discreetly changed into the gaudiest bathing trunks Shanna had ever seen, in lime green, orange and black. Nothing could detract, however, from the way they fit his splendid male form.

As Alicia slept and Shanna read, Derek waded to some reeds and cast out patiently for more than an hour, without so much as a nibble. He was kept busy untangling numerous snags, though, which Shanna pretended not to notice from her vantage point on the beach.

"Don't say a word,'' he warned when he rejoined her. He deposited his rod and looked down at her, or more accurately at the high-cut lines of her black one-piece suit.

"Have a seat.''

But he ignored the old lounge chair she'd carried down for him. "I think I'll have a swim instead.''

"Go ahead.''

His arms bent to scoop her up, causing her book and sunglasses to drop into the sand. "Derek, I'll go in when I'm ready. You wouldn't be so juvenile or unoriginal as to throw me in, would you?'' She kicked out in case her confrontational strategy didn't work, but his arms only tightened their hold.

"Don't worry. I'm not throwing you anywhere," he said, as he determinedly carried her through the shallow waters until he was submerged just below his shoulders. He eased her down then, letting the cool clear water flow around them, his smoldering eyes locked with hers. Her legs felt weightless as he guided them around his waist.

Because her arms had remained about his neck, it was only natural that she now nudge his head toward her as he bent to kiss her. His lips rested lightly against hers as he continued walking outward, and soon they were both underwater, their mouths pressed together in a shared smile.

Shanna kept her eyes closed so her sense of touch was intensified; both he and the water stroked her with the delicacy of a paint brush. His skin felt like soft leather under her fingers with rougher suede patches where the hair grew thicker. They floated and clung for a prolonged breath's length, then rose to the surface in a burst of bubbles and gasps that shattered the underwater stillness.

Treading water, they blinked at each other through water-spiked lashes. Suddenly Derek was gone, arcing his back as he swam away with powerful strokes. Shanna could almost swear she heard a boyish whoop over the noise of the splashes. Dazed, she rolled onto her back to catch her breath and invite the sun's heat to further enliven her body....

Before long, Derek's hand was at her ankle, though, and they were playing in the water—chasing, diving, splashing with youthful abandon, except that the very adult and decidedly sensuous nature of the game was never far from mind.

Even after Alicia had woken up, their high-spiritedness continued throughout the afternoon and into the early evening. Occasionally motorboats roared by and passengers waved politely at them, but Shanna somehow felt that she and Derek were cut off from the rest of the world.

He insisted on initiating Alicia to the joys of dunking. To Shanna's surprise, her pudgy, bikini-clad daughter was soon squealing with delight, but whether from the security of his firm grip, the late-day warmth of the water, the exuberance on Derek's face, or a combination of all three, she couldn't be sure. She had previously immersed Alicia so timidly that some of her hesitation must have passed to the child.

Afterward, Derek held Alicia in a huge beach towel while Shanna ran to fetch dry clothes for her and to change into jeans and a T-shirt herself. When she came up behind them, he was showing his charge where he figured the biggest fish in the lake lived and detailing how he was going to nab them. Alicia's round head with its faint new growth of fair hair was bobbing as she looked up at him, seemingly engrossed.

Derek looked up in embarrassment when he noticed Shanna watching them. "She's a good listener, and she doesn't talk back. My kind of companion."

"Maybe she likes the deep rise and fall of your voice."

"It wouldn't have anything to do with my golden words of wisdom?"

"I doubt it," she teased back, eyes dancing.

He sighed. "Why do I put up with such abuse? Unfortunately I'm too hungry to fight back." On a sudden serious note he added, "She has your eyes, you know."

"It's too soon to tell."

"I can tell. They're your eyes. Your beautiful green eyes."

As his gaze penetrated hers, a sensuous pressure enfolded Shanna's body. She took Alicia from him, needing the distraction as they headed back to the cottage.

They'd only snacked on plums and crackers since breakfast, so they were both ravenous. Derek unveiled two T-bone steaks from his cooler, as well as some fresh lettuce and crusty bread, and they each pitched in to prepare dinner, taking turns amusing Alicia. They ate on the deck in the "Cedar Room," as Derek coined it after a dangling bough kept tickling his arm until he wrestled the greenery off.

Every time that Shanna looked out toward the horizon, the flaming red-orange sun had settled lower, creating a dazzling display of colors on the cloud-streaked sky. She was filled with the same exhilaration she used to feel on New Year's Eve, watching, on television, the famed ball drop at Times Square—that sense of past, present and future blending gloriously.

However, after the hearty meal and a few sips of the vintage French burgundy, also compliments of her guest, the day's activities caught up to her. She leaned back in her chair, and no power on earth could stifle the yawn that came from her, nor could she hide it from Derek. He yawned back.

"You'll have to tuck me in early tonight," he said drowsily.

Shanna just nodded, not having given any thought to sleeping arrangements. But while she was gathering up the dishes, Derek disappeared outside. She peered out the window to see the wind puffing up a bright blue nylon tent and Derek hammering the stakes with a rock. He'd found the only flat spot on the lot, next to his car.

"You really brought a tent?" she murmured when he returned.

"Yup, and I really intend to sleep in it. If that's okay with you?" His look was guileless, suspiciously guileless. A tiny pulse beat along his neck.

"Ah, that's fine. There's room in here on the couch, bumps and all, but at least there's no wild animals."

"I think it's safer outside." He turned quickly from her.

He didn't raise the subject again. When darkness fell, they sat on their old log once more, a blanket over their laps, and watched the fire Shanna had made within a circle of rocks in the sand. They didn't talk much, but that didn't matter. Shanna felt comfortable, mellow. Suddenly Derek asked if Michael had worn a tuxedo at their wedding.

"Why?" she replied, taken aback.

"I just remember his long hair, moccasins, Indian shirts, gold-rimmed glasses, the perpetual poetry notebook. No matter how hard I try, a tux refuses to fit the image."

"You're right," she said, surprised she could smile in agreement, without the knifelike stabbing of her former pain. "He wore a regular suit, his first. Tieless, though. That came later, as did the hair cut, contacts, briefcase, *real* shoes."

"Alas, another hippie-turned-yuppie. And you. What did you wear?"

A soft, wistful look crossed her face. "A simple white dress, knee-length. We chose a small civil ceremony."

"No big hat or flowers growing out of your pretty hair?"

"No."

"Good. That's what I imagined, your hair loose, tears of emotion in your eyes...." He stopped, knowing she was eyeing him curiously. "I want to have the whole pic-

ture of you inside me, Shanna. The beginning, middle
and . . . now. And I guess I've finally got it through my
thick head that Michael is a part of all that.''

They moved onto another subject, as naturally as wisps
of smoke drifted away with the wind. Soon they simply
stared at the crackling spires of fire that reached toward
the black, star-spiked sky.

Watching the flames slowly turn to glowing embers,
Derek was filled with a great melancholy. He did not
want this special night nor his time with Shanna to end,
as he knew they would. Fighting this feeling, he held her
hand as they finally climbed the steep hill to the cabin. He
kissed her good night and waited for her invitation, but
none came.

As he zippered up his tent, he knew that his resolve to
keep himself from her until he was sure she was ready was
as frail as the nylon flap. He lay in the darkness, the night
sounds of crickets and rustling leaves droning in his ears,
wondering how he would know when the time was right.
He could not bear another rejection from her.

Sleeplessly Shanna stared at the swaying branches
outside her window, listening to the whispering winds and
the rhythm of Alicia's breathing. Derek's deeply moving
kiss still lived warmly on her lips, and she wondered how
she would know when the time was right for more.

Minutes later or perhaps hours, the cottage door
creaked. She felt no fear as the shadow moved toward
her. Slowly she sat up. Derek's face, illuminated by the
cabin's night-light, seemed like a fine sculpture of angles
and planes.

"I wish I had a thunderstorm as an excuse," he whispered throatily, lowering himself to the edge of the bed.

"You don't need one," Shanna admitted, exhaling
softly.

The back of his trembling hand caressed her cheek with an intensity of emotion that made her heartbeat accelerate. "There are parts of you that will never be mine, but more than anything, I want to be with you, Shanna." He pulled back the covers and his hand stilled. A slow grin broke across his face.

"What's so funny?"

"Your, ah, pajama top. 'Thirtysomething, still looking for a little dirtysomething,'" he read with delight.

"A present from my friend Talia," Shanna mumbled, unsuccessfully hiding her embarrassment. "I didn't expect company and—and I hardly go around displaying it to the world."

"I should hope not." He buried his face in the crook of her shoulder, his moist breath heating her neck, sending tremors along her flesh beneath the pink nightshirt under discussion. "Besides, I'd like to be personally responsible for ending your search."

"Hallelujah." And a smile once more mingled with the desire that always ran through her when she was with Derek Morgan.

From the place where hearts yearn and bodies crave, her arms reached around his neck and pulled him down beside her. He pressed his mouth to hers, kissing her with a hunger that could not be satisfied, a gladness that knew no bounds. Then he slowed down. The tip of his tongue lightly teased hers; he traced a delicate path to her ear, where he sucked gently, first one lobe then the other on his journey back. His hands slid down her body....

Shanna sighed and turned her face into his chest, feeling the wiry hair, the soft texture of his flannel shirt, his thundering heart. But it wasn't enough. Her own hands slipped beneath the fabric to seek more warm skin. The shirt was hastily, carelessly unbuttoned and thrown away by two pairs of eager hands. Her fingers luxuriated in the muscle-hard expanse of his back, the wide smoothness of his shoulders, the taut roughness of his abdomen, stopping at the leather rim of his belt. At her nearness a soft moan erupted at the back of his throat.

His own hands were busy exploring her with the same urgency. He reached beneath her nightwear to cup her breasts. Fiercely. Possessively. With searing familiarity, he rolled each nipple between his fingers, then bent to taste them. She was certain she could not stand the white-hot, exquisite torment any longer, but how she wanted to....

His touch edged along the swell of her hips. She shifted her weight, arching toward him, instinctively seeking more.

He started to pull away from her, and her eyes shot up to meet his. "I'm just getting undressed," he said, amused by her dismay.

She slipped her own clothing over her head, and because she had less to remove she was able to watch his jeans drop to the floor with a jangling thud. His perfect male body, swollen hard with need, turned toward her. A primeval longing roared down her spine, bursting into fragments of pleasure in the very center of her being.

Derek witnessed her desire, pure and primitive, and the soft womanly smile that crossed her face, and thought he had never beheld such a powerful sight. Hot blood was surging through his veins. He craved release, but he drew a deep ragged breath to maintain control. His own desire had escalated, not just from the high eroticism between them now, but from all the wanting and waiting he'd endured before tonight. Strangely, knowing his goal was within his reach made him want to prolong the sweet agony as much as possible.

He dropped beside her again and held her warm, naked length to his for the first time, her breasts nestling against his chest, his legs entwining with hers. Their bodies meshed in astonishing perfection. A strange urge to shout in reckless joy nearly overwhelmed him, and a quiet laugh escaped from him at the ludicrous thought. Above all, he wanted to hear Shanna cry out with the ultimate pleasure they would share, while he was as close to her as was humanly possible....

Shanna heard the mysterious chortle erupt from Derek's lips and thought it was the most natural sound in the world. His restless mouth closed over hers, drinking the moist depths with an endless thirst. His lips never ceased their magic on her as his hands began to explore at a halting pace, stopping to play with a knotted nipple, pausing to stroke a curve of flesh, moving on to something new, then returning to relive a particularly pleasing sensation.

With excruciating slowness, his hand inched up her thigh, where it lingered to become acquainted with the silken folds of her femininity. His fingers danced lightly there for breathless moments, before they entered her in a liquid, languid motion. Shanna's response was piercing, incredible. She clasped her arms around his neck as her hips began a sinuous dance of their own. His other hand found her nipples again, connecting her pleasure centers until the tension was almost unbearable. A low whimper was wrenched from her.

Their mouths separated as they both tried to regulate their gasping breath. Derek shifted his weight until he lay partially over her, his hardened sex against her leg, taunting, teasing, seeking. Their eyes met, serving only to increase the passion gripping them, clamoring for release. Derek moved again, so that his hands and lips could touch her in new ways, and suddenly her finger-tips encountered the source of his manhood. She encircled him, lightly then firmly, while moving in a timeless rhythm.

She felt his deep groan as if it came from her own throat. Then suddenly he was sitting on the edge of the bed, rifling through his clothing in the pale light. Without asking, she knew why. A wave of profound tenderness washed over her. He returned to fold her tightly in his arms and kiss her thoroughly as if they'd been parted far too long.

"Are you okay, Shanna...after the baby? I don't want to hurt you."

"Everything's fine," she murmured softly, impatiently, her arousal intensifying because of his concern for her.

"Good, now where was I? Here?" His hand scorched a path down her already heated body, lingering on her breasts, tugging tenderly, then roughly. "Or here?" Wantonly, his fingers slipped inside her. More heat, a fire that craved to be doused, but was only heightened by the fresh moistness overtaking her.

Their mouths met and opened wide, instinctively begging for further intimacy. Two hands were suddenly anchoring her head, tunneling through the wildness of her hair, as he lowered himself upon her. His chest brushed tantalizingly against hers before she welcomed the warm pulsing weight of him. As he nuzzled into her neck, her breath escaped in a serrated rhythm, as uneven as his.

Slowly, gently, he entered her. She guided his passage, although her assistance proved unnecessary. She'd opened for him naturally, invitingly, surrounding him with a warm tidal rush, her arms locked around his waist.

It had been so long since Shanna had made love that it felt as wondrous as her first time, yet infinitely more enjoyable as she was bathed by familiar, long-forgotten sensations, their renewed intensity almost overpowering.

With his lips melded to hers, they began to move together in a relentless synchrony. Again and again, Derek thrust into her. Wide, all-encompassing spirals of pleasure radiated through her, then Derek's movements would cease, letting her seek out the most sensitive place of all. She tightened her legs around him, urging him to press harder. He rose up, then drove deeper, whispering her name with a profound, uninhibited joy. A wordless sound escaped from her, too. On a primitive level she responded to his sheer boundless enthusiasm. Her fingers dug into his back, then the powerful ripples crested inside her, resonating with mind-blackening, breath-robbing force along every nerve she possessed. Slowly the pinnacle of intensity faded....

Derek felt her quivering heights and her calming. His breathing, his senses, became one with hers. Nature ordained that he quicken his pace until heated life rushed through him at last. The air was pressed out of his lungs as he erupted within her, like a man possessed. He cried out her name again on a long expelled breath, then clung to her fiercely, his life-saver, his life-giver, as the eruption subsided.

The thing that was woman in Shanna responded to his powerful male surge. Once more, convulsive shudders rocked her body. Her climax started before his had ended, and the two merged into one glorious vortex. They held each other until their heartbeats slowed. Joined thus, in the aftermath of their selfless union, Shanna was struck by a single thought. It was as if they were two faces of a dazzling prism, two sides parallel to one central axis that she was afraid to call love....

As languor turned to drowsiness, they resettled into each other's arms, and the last sound Shanna heard was Derek's low murmur of satisfaction. "Much nicer than the tent. Thought you should have me before the bears did."

Thankfully Alicia slept through the night, never one to be roused by background noises, but at dawn her demanding cry of hunger awakened them both abruptly. Derek buried his face in the pillow they'd shared and grumbled that he had to admit the truth at last. He was *not* a morning person. Eventually he rolled sideways to watch Shanna, who had retrieved her nightshirt and donned a pair of white gym socks to warm her against the morning chill.

His gaze was fixed on her so unabashedly as she heated Alicia's bottle that she finally asked in playful exasperation, "What?"

"Nothing."

"You've never seen a negligee quite like mine, right?"

"Hmm...nor such wonderful legs."

"Thank you." She dipped in a pert curtsy, then sat down with Alicia on her lap, the springs of the old chair squeaking loudly.

"You also make me reconsider the sweet benefits of mornings." His low husky voice was like a caress upon her body, still sensitive from their lovemaking.

"Hold that thought," she murmured back, lowering her eyes to give Alicia her bottle, trying to feel matronly.

"I intend to."

If Shanna had any fear that last night's culmination of their attraction would dampen their appetite for each other, she was wrong. Their mutual need grew stronger because of the heightened awareness. Every look, every touch, was filled with sensuous meaning and promise. Even after he'd stepped outdoors, she still felt attuned, linked to him. She couldn't help but notice that their mugs touched cosily on the counter, their mingled scents lingered on the bedding, his jacket lay carelessly over hers.

He returned, bearing a bouquet of flowers. "From the roadside florist," he told her, lightly brushing her lips.

Wild lilies of the valley. Their tiny, sweet-scented white flowers and heart-shaped leaves pleased Shanna more than a dozen boxed roses, delivered impersonally, ever could. She put them in a coffee jar on the steel-legged kitchen table, delighting in their pretty simplicity amidst the rustic decor.

The day was once more warm, sunny, inviting. After breakfast, they walked farther along the tree-shaded back roads than Shanna had ventured on her own. Derek volunteered to carry Alicia in the backpack. The pleasant stroll lulled her to sleep, though. She was awake by the time they returned, so the two lovers could not be alone until she was ready for her afternoon nap.

After lunch they swam briefly, then came to each other determinedly, urgently in the unmade bed, swiftly shedding their wet bathing suits. Their desire was already fueled by anticipation, by the sweet private thoughts that they'd each indulged in all morning. This time, however, they stayed awake afterward, exploring each other in the light of day with the shamelessness and lightheartedness of satiated lovers.

They returned to the water long after darkness had fallen. As they cavorted through the warm and cold currents, aftershocks seemed to reverberate along their unencumbered, overcharged flesh. Hand in hand, they finally ran back to the cabin to finish stroking each other to fulfillment. Derek then surprised Shanna by challenging her to a card game called Concentration. They matched pairs, alternating fun with sensuality, not being able to resist a playful touch if the sought card rested near a leg or an elbow. Finally they slept, burrowing close to each other, marveling at their newfound intimacy.

They spent the following days and nights in the same leisurely, lazy, provocative fashion. Shanna had discovered in Derek not only an exciting, innovative lover, but a deeply passionate one. She realized that because Michael had been a more restrained person he had never uncovered the rich layers of sensuality that Derek could evoke so easily from her.

With the emotional fulfillment she received from her daughter and the physical satisfaction that Derek provided, Shanna started to feel happiness again—a tempered happiness, though, because she never took anything for granted with Derek Morgan.

On Thursday, the sixth afternoon of his visit, they were floating in the dinghy, anchored close to shore. Shanna's legs were atop Derek's as they faced each other in the small, but comfortable quarters, clad only in their bathing suits and T-shirts. The sky was hazy, the air muggy, so being able to splash intermittently in the lake was welcome relief. And nothing was more relaxing than rocking in the gentle swell of the waves.

Shanna was reading; she thought Derek was dozing, a towel over his eyes, when suddenly he began to speak. "You know, this is kind of how I've felt my whole life."

From beneath her visor-cap she peered at him through her sunglasses. Something odd had crept into his voice. "How?" she asked.

"I don't know—adrift, pampered, my reasons for being here somewhat vague. I mean, it's all great, and who could complain with a companion like you...." The towel fell from his face as his fingers lightly slid up one of her legs.

"But this isn't life, Derek," Shanna was compelled to say slowly. "It's part of the rest, but still just a sanctuary, a holiday."

"I know," he stated in a rare, serious tone. His arm dropped into the water, and idly he watched it glide below the surface. "You know, for a long time I've dallied with the thought of buying land, not in a prime real estate area, as Ray's always pushing me to do, but somewhere quiet, out of the city. Maybe before I'm old and gray, I even thought it would be neat to build my own house there, or more realistically, to supervise someone who could use a hammer better than I. Then I'd have somewhere to call home before I *am* old and gray."

"It doesn't sound like an impossible dream."

"No, I don't suppose it's impossible, but dreams are dreams. They don't always fit into reality. My day-to-day practical side tells me I barely spend enough time at my condo to justify the high price I paid. What do I need with a big empty house, anyway?"

Shanna couldn't answer the question for him. The swish of water became more pronounced as silence fell between them. She stared at her book, pretending to find her place.

Suddenly he fell forward onto his knees to lean closer to her, which made the dinghy rock precariously. "Hey, don't look so serious. It's no big deal," he said. "I'm happy with things the way they are, especially with you. Aren't you?"

"How *are* things?" she asked pointedly, the first time she'd questioned him about their relationship since they'd slept together. The answer had taken on a new, frightening importance.

"Good," he murmured, pushing back her sunglasses to see her eyes more clearly. "Very good. Too good, if that's possible."

And she was lost in a sea of blue, his lips drawing closer. "I want to finish this chapter," she protested weakly.

His hands began working their magic upon her. "There's a chapter in my life that needs some attention."

"Not here."

"Why not?"

She knew he was perfectly capable of taking her there, in broad daylight; the more dangerous the situation, the more appealing. "Because I like to be on solid ground." He didn't seem to be listening as he began to rain kisses upon her neck, despite the boat's tottering. She broke free and climbed out none too gracefully, wetting both herself and her paperback. She only made it about halfway to the refuge of the cabin, when he caught up to her. He led her to a sheltered nook beneath a canopy of conifers, well-hidden from the lake or the adjoining property. He spread out his towel, and without much more sensual persuasion, Shanna lay there with him. In the pine-scented, humid den, they became one, their muffled cries mingling with the screech of gulls and the soft friction of fallen leaves, needles and moss beneath them.

"I HAVE GOOD AND BAD NEWS." Derek gazed out at the faraway gray clouds that were moving closer, his elbows leaning on the deck.

Shanna tensed. From the minute he'd informed her, just before dinner, that he should drive to the nearest phone to check in with his office, she'd suspected their idyll would be coming to an end. Especially when he'd been gone longer than she'd expected. She was holding Alicia on her hip as she, too, rested against the railing, facing him. "Okay, shoot."

"Jalsevac wouldn't say much over the phone, but I gather he has some good evidence in Roger's favor. I have to go back."

"That's what I figured."

"Tonight."

"Oh." She swallowed. "There's a storm coming...."

"I want to be there first thing in the morning. Plus, there's some other crises, the usual kind. You do understand, don't you?"

"Sure," she said quickly. "But we won't have one last night...here," she added, fighting the insecurity that wanted to well up inside her at the threat of change. They'd only spent six nights together, but already she'd grown accustomed to his warm body beside hers. And she hadn't had time to examine her deepest feelings for him....

"We'll have lots of nights." He smiled unconvincingly as his eyes focused beyond her. As an afterthought, he murmured, looking around, "Oh, I went for a walk on the way back and I found some different flowers by a stream. Where'd I put them?"

Shanna saw the tall wildflowers, lying on the table, already in need of water. The delicate, pinkish-purple petals were heart-shaped. "Blue hearts," she murmured, remembering how much her mother used to like them. She felt sad and happy and confused.

"When are you heading back?"

She continued to stare at the flowers. "Oh, in a day or two, I guess. I have to get ready for school."

"I'm going to miss you, Shanna," he said suddenly, reaching over to stroke her cheek, his eyes strangely troubled. Alicia grabbed at his finger. "Mind your own business, squirt," he teased, tweaking her toe, then adding, "I'm even used to having you around, too, if only you'd let me sleep in longer. But at least you gave me lots of time with your mom."

Shanna exchanged a long look with him, loaded with sensuous memory, all the more poignant because he was leaving. "We're going to miss you, too."

"Hey, you've got those little worry creases between your brows. I want to remember your face breaking into a secret smile or overcome with pleasure. Okay?"

He spoke in low tones, slowly, deeply. She studied his face, the rugged tanned lines that had grown so familiar. Maybe she'd imagined the distant look that had strayed into his eyes. "Okay. But call me in a few days." She fought to keep a pleading note from her voice.

"Of course," he replied swiftly. "Why wouldn't I?"

"I don't know." She held his gaze, feasting on it, afraid to let him go, knowing she had to.

His eyes broke contact first. "I should get ready."

He decided not to stay for dinner, hoping to beat the storm. It didn't take him long to pack his few belongings. He kissed Shanna goodbye fondly, winked at Alicia, then drove off in the traditional dust cloud of old western movies.

As she watched him go, Shanna felt a deep wrenching inside and realized how attached she'd grown to him. He waved and honked farewell in the high-spirited Derek Morgan style, and she stared at the empty road a long time afterward, finally facing the fact that not once during their passionate interlude together had he mentioned love.

In the morning she found the abandoned blue hearts, battered by the rain that had fallen hard throughout the night. She placed them in a jar with water, trying to ignore the ancient verse that kept drumming at her brain—"Loves hopes all things...."

CHAPTER THIRTEEN

"So, WAS THAT SLEUTHING great movie material or what?"

"Sure was." Derek couldn't fault Jalsevac for looking and sounding so self-important. In fact, he felt pretty good about himself, too. His hunch had been correct. Roger had been proven innocent.

Smiling, Derek leaned back in his office chair and loosened his necktie. "The script's not bad and the ending's great—you got your man, or rather men, but I'm a little disappointed there were no hair-raising car chases or beautiful women lurking in the shadows."

Jalsevac grinned back. "We're talking A-class movie stuff, not B-grade."

"All kidding aside, you did a fine job, Jalsevac. I'm sorry I missed the action, though."

"You wouldn't have wanted to be around when your old man heard about another botched shipment. Maybe that's why I decided to get the hell out of here and check out the Toronto firm claiming to be short those high-tech electronics parts. When I saw Burns there, working the dock, I got those little chills that tell me everything's falling together."

Derek couldn't picture anything little about the hulk of a man facing him, but he just listened encouragingly.

"He'd quit Morgan's just after the last heist, but when I looked into it, he had a perfectly legitimate reason for moving away. His wife had a new job in downtown T.O., but that was likely planned out in advance to divert any suspicions. When I checked further into his previous employment record, I found he'd lied about how long he'd spent at each company. The same applied to Greene, your new driver, who happened to be working the night of the latest problem.''

Derek had heard a similar version of this story before, but the least he could do was let Jalsevac relive his moments of glory. The bottom line was he'd done the job for which he'd been paid—handsomely. As it appeared, Burns and Greene had been running their undercover operation for years. While working for different employers, one as a dockworker, another as a driver, they would each sign for the wrong number of goods shipped then received, so neither could be blamed. Usually they stole valuable merchandise that they could sell "hot" as quickly as possible. Surprisingly, or perhaps not too surprisingly, depending on one's degree of cynicism, Derek reflected, they must have found buyers who were willing not to ask any questions in return for a good deal. When the discrepancies started to become noticeable, they would lie low for a while, then one or both would move to different jobs. Unfortunately they'd not been able to resist the particularly lucrative shipments at Morgan's, which alerted the Morgans and then Jalsevac to their scam.

After Derek had returned to work last Friday, he and the security consultant had quickly obtained search warrants. With the help of the police, stolen merchandise had been found hidden in the men's homes, including some with matching serial numbers to the missing cargo. Merchandise was even traced back to lost or unaccountable inventory from Burns's and Greene's former employers.

The men had been charged with theft, possession of stolen goods, falsification of records and fraud. They were awaiting trial. With such a stack of offenses, their sentences would likely be lengthy, even if some plea bargaining was involved.

All this had occurred with amazing rapidity during the week or so that Derek had been back.

"I'll see to it that our account with you is settled up as soon as possible," Derek said, standing to signal the end of the Thursday meeting. "I hope you'll be taking a well-deserved holiday."

Jalsevac shook his head. "My wife would rather redecorate the house than sit on a beach somewhere, which always means more work for me. I'd almost prefer to be out in the field, but we'll see. How was your own time off? In all the confusion I never even asked."

"It was fine," Derek answered smoothly. Nothing in his look showed the nature of the disturbing thoughts that had plagued him since his return.

The two men shook hands, knowing they'd be meeting again with regard to the pending case. As soon as Jalsevac left, Derek ambled toward his father's office, the next task on his list of unfinished business—and a more difficult one. He chatted with the dispatcher until Leo was off the phone.

The senior Morgan finally greeted him with the strained politeness that had existed between them since he'd been back. Leo had also chosen to stay completely out of Derek's dealings with Jalsevac.

Gearing himself up for the expected battle, Derek stood by his father's big desk and immediately began, "I'm going to give Roger Hartly his job back."

To Derek's amazement, Leo shrugged in silent acquiescence. His gaze was fixed on a truck that was reversing toward the dock outside his window. After a minute he asked, "Do you really think he'll take it?"

"I'll do my damnedest to convince him he should. We're all behind him, aren't we?"

His father neither agreed nor disagreed. "Would *you* come back under the circumstances?"

His unwavering blue gaze met his son's. Not a muscle moved on his rigidly held, dark-suited body. Then Derek saw the barely perceptible motion of Leo's index finger sliding up and down the fine pen in his hand. "I'll let you know what happens," Derek said quietly before leaving. He would have to accept the fact that his father had too much pride to ever admit he'd been wrong about Roger.

However, Leo had been dead-on about one thing. When Derek finally reached Roger on the telephone two hours later, his offer was turned down immediately.

"I could never work for your father or his company again," Roger elaborated, his voice filled with pride. "I appreciate all you have done on my behalf, Derek, especially since my name has been cleared, but I can never go back."

"If a raise would help—"

"That's not it. I really need to start clean somewhere else." His bitterness was gone as he went on haltingly, "I want to be someone my son can be proud of some day. I almost went off the deep end again, but coming so close made me realize I am *not* going to give up until I find another decent job. I know I've got to be honest about my past this time, but I'll tell whoever will listen that they won't find anyone who'll work harder. There has to be someone out there who'll see I mean it and let me prove it."

"I'm sure there is," Derek said, moved by Roger's newfound determination. "Look, I may be able to help you get a foot in the door, at least. Will you let me check some of my contacts for you?''

"I may be stubborn, but I'm not stupid. Sure. You can do some legwork for me."

"Good." Derek heard a young voice screech in the background. "I should let you get back to your family. How are they keeping, anyway?"

"I don't think I could have got through this without them," Roger said so fervently that the finger that Derek habitually tapped when he was on the phone stilled. "Kim's been full of support, and when I hold Teddy...man, I feel like the luckiest unemployed ex-con alive."

Roger's heartfelt words about Teddy rang in Derek's ears later that evening, as he unwound from his day's work, alone in his condo. He, too, had been surprised to feel similar changes in himself. His day-to-day exposure to Alicia at Maple Lake, more time than he'd ever spent with a child, had been more enjoyable than he'd expected. He'd even gotten up early one morning to care for her, so that Shanna could sleep in. Wonder of wonders, what he'd first viewed as a major sacrifice, had turned into a pleasant and rewarding experience.

He knew he *should* call Shanna, who was undoubtedly back home now. He'd been avoiding calling her all week, but now that the crisis at Morgan's was resolved, he no longer had any excuses for his procrastination.

He felt like the world's worst creep because he was actually contemplating never seeing Shanna again. From the moment he'd learned he had to leave their idyllic cabin, he'd realized they were entering a new phase of their relationship. The phase he'd always failed at in the past. The one he'd always botched whether it took a month, a year or longer. He'd never really believed it could be different this time, but neither had he expected to be drawn to her so forcefully, as if he'd been swept up by a hurricane, by a power greater than himself.

Never had he grown so close to a woman. Never had he felt so awed, yet so petrified at that closeness.

Like a refrain from a sound heard in passing that would not leave his brain, he remembered how Shanna had accused him of wanting to control her when he'd resented her frankness with Leo at the party. She was right. He hated being compared to his brothers, but he finally had to admit that in his own way, he, too, had always controlled the barometer in his relationships with women. He was losing that control with Shanna. Perhaps he'd already lost it.

He no longer knew if his *feelings* for her or if Shanna herself were starting to dominate his mind, his body, his soul. But it didn't matter. He was terrified to his very core, and he despised such weakness in himself.

He wanted desperately to talk to her, to explain, but he couldn't bring himself to do it, not until he was back in control. . . .

SIGHING INWARDLY, SHANNA greeted her father at the door. She would just have to get used to the idea that some things in life might not be controllable. Since she'd returned, two long pensive days after Derek had left the cottage, her father had been at her house *daily*. Her vacation had been infinitely therapeutic for herself, but it had not made her father any more independent. In fact, he'd missed her and Alicia so much, he'd said, that he was more than making up for lost time.

Every morning for the past few days, he'd insisted on wheeling Alicia to the small park and playground nearby to give Shanna a break. Today, though, she didn't want or need a break. She was growing increasingly perturbed that Derek hadn't called, and the last thing she wanted was to be alone to brood. It was critical that she wait for him to call her, though. She felt she had to test Derek's emotional fidelity—as long as she could last *and* keep her sanity.

"I think I'll come along for the exercise, Dad," she said, grabbing her jacket since the late August air had cooled.

"There's no need, dear," he replied hastily. "You must need to get yourself ready for school next week."

"I *am* ready. That's all I've been doing all week. No curriculum is in better shape than mine. I have to keep myself in shape, too. Let's go."

"If you insist..."

At the park, several blocks away, a dark-haired girl of about four or five years old was pushing her toddler brother on the baby swing. Alicia, who was propped up in her stroller with the help of a head rest, was certainly not ready for any of the playground equipment. Shanna looked around for a bench, so they could at least watch the other children play. Her father was already heading to one, though, nodding and grinning at the occupant, an attractive strawberry-blond-haired woman who was wearing a classic navy pant suit with white accents. Slowly Shanna followed him.

"Another lovely day, but a little crisp, isn't it?" He beamed at the woman. If he'd been wearing a hat he probably would have tipped it.

"Yes. Before you know it, summer will be over." The woman smiled at him. She was not unfriendly, but not exactly warm, either, somewhere in between, as if she hadn't quite made up her mind about him.

Her short perm had that perfectly shaped look of a hairdresser's styling. Tall and slender in build, her manner poised, she reminded Shanna at first glance of a retired prima ballerina, but her deeply melodious voice could have made her an actress who'd performed Shaw or Shakespeare, perhaps. Her skin appeared flawless, as if pampered by many a facial. Only her long and graceful neck showed the telltale signs of age, which Shanna placed in the mid to late fifties.

"Is this your daughter, Ned?" the woman asked, her light gray eyes more inviting, less guarded toward Shanna than they had been toward him.

"Oh, yes." He turned jerkily toward her, as if finally remembering her presence. "Shanna, this is Phyllis. Phyllis Groves. And those are her two grandchildren on the swings."

"I'm delighted to meet you," Phyllis said. "I feel as if I know you already, though. As is often the case with dotty souls like your father and me, we seem to chat most about our children and grandchildren."

Phyllis Groves seemed anything but dotty. Her eyes sparkled with gaiety, self-assurance and intelligence. "I'm pleased to meet you, too." Dazed, Shanna stared from the other woman to her father with undisguised curiosity.

"Phyllis has two other grandchildren in North Bay. And a fifth on the way." Ned seemed anxious for Shanna not to voice what was plainly on her mind. "She's been staying at her daughter's here for a few weeks until number five comes along, which is any day now, and then she'll help out for a while longer."

"You're not from Kitchener-Waterloo, then?" Shanna asked.

"No, I'm living in Guelph at the moment, which isn't too far away, but Vicky, my daughter, is hoping I'll move in with her permanently," Phyllis confided. "She knows three children is going to be a handful—and she's right."

"So . . . are you going to move in?" Ned asked with a forced casualness.

Phyllis shook her head firmly. "As much as I love Vicky and my little ones, being a full-time nanny is not in the stars for me. I'm busy enough with my own life. I spread myself thin for too many years, pleasing everyone else. I decided these are *my* years."

In another woman this proclamation might have come across as selfish. But Phyllis was smart and refined; her independence seemed to have been hard-won and Shanna could not fault her for it. If only her own father exhibited more of that quality. "Are you currently working?" Her interest was definitely piqued.

"I work *at* many things, but no, I don't work in the sense of taking home a regular paycheck. I used to work as a receptionist in a modeling agency after I raised my children." She glanced in the direction of the swings to check on her charges before she went on. "My husband died five years ago and fortunately left me well-provided for. I finally sold the house and decided to do everything I'd kept putting off. I travel, take courses at the university, do volunteer work, that sort of thing. I even formed a seniors' group in Guelph, and I publish a monthly newsletter for it, which I quite enjoy. I've been trying to get your father to come to one of our meetings—it's my job to build membership—" she hastened to add, "but he hasn't run out of excuses yet."

"Tell me about it," Shanna said dryly, and the women exchanged a knowing smile.

Ned jumped in to defend himself. "I've always been a homebody. I've never been one for group powwows or outings."

"Dull, dull, dull, darling," Phyllis joked.

"Not necessarily." This time Ned held her gaze as he spoke, his expression suddenly serious, and Shanna felt as if she'd been caught in an intensely private moment where she did not belong.

The toddler wanted down from the swing then, and Phyllis rushed over to help him, but not before Shanna had noticed the faintest rosy tint that had crept into her cheekbones. The pretty widow was perhaps not as indifferent to her father as she appeared to be, though she seemed ambivalent about pursing the budding friendship. Shanna became more convinced of this as she watched them interact together. She surmised they'd seen each other on and off at the park during the summer, but they'd talked most during the last week or so.

Her father would have stayed indefinitely, barring an uprising from Alicia, but Phyllis soon gathered her two grandchildren together, insisting they make their way homeward to check on their mother. She waved goodbye cheerily. It wasn't clear whether she heard Ned call out, "See you tomorrow," amidst the children's protests at leaving.

"Why didn't you tell me about her?" Shanna asked when they, too, were leaving the deserted park. While she held a fussing Alicia, Ned pushed the empty stroller.

"Nothing to tell. Yet."

"But you'd like there to be?"

He hesitated. "Maybe. Does that bother you, Shanna?"

This time Shanna hesitated, trying to be honest with herself and him. She was happy he was enthusiastic about someone else. On the other hand, she couldn't deny a certain loyalty to her mother's memory, an inner resistance to seeing her father romantically linked with another woman, no matter how much she liked Phyllis Groves. "It'll take some getting used to," she admitted quietly. "But don't let that stop you. Have you asked her out yet?" She tried to be as nonchalant as she could about the question that sounded so odd to her.

"I'm trying to get up my nerve. It's been a long time."

She wondered if her father sensed Phyllis's ambivalence toward him. Another unfamiliar emotion hit her— protectiveness toward her parent. But she couldn't destroy the boyish, hopeful look of infatuation that lit up his eyes.

"You'll do fine," she said, squeezing his hand atop the carriage.

That look haunted her, though, as if she'd looked into a mirror of her own irrational fascination with Derek Morgan. When she got home, she decided to go out on her own, after all. Shopping. To a mall. The bigger the better.

Ned gladly agreed to baby-sit Alicia, which gave him the excuse he needed to stay longer. Shanna didn't realize, though, how troubled his eyes were when he watched her leave. She'd roamed the stores a lot after Michael had died. Wandering aimlessly in the impersonal atmosphere of the malls had been the perfect antidote then and it was what she needed now, to sort out her thoughts. She would try to restrain herself from overbuying, though. She'd never worn any of the darkly unattractive outfits she'd rashly purchased while mourning Michael.

She hadn't been aware how much tension had built up inside her until she started walking, with increasing restlessness. Summer sale signs, severe-looking mannequins and store windows decked out in the fall's new colors all passed by in a blur. The lake seemed more fantastic than ever.

Finally her steps slowed at a table of reduced sandals. She started digging through them for her size, hoping to find a more neutral color than the mustard-yellow ones she'd already seen, growing increasingly agitated at her lack of success....

She felt as if she had a split personality. In one sense she was furious Derek hadn't called. But in another she was actually relieved he hadn't. The niggling doubts and questions she'd ignored while luxuriating in her sensual rebirth had slowly risen to the surface. Even though she was ready to let a new man be part of her life, was she ready to love again? Was Derek simply filling a certain void of intimacy? After all, he was the first man she'd become close to since Michael's death. She wasn't looking to audition a series of eligible bachelors to take Michael's place, of course, but she had definitely arrived at the point where she had to decide what to do next about Derek.

Perplexed, she bought the yellow shoes.

Swinging her parcel, she started walking again. She wandered into the children's wear department of a major store chain, drawn to the most adorable jogging suits, featuring Winnie-the-Pooh. She still felt guilty about giving Alicia her divided attention at the cabin, even if her heart had *seemed* big enough to encompass both her daughter and Derek.

Her inner voice continued pestering her.... Granted, Derek had warmed up to Alicia considerably during the relaxed interlude. But would he make a good full-time father for her child... down the road? What road? She pictured Derek Morgan zigzagging his way through life, never content to pursue one goal in one direction. Would he ever choose to settle down with a ready-made family, with all its inherent responsibilities and challenges? Surely she couldn't ask him such a question. He knew her situation. If that was what he wanted or didn't want, then he'd let her know, wouldn't he?

He hadn't called her, and he'd acted strangely before leaving the lake. Was that his way of letting her know? Maybe he was retreating, surrendering, like an enemy who'd given up on the battle. But they weren't enemies, her heart protested. They'd been as intimate as a man and woman could possibly be.

In this day and age *she* could certainly call *him*, but she knew how that would turn out. She would be defensive, vulnerable, feigning indifference, salvaging her pride... when it could all be so different. Maybe she was overreacting by thinking the worst. Maybe there was a good reason why he hadn't called yet.

No, not after what they'd shared. He could find the time.

Now carrying two shopping bags, she descended the escalator and caught a glimpse of herself along the mirrored ramp. Her face was drawn, her lips clenched in her classic worried expression. No denying it. She looked terrible. From her elevated vantage point she scanned the aisles of jewelry, lingerie, handbags, scarves, hats. Determinedly she headed to the hats. She needed to feel independent again, whimsical, daring, not afraid to be different or to stand out from the crowd. She set down her parcels and started trying on the head wear, comparing the most outlandish to the simplest, pushing them back, tilting them forward, sideways, brims down, up. She couldn't make up her mind. It wandered again....

In the depths of her heart, she couldn't believe that Derek was copping out already. But then again his personality had been shaped by his unemotional, male-dominated family long before she'd met him. The passion between them at the cottage had soared beyond her wildest dreams. Maybe such passion was doomed to fail the test of time, given their differences and Derek's love-less history.

She reached for a silver sequined cap. Frowning, she wondered if it suited her. It was absurd, right out of this world. Had she really been living in some kind of never-never land where Derek was concerned? Suddenly she remembered a talk show she'd seen once about men afflicted with the Peter Pan Syndrome. According to the theory, certain narcissistic males refused to grow up; they were masters at having fun in a magical world, but they would never commit themselves to a woman. Try as she might, Shanna could not fit Derek into that mold. He was self-involved to a degree, but he had revealed layers of vulnerability to her. He had a caring, nurturing side. Would he ever find a balance between self-love and other-love? Could he ever overcome his emotional barriers?

In the end, she defiantly chose a black hat that was mysterious, alluring, coquettish. It made her feel good. Her satisfaction with her purchase lightened her step as she left the mall, but she knew she still hadn't resolved the major issues weighing upon her mind.

That night she broke down and called him. He was out. She left a clipped message on his answering machine to call her when he got a chance.

The early days of September crept by. Derek never returned her call. She called his office, left another message with his secretary, who told her he'd just returned from the West Coast. With such a backlog to attend to, it might be a while before he could get back to her, according to the other woman.

Trying to keep busy, Shanna visited Kim Cho Hartly the afternoon before school began. Alicia and Teddy stared curiously at each other from opposite ends of the playpen, while their mothers sipped iced tea on the couch.

"I am very nervous about leaving Teddy tomorrow," Kim admitted as she watched the two children. "Do you feel the same about Alicia?"

"Of course. But at least I know the staff at the school's day-care center. They are well-trained, but most importantly, very warm people. It's not just a job for them. They truly love children."

Shanna had already relayed that information to Kim when she'd persuaded her to enrol in the full-time, advanced ESL program that she herself was teaching. Clearly the Korean mother still needed reassurance. And Shanna would never admit how daunting the thought of being separated from her own child really was to her, no matter how much faith she had in the caregivers. For financial reasons though, she had to return to work and she did love her job. Hopefully, by seeing Alicia as often as she could manage during the day, she would have the best of both worlds.

"Another person can be very nice to my Teddy," Kim said, her dark brows still knit with concern, "but no one is *me*. You know?"

"I know," Shanna softly replied.

The telephone rang, and Roger, who had been in the bedroom, burst through the door, calling out loudly that he would get it.

"Is he expecting an important call?" Shanna asked quietly.

"Always." Kim lowered her voice even more. "After talking to another man at the employment agency, he is writing his résumé again. This is six times. He says is better now. I say just different. At least it makes him busy and he is not as sad as before. He want to work very badly."

By the animated expression on Roger's face and his rapid firing of questions, Shanna guessed he was discussing a favorable prospect. But when he approached them after the call, his face wore a carefully schooled nonchalance, perhaps because he'd been disappointed so often.

"Good news?" Kim asked eagerly.

Roger shrugged. "Maybe. I have an interview tomorrow. They're looking for a dock foreman at Redding Transport. Morgan's main competition out this way," he added without any smugness, and the reason soon become clear. "Derek Morgan lined it up."

At the simple utterance of the name, Shanna felt herself grow warm. "Does he think you stand a good chance?"

Roger's eyes gave away his building excitement. His expression was keen, speculative. "He says that the company was bought out by a guy who's an ex-con himself, although it's not common knowledge. Fifteen years in, fifteen years out. At least this Clapton fellow may listen to what I have to say."

Kim's hands met for one sharp clap. "Tomorrow is my first day at school in Canada, Teddy's, too, and the day you get new job. I feel it here." She pounded her heart.

"Don't get your hopes up, Kimmie."

"Sorry, too late..."

Shanna wished Roger luck before she left. The image of the couple, arm in arm with the child between them, tugged at her heart, refusing to fade. And another seed had been planted by the mention of her lover's name.

Later that night she finally made up her mind to call Derek yet again. It was two minutes after ten o'clock. She'd given him until ten to spare her this final humiliation. She didn't know what she would say. Nothing short of a magic wand could make her forgive him for his actions, but she *had* to talk to him. She wanted to start off the school semester with her usual energy and enthusiasm. She couldn't do that properly with Derek Morgan a big ugly question mark in her mind. Actually he was in danger of being demoted from an exclamation mark in her life to a period. Her fingers were shaking as she dialed.

The phone rang only once before Derek picked it up. "Expecting my call?" Shanna asked icily.

"Not . . . exactly. But I'm not one of those people who waits for the socially acceptable second ring." A scuffling sounded as he shuffled some papers or sat down or both. "How are you?"

"Oh, all geared up for school tomorrow, but never ready enough." She was amazed at how civil she could sound.

"Is it that time already? This summer just zoomed by."

"Hasn't it, though?" Shanna could hear him breathing in the silence that fell. She felt as if she were buried in a time bomb, ready to explode.

"Shanna, I'm sorry I didn't return your call right away—"

"Calls."

"I've been meaning to, really. Let's go out for dinner soon, to catch up, talk. Say, Friday, next week? You'll want to get settled at school first . . ."

She heard the ambivalence in his voice, and something snapped inside her. "I'll save you the effort," she retorted. "Why don't you just say what you have to say now?"

"This isn't the right time."

"Yes, it is. It sure as hell is." She waited, a maelstrom of emotions assaulting her before his next words finally left his lips.

"Shanna, I think we should cool things for a while..."

"That's obvious. I want to hear why."

"I—I know you must think I've been a coward for avoiding you, and maybe you're right. But I've been waiting until I understand it all myself, so that I can find the right words. I owe you that much, I owe you so much more, but I can't pay up. I—" He stopped, exhaled in frustration. "You deserve someone who can go the distance with you. It's not me. It never was."

Suddenly the anger drained from her, leaving her weak. "You can't be sure of that, Derek," she finally said haltingly. "What we had—at the lake—may be worth starting from, building on."

"The lake will always be a wonderful memory, Shanna." Relegated to past status already.

She tried again. "Derek, why are you doing this, destroying everything we had? You even admitted it was good, too good."

"It was. I'm just saying we should step back—"

"No, you're running in the opposite direction. At least meet me in the middle, Derek. Talk to me. I'm just as scared—"

"So we both need a little breathing space. Shanna, this isn't easy for me. You have to realize that. But I know now is the best time to reassess. It'll only get harder."

"Derek, I'll never believe I was wrong about you. Never. But I have to hold on to the truth—the sad and frightening truth—that you are so wrong about yourself."

He said nothing. Finally she took the graceful exit. "Goodbye, Derek," she said and hung up quickly.

She sat by the phone a long time. The worst part was his lack of emotion. She remembered how he'd told her he'd felt a great emptiness after his mother's death when he was young. He'd received no loving substitute since that time. Hiding behind a wall of remoteness, blocking intimacy, had clearly become second nature to him. He'd come a long way with her, but he was determined to sabotage their relationship before it progressed any further.

She felt the futility of fighting something so deeply engrained in him. She'd tried, she'd tried hard...and failed.

Thank goodness, she had the demands and rewards of teaching to occupy her from the next day onward. She was called Mrs. Rhodes by her new pupils, and that strangely was a comfort. She found herself slipping into the complacency of widowhood. Knowing she'd lost her beloved husband through the tragedy of his death, however wrenching, was almost easier to deal with in some ways than the complex psychological barriers that had separated her and Derek.

HER CLASS SIZE was larger than ever, and many of her students needed extra personal attention. She often stayed late or gave up her lunch hour for private tutoring, developing weak pronunciation, reading or listening skills, as required. Alicia seemed to have adjusted well to her new daytime routine, so at least Shanna didn't have that worry. And the day-care staff were flexible about keeping Alicia if Shanna was tied up.

The advent of school didn't alter Ned's patterns, however. He showed up bright and early the following Saturday morning to escort Alicia to the park, sporting a new outfit, a fresh haircut and the serious demeanor of a youth going courting for the first time. If Phyllis wasn't at the park, he confided to Shanna, he was going to drop by her daughter's house to have a peek at the new baby who'd surely arrived by now. He set off, steering the carriage with steely determination.

He returned less than half an hour later, dejected.

"She wasn't there?" Shanna ventured, setting her pen atop the pile of short essays she'd been grading on the kitchen table.

He handed Alicia to her then ran the cold water tap, his empty glass poised. "I saw her at her daughter's place. The baby's fine. A boy."

"Good. So you had a chance to chat?"

"Some. She has to go back to Guelph tomorrow—to straighten out some business." The tap continued to run, but he'd forgotten about it. "She turned me down."

"Dad, turn off the tap. What did she say?"

He filled his glass and drank the entire contents in one swallow. "It doesn't matter. I asked if I could take her out, as eloquently as I knew how, and she very nicely turned me down."

"She must have given a reason..."

"Oh, she said that was very sweet of me and something about being beyond all that. It's probably a bumbling idiot like me that she's beyond," he added grimly.

Shanna ached for her father because she knew how much it had cost him to even approach Phyllis. To be spurned was even harder for him to deal with. "I still think you're the handsomest, nicest man *I* know." His eyes flickered disbelievingly. Softly she added, "Maybe it's better this way. Better to know how things stand up front, before it's too late." She didn't have to mention her fiasco with Derek, but they were both aware of it.

He touched her shoulder before he sat down beside her at the table. "To soften the blow, Phyllis very tactfully mentioned her Over Fifty-Five group again. She probably thought I'd refuse, but I didn't this time. I'm going next week. Might as well get in there with the rest of the old fogies. At least I'll get to see her."

"Hey, it won't be so bad. You can be the new kid on the block, the baby in the group." All Shanna could do was smile at him in comfort.

He smiled back sadly. "We're not doing so well in the romance department, are we, kiddo?"

"No, I guess not. Maybe ill-fated love runs in the family."

Alicia, who'd been watching her mother's mouth closely, started babbling a string of syllables, a series of ahs and ohs, which she modulated in tone. She looked quite satisfied with her results.

"Looks like it's up to you to break the chain, 'Licia," Shanna murmured.

Alicia answered something indistinguishable. It sounded optimistic, but it wasn't enough to ease the deep ache in Shanna's heart.

CHAPTER FOURTEEN

"ARE YOU FREE for lunch today?"

Stunned, Derek looked up from his overcrowded desk and stared at his father. He couldn't remember the last time he'd heard that question. "I can be."

"Good. I'll stop by around one."

He thought he'd imagined the invitation in his overworked condition when one o'clock passed and his father didn't appear. At one-fifteen Joan relayed the message that Leo had been detained. Lunch was changed to dinner.

At six o'clock Derek found himself sitting opposite his father at an elegant steak and seafood restaurant in Waterloo. Leo ordered them each a Scotch on the rocks, took one sip from his, then leaned forward, immediately set on discussing the purpose of the meeting. There had to be a purpose, Derek knew. Leo never did anything frivolous.

"I'd like to talk to you about the Hartly business."

Derek sipped his own drink. "Sure."

"I owe you a long-overdue apology. I should have listened to you about not jumping the gun. You were right and I was wrong." His elbows resting on the arms of the chair, Leo tapped his knuckles on the rustic wooden table. "There, it's said. Those are tough words for a fellow like me."

It took a few seconds for the unexpected apology to sink in, especially since Derek had been gearing himself up for some sort of unwarranted reprimand. "Apology accepted," he said simply at last.

"I don't blame Hartly for not coming back to us," Leo went on, his dark eyes unreadable in the dimly lit room, "but I've sent him a personal letter of reference. Maybe it'll help him find a new job."

Derek took another mouthful of Scotch, then waited for the slow burn inside to end. "I hear he's going to be the new dock foreman at Redding Transport."

This time Leo looked at him in surprise. "Who'd you hear that from?"

"From Clapton himself. You might say I was... instrumental in bringing the two together. Did you know Clapton did time, as well, fifteen years ago?"

"No... Once more, you're one step ahead me all the way, son. You're going to keep me sharp in my old age."

"It's a tricky job, but someone's got to do it," Derek joked, feeling an unfamiliar surge of affection for his parent well up inside him. Because most of their dealings were business-related, Leo almost never referred to him as "son," as he'd just done.

A bread basket arrived and Leo ripped his roll apart, not bothering to spread the curl of butter he'd dropped into it before taking a bite. "Do you think you're ready to take over for me?" he asked as he finished chewing, reaching for another roll. "As head of Morgan's."

Derek dropped his own roll. "Come again?"

"You heard me. Since my birthday, I've been thinking that I ought to step down over the course of the next year or two. It's time. And you're the most capable one to fill my shoes."

"What about Ray?" Derek asked carefully. He'd known that Leo would retire eventually, but he hadn't expected it so soon. And he'd always presumed he would share the helm with his older brother, similar to the way they were dividing the position of vice president now.

"You've got more of a head for business than Ray. You've also got good instincts. You stand up for what you believe in. You're a doer, not a follower. You're rational, fair and even-tempered. Usually. You want another drink?"

"No..."

"You want the job?"

"Do you want your answer now?"

"No rush. The morning will be fine." Leo's face split into a controlled smile. "Or the next month or two. I want a man at the top who's prepared to give it his all."

"As you did?"

"Damn right," the elder Morgan answered swiftly.

"And if I don't want the job or if I don't want it on your terms?"

"Then I'll offer it to Ray on the same terms or we'll sell the company. I worked too hard to see it all go down the tube."

Leo folded his menu, gestured for the waiter and ordered a T-bone steak, well-done, making it clear all hell would break loose if there was a trace of pinkness left to the meat. Derek ordered the prime rib, rare, the way *he* liked it.

So Leo hadn't been secretly grooming him for the job all along; he'd been waiting for Derek to prove himself, with a few tests along the way. Yet he wasn't bluffing about selling the company if Derek or Ray weren't willing to give one-hundred-percent dedication. Derek also suspected Leo would have a harder time letting go of the reins than he thought. He had to be brutally frank.

"Dad, we're two different people. I could only consider the job if I was free to use *my* best judgment, apply some of my own ideas. It wouldn't work with you always looking over my shoulder."

To Derek's amazement, Leo nodded. "I know. That's why both you and I have to be sure of your commitment up front." He looked down, meticulously straightened his cutlery. "Are you still seeing that teacher?"

"Oh, off and on," Derek said vaguely, then adding truthfully, "Off at the moment. Probably permanently. But you can't be implying that I should never have a personal life?"

"On the contrary. I've come to think that maybe you would be happier if you settled down. You seem to be having more of those 'off' times lately. You've been ready to explode at any moment, which isn't like you."

Derek's narrowed eyes met his father's. The two men rarely discussed anything so personal. "I thought you didn't like Shanna."

"I never said I didn't like her. You must know by now that I don't take kindly to being disagreed with, especially about how I run my business, but generally I admire gutsy women. Your mother was like that. Her only problem was that she checked out on me too early."

Derek had rarely, if ever, heard his father mention his wife. He certainly had never seen the softening of expression that accompanied the words. "You could have married again. Why didn't you?" he asked quietly.

"Oh, for a couple of decades I didn't think anyone could take the place of my Katie. And now I'm too set in my ways—some might call it pigheaded." He busied himself folding and unfolding his napkin. "Sometimes I wonder what it would be like if things had turned out differently."

"If the spirit is willing . . ."

With great care Leo spread his napkin over his lap. He shook his head self-consciously. "I tell myself I'm lucky to have loved once in my life, however imperfectly at the time. Why be greedy?" He attempted a weak smile. "Besides, I'm a miserable old cuss if things don't go my way. So maybe you get that honestly enough."

Derek blinked, about to protest, deny, joke, but something in his father's eyes and nervous manner made him remain silent.

"I was sorting through some of my personal papers last night," Leo went on, "and I came across my old wedding ring in an envelope. I haven't worn it for about thirty years, not since your mother died. It made me too angry." For the first time Derek noticed his father was wearing it now. "I stared at that simple gold circle a long time. I came to realize that that ring joined not only her and me, but that it grew to encompass all of us, my whole family. I had lost sight of that." Leo met his gaze. "I have three sons, two grandsons and a daughter-in-law to get to know properly. I haven't been doing such a good job, have I?"

Derek wasn't sure how to answer this as he stared at the man he was just starting to get to know himself. Finally he said, "It's never too late."

Leo studied his weathered hands, spread flat on the edge of the table, then he wiggled the finger bearing the unfamiliar ring. "We've all been existing like little islands, and I haven't known how to pull us together."

"We should all be doing the pulling." Out of the corner of his eye Derek was conscious of the waiter's approach.

"I may need a little help," Leo admitted, his voice gravelly, lost in the shuffling of his chair as he allowed the young man more room to set down his soup bowl.

But Derek heard him. "Sure..." Suddenly he understood what had prompted the earlier apology about Roger.

They set about the business of eating, then. Leo sent back his salad because it didn't have enough dressing. His steak arrived, grilled to perfection, and he gruffly told the waiter to thank the chef.

When they'd finished, Derek waited for their dishes to be cleared before saying, "I'll give serious consideration to your offer. I'm as proud of Morgan's as you are. But it's critical that we figure out how Ray would fit into the whole picture."

"As senior vice president."

"But we *all* have to be comfortable with any changes." Leo nodded. "I'm going to call him," Derek added, pushing back his chair.

"Now?"

"Why not? But you should be the one to fill him in. We both know he's not going to be happy." Again his father nodded.

Ray suspected something unusual was going on by the tone of his younger brother's voice, but Derek refused to discuss anything over the phone. Ray left home immediately and joined them in the licensed lounge of the restaurant, impatient while they ordered coffees. He requested a rum and Coke.

"So what's up?" he asked as soon as the beverages arrived.

Derek looked toward Leo, who was stirring sugar and cream into his coffee with deliberate slowness as he pondered his words. "Above all, I don't want any hard feelings between you two,'' the elder Morgan began. ''This can only work if you are both in perfect agreement about the arrangement.''

''What arrangement?'' Ray's eyes became wary blue slits.

''I want you to know I thought about this a long time, and I thought hard. If Derek agrees and is willing to be wholly committed, I am appointing him as the new president of Morgan's. In turn, you will become senior vice president, operations.'' He sipped from his coffee, ignoring the stiffening of Ray's jaw. ''You two will have to divide certain responsibilities and you will certainly have as much input as you do now, Ray, but there can be only one figurehead who has final authority and who oversees the entire operation.''

''And where are you going to be when these... appointments take place?'' Ray's voice was dangerously low.

''Oh, I'll be around,'' Leo said evasively. ''Not too close, but not too far away, either.''

''Dad's thinking of retiring,'' Derek clarified.

''This is going to be an adjustment, a big one, for all of us.'' Leo reached over to touch his eldest son's sleeve. ''So if you've got any gripes, lay them on the table, Ray. That's why we're here.''

''Gripes!'' Ray shouted, oblivious to the stares of the other patrons. ''You insult me and everything I've ever done for you, working like a horse all these years, by telling me to just sit here and take it—''

''I'm not insulting you,'' Leo cut in. ''I'm recognizing your strengths and Derek's. I want you out in the field, handling all the nitty-gritty problems, and Derek at home plate, so to speak, where you each manage best.''

Ray's face reddened, contorting with anger; his eyes gleamed. "We can sit here all night and debate your pretty justifications, but there's a world of difference between president and vice president, and you both know it. Use a dictionary if you need to refresh your memory."

"Ray—"

"I don't want your condescension, little brother." Ray shot Derek a scathing look. "I'm the oldest. All my life I've been the one who's always had to break new ground, and I'm not about to be demoted now." Ray abruptly stood, throwing a crumpled bill on the table. "Thanks, but no thanks, to your appointment, Dad."

"Now don't go flying off the handle," Leo warned, barely checking his own rising anger. "Give it all some serious thought first—"

"You know, I've actually been able to turn a blind eye to your faults and admire you." Ray made a conscious effort to lower his voice, but his outrage remained strong as he stared at his parent. "I looked forward to *being* like you, in a position where I didn't have to take crap from anybody, knowing I've paid my dues. Well now maybe I can, on my own."

As Ray moved away, Leo grabbed his arm. "This is precisely *why* I made my decision, son. You've listened with your ego, not your brains. You're acting like an adolescent, not a man." Ray shrugged him off, glowering. "Don't do or say anything rash now because I guarantee you'll live to regret it. We'll talk again at work on Monday, okay?"

Ray didn't reply before he stormed away.

Several long minutes passed. Finally Derek murmured, "Do you really think he'll show up?"

Leo stared off wearily in the direction Ray had fled. "I hope so. I sure as hell hope so. Maybe by then he'll have cooled down. In any case, I'll probably give him a few weeks to get used to the idea before forcing any changes, no matter what your decision will be. It won't be the first—or last—time I've faced what looked like a no-win situation."

Derek said nothing, his fingers drumming an irregular beat on the table. "Let's get out of here." At his father's nod, he threw down another bill that landed beside Ray's abandoned one. As they were walking out, Derek asked, "Are you tired?"

"Not physically."

"Let's drive to Toronto. To Terry's bar."

Leo shot him a startled look. "That's awfully far."

"It's only about an hour's drive. Besides, my car needs a good highway run."

After pushing open the heavy, ornate door, Derek looked back at his father, overcoat in hand, standing under a silver sword and shield in keeping with the Old English decor. "Coming, Dad?"

Leo held his ground for several seconds, then he slowly moved forward, shaking his whitening head in resignation.

The night sky was turning to a dusky gray as the car wound along the local expressway, then turned onto Highway 401. Derek couldn't remember the last time he'd ridden in the same car as his parent. He switched from his rock radio station and they listened to the news before the slow, melodious voice of the evening announcer took over, followed by some "easy listening" music.

"Why do I have the feeling that this whole presidency issue may be theoretical, or at least highly premature?"

Derek finally ventured. "Somehow I can't see you letting go . . . yet."

Leo stared fixedly out the window at the dark sweep of fields. "I want everything in place for when the time is right. You boys have to set your goals, too."

They drove quietly. Soon the rural stretch of road was lined with towering lights that shed an orange glow across the city outskirts. What seemed like distant memories suddenly flickered in Derek's brain and he let himself grasp them, giving them shape and texture and taste. In vivid detail he remembered the nights he'd spent with Shanna under a northern sky—frolicking in the cool lake, holding hands by the fire, tumbling into their tousled bed.

The experiences seemed clearer in recall, as if he were an artist perfecting a painting, adding the right finishing touches, a shading here, a speck of color there. He wished he could be with her one last time. He'd never felt that so strongly before. His unexpected yearning for the young widow wasn't entirely sexual, either. In fact, after this trying day, lovemaking was not a priority. He just wanted to be with her again.

But like a drug, Shanna had a mind-distorting effect on him. She sometimes fooled him into thinking he was a different person. She made him dream up crazy, impossible possibilities.

Needing to talk about her, he found himself telling his father where, how and with whom he'd spent his holiday—a censored version.

SEVERAL HEADS TURNED as the two men entered the crowded bar. Perhaps the observers noticed the younger one, who had an air of authority and confidence, saunter past the long Friday night lineup, chat briefly with the formidable-looking employee protecting the door as if maximum security clearance would be required, then gesture to his companion to enter with him. Any on-lookers might have been curious whether something more persuasive than words had passed between the two men, but no one could be sure, not even the annoyed would-be patrons left standing in the line that snaked through the lobby and along the busy downtown Toronto street.

More than one pair of female eyes, in particular, ob-served the new arrivals, noting not only the striking re-semblance, but the effect of the blue-eyed sophistication in duplicate. A more perceptive eye might have been in-trigued by the different dynamics exhibited by each man. The door negotiator, wearing a double-breasted gray suit with a distinctive flair, as if he would be comfortable on a fashion runway, appeared to be set on a mission as he scanned the crowded room. Any expectant female who looked his way would have been disappointed, because his sweeping glance seemed disinterested. She might speculate that he was either there on business—a friend of the owner or a prospective investor—or that he was looking for a particular person.

The elder gentleman, clearly the other's father, ap-peared mildly interested in the surroundings—the ultra-modern decor, the prevalence of chrome and glass in the multilevels, the T-shirts that hung above the huge stand-up bar, the trays of sandwiches or pizzas that came from behind the kitchen doors. He seemed uneasy, but some-thing in his proud bearing indicated that the reason had nothing to do with feeling out of place in the youthful crowd. When his son touched his arm in a conciliatory gesture, it became obvious that the elder man was there, almost involuntarily, at the other's bidding.

If one believed that the decibel level of music increases with each generation, then one might have thought the noise would have also bothered him. But his expression grew even more perplexed when the raunchy Rolling Stones song faded and the new disc jockey, Terry Morgan, took the microphone to chat in the laid-back, witty style of a stand-up comedian that had made him one of the club's main draws.

Father and son made their way toward the elevated platform where Terry sat like a pilot before a dazzling board of lights and controls. He was introducing the next song by INXS, pronounced in excess, deliberately mixing up the syllables, recreating some new combinations, and making snappy jokes about his results, when he saw them. He faltered as he tried to say "sin-dexes," quickly recovering as he added that he had some extra copies, which were hotter-selling items than the album. Amidst the scattered titters, he finally got his introduction of the group right and let the sounds of "Never Tear Us Apart" fill the room.

Terry hailed a waiter. A table seemed to float out of nowhere and landed just below his ministage, kitty-corner to the hardwood dance floor and strategically away from the main speakers. Finally he approached the men, looking like a specter in his casual all-white outfit that glowed under the spotlights. He greeted them warmly, turning to the older man last. At first glance, no one would have noticed the resemblance between the fair-haired Terry Morgan and his father, but it was there, in their strikingly handsome features. After a second of hesitation, their two hands met in a gesture that might have been formal in such a congenial place had the look that passed between them not been so weighty.

After the affable deejay leaped back onto his platform, the two new arrivals sat quietly, unobtrusively, sipping on drinks that had appeared with minimal delay by a tall brunette waitress who appeared to have followed the exchange quite intently. Whoever else had been watching the men would likely have lost interest at that point, had a particularly exuberant Terry Morgan not drawn it back to them several songs later....

DEREK FELT HIS MUSCLES loosening with his second, and last, Scotch of the night—knowing he'd be driving home. Talking was virtually impossible during each set, but they hadn't come here to talk. For his part, he was simply enjoying the mix of music that Terry had chosen for the excellent sound system. He avoided staring at the swaying couples and refused to examine his reason why.

He did note that the waitress who had served him and Leo their drinks seemed to be eyeing them closely. Also, she never passed by Terry's post without smiling his way or acknowledging his look. Derek was no stranger to that look of vital awareness; the same look had passed between himself and Shanna many times. So Terry has a new girlfriend, he mused. But something here was different from his brother's previous relationships. The longer he watched the two he was certain that the caring, *the connecting,* that he sensed between them were not products of his imagination.

He was further surprised at how outrageously his younger brother was lip-syncing and dancing to the music, enjoying himself wholeheartedly, an endless source of motion. Clearly the patrons loved him, many waving at him or imitating him from the dance floor. The room seemed to crackle with the energy he created. Derek's worry about his brother's depression was alleviated; at the same time he recognized how difficult Terry's passage out of remorse and self-incrimination must have been. His brother would never be the same.

Even Leo smiled more than once at Terry's antics. But soon Derek could tell his father was ready to leave.

Strangely the last song ended and the loudspeakers grew silent. Terry seemed intent on pushing dials, but Derek had watched him enough during the past few numbers to know it was just an act. Terry was playing for time. His waitress friend also stood by a wall, empty tray in hand, as he finally took the mike and walked to the edge of the stage.

"I'd like to dedicate this next song," Terry began, "but not for your run-of-the-mill birthday or anniversary celebration." He waited for the roomful of voices to quiet even more. "The dedication is from me, but that's not why it's special. It's for my father who happens to be here for the first and probably last time. This isn't the quietest place on the planet."

"Give him some earplugs," someone yelled out.

"Good idea," Terry retorted, smiling. "But the main thing is he's here tonight. He's a guy I admire a lot because he taught me to think big. We may have different definitions of big, but I hope we agree that what matters most is that you're reasonably happy where you end up, despite the knocks you took to get there, and that some of that happiness rubs off on others. The song is 'Big League' by Tom Cochrane and Red Rider. My dad may never have heard it, but help me show him what it does to you!"

Sound blasted forth and the bodies on the dance floor came to life again. With Terry singing along, it was easy to distinguish the lyrics about a father's expectations for his boy to play in the big league, turn some heads and knock everyone dead. However, the son is tragically killed before he can live up to all his father's dreams.

Leo didn't take his eyes off Terry. Just as the song was segueing into the next one, he folded his arms and slowly nodded at his youngest son with the utmost gravity. Terry responded with a thumbs-up signal.

The exchange may have been understated, Derek thought, but it expressed a new understanding between father and son. And even though the song was about thwarted hopes, the message Terry and Leo communicated to each other was optimistic.

By quitting tennis, Terry had stopped trying to prove his worth to his father. And by coming tonight to see Terry at a job Leo disapproved of, but one to which his son was eminently suited, Leo had finally acknowledged his son's worth. Most importantly, he'd forgiven Terry for the crime he'd been paying for all his life; the crime of being a living reminder of his blond-haired mother.

CHAPTER FIFTEEN

AS DEREK RODE the elevator to his condominium, he knew he had a restless night coming up. He had a lot to mull over, particularly his future as president of Morgan's. Why didn't he feel as excited about that as he should? It was what he'd always wanted, secretly—to be at the helm, the benevolent, well-liked boss who inspired unshakable loyalty.

He sensed, even now, that a rude awakening awaited him. Already his own brother had been alienated. And the reality of managing more than two hundred employees was not going to be easy. He hadn't always agreed with his father's tyrannical tactics, but there was no question Leo had run a tight ship. Of course, he *should* accept the offer, however challenging, with or without Ray. Morgan's was a part of him. It was the other parts of his life he couldn't seem to piece together so well . . .

His phone was ringing as he entered his door. He stumbled in the darkness as he lunged for it, hoping to pick it up before his answering machine intervened. "Hello."

"Derek? It's Ned. Ned Bennett. Did you just get in? I've called a few times."

"Sorry, I—I must have forgotten to turn on my machine this morning."

"I'd rather talk to you directly, anyway. It's about Shanna."

Derek sat on the arm of his leather couch, rubbing his temple. It was late. He had enough on his mind, without Ned's advice for the lovelorn, however well-intentioned. "How is she?"

"She's at the hospital." Derek's fingers froze. "Alicia's the one who's sick, though. Severe croup. She may have to have surgery to help her breathe."

Derek felt as if the air was being sucked from his own lungs, and he was afraid to ask how serious such an operation was. "Is she getting the best care?" he heard himself ask.

Ned gave a short laugh of derision that penetrated the numbness spreading through Derek. "I only talked to Shanna briefly on the phone, but I assume so. Look, I called because...I wasn't sure whether you'd want to know or not. Shanna would never call you herself, but she's mighty upset." His own voice unsteady, he stopped. "She'll get through this somehow, like she always does."

"Which hospital?" The question was barely audible.

"Kitchener-Waterloo Emergency." Neither spoke. "Derek, if you care anything for my daughter, now is the time to show it. She needs you, not me."

Already Derek had stood, mobilizing his inert limbs. "I'll be there."

"If you change your mind, let me know and I'll get there so damn fast—"

"I won't change my mind. Thanks for calling—"

"And Derek?" Ned cut in sharply. "Make sure you've got a few quarters with you. Keep me posted."

"We will."

Derek didn't dwell on the "we" that had spontaneously left his lips. He raced to the hospital, cursing the speed limits, even though he barely complied with them. Despite his single-minded frenzy, he recognized the slow, twangy bars on the radio. Oddly he was hearing the song "Never Tear Us Apart" for the second time that night. The words about the indestructibility of love hit closer to home than they had at the bar after Terry's wacky introduction. Alone in his car, all he could think of was the depth of his concern for both Shanna and Alicia and his desire to be with them.

Pacing in the emergency ward while their whereabouts were being traced, he recalled his previous visits to the same hospital to see Megan and Shanna, then he relived the horror of Alicia's kidnapping. His destiny seemed to be inexorably entwined with theirs. He'd tracked Shanna down at the cottage, like a man possessed. He'd run from her since then, but Ned had called to give him another choice. What he'd chosen, he didn't know—only that he had to share this crisis with Shanna.

SHANNA'S EYES WERE CLOSED as she sat beside the heavy plastic tent that encased the crib, but she was fighting her fatigue. One hand touched the crib, her only link to her daughter who was inside the cool, misty interior, breathing noisily yet sleeping at last—thankfully.

She heard the door creak and her eyes fluttered open. Derek Morgan entered the darkened cubicle. He was too real to be an apparition, but she had the sensation that she'd conjured him up somehow from the dream world she'd been slipping into. She didn't care why he was there or how he'd found her. It was enough that he'd showed up at all to lend his support.

"Hi," she murmured groggily.

"Hi." He crouched beside her. Anxiously he peered at Alicia's tiny form in the center of the bubblelike covering. "How is she?"

"Improving. The nurse just removed her oxygen mask, which had been connected to a medicated mist she'd been inhaling for about ten minutes. It seems to have opened up her bronchial tubes."

"Your father said something about surgery."

"He shouldn't have called you."

"That doesn't matter. Does she need the operation?"

Shanna exhaled slowly, the only evidence of the incredible strain she'd been under since Alicia's croup had begun twenty-four hours ago. "We hope not. The thought of putting tubes down her throat..." She shuddered. "But I'm afraid of a relapse. I'll never forget watching her struggle for air, that horrible inhuman barking sound..."

He took her in his arms then, his own relief that Alicia seemed to be over the worst as strong as Shanna's. His lips brushed hers, then deliberately moved away. He kept his arm around her, though, so that she could lean against him. Soon her lids drooped. "Up with Alicia last night, too. Just want to rest my eyes...."

"I'll watch her," he promised. Within seconds, Shanna was fast asleep, a trusting smile on her lips.

As night journeyed toward day, Derek managed to stay awake. He watched not only Alicia, but Shanna, too. On the hospital wall he saw the shadow of her head fitting into the crook of his shoulder and he stared at their joined hands. The images would not leave his mind, even when he briefly closed his eyes. At some point during the long night he realized that he didn't want to end up like his lonely father. He didn't want to be marooned on a loveless island of his own making.

Alicia had only one bout of coughing, but not severe enough to awaken her. By morning, she woke up with her usual feisty cry and didn't appear sick at all, except for some mild congestion. She was discharged—to Shanna and Derek's profound relief.

Shanna drove Alicia home, while Derek went on to the drugstore to pick up the medication the doctor had prescribed and to purchase a cold-mist humidifier to use in Alicia's room for the next few days. Shanna had also asked him to buy a supply of diapers and tissues.

Standing impatiently, distractedly, in the checkout line with his full shopping cart, he finally realized the man behind him was talking to him.

"I see this isn't your favorite hangout on a Saturday morning, either."

Derek focused, heard the words like an echo. "No, it's not." The other man was about his own age, wearing an old cracked-leather Wilfred Laurier University jacket. He carried the same brand of diapers as Alicia's, but large-sized.

"How old is yours?" the man asked.

"Mine?" It was less complicated to play along. "Oh, about four, no closer to five months, I guess."

"You look like you've had one of those rough nights." Derek nodded dully. "Don't despair. It gets easier...in some ways. In others, well...you'll find out. But it's all worth it, isn't it?"

"Yeah..." Derek's turn finally came up and he automatically charged the items to his credit card. He threw a quick wave the stranger's way, smiling at the mix-up, then went searching for a restaurant.

Armed with his bulky purchases, two large cups of coffee and a bag of pastries, he arrived at Shanna's doorstep, pressing the doorbell with his nose.

Finally she appeared. "Sorry, I just got off the phone with my dad."

"But you just called him from the hospital."

"He wanted to know we got home safely. Don't say it I know you're thinking that we parents are a pathetic lot of worriers, but hey, that's life." Before he could reply she added, "Come in, Santa."

"I feel just as zonked as he must by Christmas morning." He leaned over to kiss her as he passed her one of his parcels. "I brought us some hot coffee and cherry danishes."

"How did you know that's exactly what I've been craving?" Eagerly she peered into the bag.

"Because your cravings tend to match mine," he murmured. His heart ached as she refused to meet his searching gaze before disappearing into the kitchen.

Alicia was amazingly bright-eyed as they ate. But after Shanna had changed and bathed her, she was ready for bed again, no doubt from the combined effect of her medication and the fact that she'd lost sleep on the days before. Shanna put her in her crib, then rejoined him in the kitchen. She turned the monitor up to the highest level, then faced him, looking awkward for the first time.

"You must be anxious to get home and get some sleep yourself," she said. "But could you just stay until I have a shower? I'm so afraid to leave her...in case...would you mind?"

"No, not at all." The coffee may have perked him up slightly, but his body felt energized for other reasons as he looked at her. She wore no makeup, but she didn't need any. It might have detracted from her bewitching green eyes, her healthy, smooth complexion and the natural beauty of her long auburn waves. "Take your time..."

She turned swiftly, her expression suddenly clouding, and he knew he had to talk to her before he left. He sat there, perfectly still, and thought about what he would say. The shower roared to life upstairs and he imagined her standing in the steaming heat, the woman of strength and softness and warmth that he'd come to know so well.

He looked deep into himself, at the man he was when with her. She made him feel lovable and worthy. She transformed the grayness of his life into rich, vibrant colors. She understood him, not only his strengths but his weaknesses, too, and she helped to bring out the best in him. Somehow, she'd accepted him. He desperately wanted to accept himself. Completely. Including all that he needed to give, all that he needed to receive. Finally he willed that fragile acceptance into being.

He stood and slowly climbed the stairs. He looked into Alicia's room. She appeared to be sleeping soundly. With increasing urgency he removed the wrinkled suit he'd worn for days running, then dropped the rest of his clothes carelessly in the hall. He stepped through the bathroom door toward the tub, his heart hammering. He felt more nervous, more driven, than he could ever remember having felt before. For the first time in his life he was going to tell a woman he loved her.

FACING THE NOZZLE, Shanna felt the gust of cool air on the back of her legs as the curtain was pulled back. She heard Derek enter, but she didn't turn around. His large hands fanned her waist until she was pressed tightly against him. The pressure of his lips upon her neck merged with the spray ricocheting off both of them.

She had a sudden vivid memory of the cool lake water surrounding their flesh, energizing it. But being locked against him in the primeval heat stirred her deepest instincts even more. Another instinct, self-preservation, rose just as fiercely.

As her fists closed against her chest, she pivoted around and pushed against him. Water streamed down her face and beat against her back. "You can't keep doing this to me," she cried.

"Shanna—"

"I can't be here for you, whenever it suits you. Emotions aren't like toys or games—"

"Shanna, I love you." He whispered the words into her moist lips. "I love you." Into her ears. "I love you." His fingers gripped her glistening shoulders, slithered down her arms, along her back, her breasts, her hips. "I love you."

Shanna knew that more than three words were needed to meld two lives as divergent as theirs, but she let him kiss her, to seal the surging joy those three words were nevertheless bringing. They'd been uttered not in the throes of passion, but quietly, fervently, before desire had built to mind-distorting heights.

"I love you, too, Derek," she admitted for the first time to him, and to herself, as if his words had set hers free. His hands pushed her hair back, so that it fell in a long sleek tail down her back. They blinked at each other for countless moments, assimilating the truth.

"This—this feeling has been inside me, almost since meeting you again. I just didn't understand it. Or maybe I wasn't ready to understand it. I—"

Her fingers touched his lips. "It's okay. I understand."

"*That's* why I love you," he said so quietly his words were almost lost in the roar of the water.

Finally Derek reached around her to turn off the shower. His other hand found a towel. As if he were a doctor and she a patient who had to be treated with the utmost care, he gently squeezed the ends of her hair. His face was grim with a barely controlled passion; his eyes were fixed on her. The towel encircled them, absorbing moisture. When it fell into the pool of draining water, neither noticed or cared.

Shanna wanted nothing but Derek's hands on her naked flesh. Only he had the power to ease the hollow ache, the wonderfully hollow ache, growing deep inside her.

Impatiently he scooped her into his arms and carried her to her bed. No sooner had her damp head touched the pillow, than his body covered hers, rolling, taking her with him. Lips and hands and limbs became part of the mammoth fire spreading between them, through them. She remembered to tell him she was now taking the necessary precautions....

When neither of them could wait any longer, he entered her, filling the throbbing void inside her, sheathing himself in her moist sweetness. He didn't repeat his previous declaration, but she had no doubt he was finally expressing the love burning in his heart. She was overwhelmed by the fury of it as he exploded within her. Her own release followed swiftly, a prolonged, slow-burning series of waves that made time stand still.

They held each other tightly long after the fires had stopped raging....

Two hours later, Derek stirred from a deep, dreamless sleep. At first he didn't know where he was. He recognized Shanna's furniture then and jerked around, but the other half of the bed was empty. He could hear her downstairs, speaking in that higher voice she reserved for Alicia.

The events of the previous night and morning flooded back to him. He made himself relive them in minute detail, in slow motion, as if he were viewing a movie of his life, frame by frame. He froze certain other segments—his father's description of the resurrection of his wedding ring; the shadowed hospital room where he'd sat by Shanna's side all night long, drawn together by more than worry; the sweet amazement of their newborn love; their incredible lovemaking.

He fast-forwarded the film to look ahead at what he really wanted the future to hold, at what would be best there....

Smiling, he decided he would surprise Shanna. He would wait until all his plans were implemented as perfectly as possible. And heaven knew he was a longtime master at covering his most private thoughts.

SHANNA ENTERED THE ROOM, with Alicia in her arms. Derek was lying flat on his back, looking up at the ceiling so pensively that she was suddenly afraid of losing the dreamlike ecstasy they'd shared. "Good afternoon," she said quietly.

"Hi there." He smiled warmly at the two of them. "How is she?"

"A lot better. Thank goodness for the miracle of medicine."

"How are you?" And the slow intonation he gave "you" made her feel like the most revered person in the world.

"A lot better," she repeated, her voice thickening. "Thanks to the miracle of—" She stopped.

"Love?"

"Yeah." And the love was as real again as the glorious blue of his eyes. "Derek, what happened after the cottage?" She thought she knew the answer, but she had to hear it from him.

"I guess I got cold feet. But they're real warm now. Want to check 'em out?" Teasingly he pulled back the covers just as far as his hips.

She shifted Alicia to her other side in a fruitless effort to distract herself from imagining, with searing precision, what exactly lay beneath the sheets. "I'll take your word for it." She set Alicia in the center of the bed, then riffled through her drawers for a change of clothing.

"How wonderfully uncivilized not to be dressed by...five o'clock," he gasped. "Why didn't you wake me?"

"I thought you needed to sleep." Her sweater and underwear in hand, she glanced back at him and once more caught that strange disturbing look on his face. "What are you thinking about?" she dared to ask.

He stared at her for a few seconds. "How knowing I love you makes me feel."

"How does it make you feel?"

"Incredibly lucky. Different yet the same. In awe yet comfortable. Wishing time could stop, that nothing would change."

"Scared?"

"Maybe a little..."

Scared enough to run away again? But she couldn't ask him that.

"My dad offered me the presidency of Morgan's. When he retires," he said suddenly.

She studied him even more closely. "Didn't you expect that?"

"Not exactly. One never knows with him."

"And what about Ray?"

"That's a very astute question. He's furious, being the oldest and all. Ray hates to be under anyone's thumb, least of all mine. I might even have felt the same if the roles had been reversed. We have to work out a lot of things."

"Wars have been waged over such power struggles," Shanna commented dryly.

"We're going to find a truce for this one. Somehow."

"So you've accepted your dad's offer?"

"Another good question. I owe it to myself to think it all over, at least. It's going to take a high degree of commitment. Time. Energy."

"And you're wondering how I'm going to fit into all that?" she murmured.

He nodded, looking away, and she knew in her gut there was something he was holding back. Maybe it was that his work would always come first with him. She sat on the edge of the bed near him, their hands touching, and he proceeded to tell her about taking his father to Toronto to see Terry, about the men's reconciliation, about Terry's new-found wisdom and direction. She realized how much that visit had meant to Derek and how deeply he really cared about his family.

The opportunity had passed, though, to ask him for the guarantees she herself needed to hear, despite his proclamations of love, but she probably wouldn't have asked, anyway. Such guarantees had to come voluntarily, and there was lots of time, she told herself.

But love and patience were not a compatible twosome—especially in her case—because she still feared that a relationship with Derek Morgan came with an expiry date, not a lifetime warranty.

CHAPTER SIXTEEN

"DAD, I CAN'T BELIEVE you've saved all this stuff!" Shanna read the labels on two boxes. *"Reader's Digest 1985-89. Time 1987-88 . . ."*

"Just a few issues with articles I liked."

Shanna's glance swept the array of used clothing, kitchen supplies and such miscellaneous knickknacks as an old bird cage without the stand. When her father had finally asked for help in sorting through some of her mother's belongings, she'd gladly accepted. Unexpectedly the project had grown into a massive overall cleanup, prompting her father to decide to hold his own garage sale. "With some of my castaways, we've got enough here for a week's worth of sales," she told him.

Ned chuckled. "We'll just make it one humdinger of a day. Let's hope this Indian summer weather holds up for us until next weekend."

"What's all that furniture over there, Dad?" Shanna stared at a stack of old tables and chairs, some that appeared to have been sanded down.

"Oh, those. I refinished one of the neighbor's coffee tables for him. He was going to throw it out! Thank goodness I spotted it before he did. Under all the years of paint was some beautiful oak grain. He ended up passing it along to his niece who's apparently delighted with it. His wife salvaged a few other pieces then, and I've been doing some work on them. I wasn't going to take anything, but they insisted on paying me a little."

"That makes good business sense . . ."

"Actually word is spreading to some of the other neighbors, and I've had a steady stream of requests. It's quite surprising."

"I'm not surprised." Her father always took great pride in his workmanship, no matter how small the task. That pride was modestly shining in his eyes now, and Shanna had no doubt he was enjoying his burgeoning projects and doing a fine job of them.

Suddenly the doorbell rang and he jumped up eagerly. "That must be Phyllis. Don't look like that," he added as Shanna's eyebrow raised in curiosity. "She's just dropping off some of her own junk. And I asked her to help me price this female gear. I have no idea. . . ." He scurried off.

A few minutes later, Shanna heard voices descending the basement stairs. "Watch your step there, ladies," her father directed, sounding breathless.

Phyllis entered first, looking as lovely in her camel-colored pantsuit as she had the day Shanna had met her in the park more than a month ago. Another gray-haired woman, as compact and sharp-eyed as Estelle Getty of *The Golden Girls*, but considerably younger, followed her.

"Hello, Shanna," Phyllis said warmly. "I see Ned enlisted your services, too."

"I hadn't realized he had a miniwarehouse of junk stored down here."

Phyllis surveyed the room and whistled. "Ned, you don't seem the scavenger type."

"I'm full of surprises," he said boldly, meeting her eyes.

She swiftly looked away, addressing Shanna. "This is Emily, one of my dearest friends. She's going to help out on the day of the garage sale. Your father asked me, but I'm participating in a walkathon to raise money for local environmental programs."

"You can stop by if you finish early," Ned interjected, disappointment written on his face."

"I don't intend to break any records," she told him evasively. "Besides, Emily is far more efficient than I'd ever be. She has zillions of years of cashier experience at a supermarket."

"Twenty-five," Emily said proudly.

Ned didn't look as impressed as he ought to. "Well, I appreciate any help...."

Phyllis winked at Shanna. "We would have let your father wing it on his own, but when he told us he would donate the proceeds to our charity pool at the club, we could hardly turn our backs, could we?"

Shanna stifled her surprise at this news of his generosity. She knew he'd been attending the Over Fifty-Five gatherings for a couple of weeks, but he'd been vague about them whenever she'd asked.

"So how are the meetings going?" she asked slyly, looking from her father to Phyllis in order to glean any information.

Phyllis answered, a perceptive gleam in her eyes. "Your father has been a...reluctant observer, shall we say."

"I just hadn't expected the age range," he said defensively. "That T.J. fellow, for example, is over eighty."

"And he's as sharp as a whip," Phyllis retorted, momentarily losing her composure. "He knows about the Depression, the war, even the price of bread in 1952! I hate reading history books, so I chat with T.J. instead. It's a heck of a lot more interesting.''

"He does know a few things about baseball stats," Ned admitted begrudgingly.

"See! You can't lump retirees—early or late ones—nor any so-called seniors into your little stereotype boxes. We simply don't fit. A little gray hair or a pension check doesn't mean instant senility. Even T.J. asked me if you were recovering from a major operation. He said you seemed so stiff."

"You're kidding!" Ned burst out, clearly offended, prompting the three women to smile.

"That's nothing," Emily piped in consolingly. "He's proposed to me at least a dozen times. He even took me to a fortune teller who insisted I should marry a man amazingly similar to T.J. I accused him of putting her up to it, but he keeps denying it!"

This time Ned joined in the round of laughter. "Well, I guess I shouldn't be so hard on him. One of these days I might find myself over eighty, too. If I'm lucky," he added on a more somber note.

Suddenly Shanna understood with piercing clarity: her father had been wrestling with his own mortality, perhaps since her mother's death. That was why the age range had been so uncomfortable for him at the meetings, why he'd avoided attending such events in the first place.

Phyllis, too, allowed herself to study him more intently than usual. "Well," she said in a gentler tone, "I think we're a fascinating mixed group, don't you, Emily?"

"Why, certainly. As long as we keep looking past the surface to the rich lives we've led. We all have a lot to share." She spoke in generalities, but she was Phyllis's ally in kindly reprimanding Ned for his patronizing attitude toward the older group members. However, she swiftly made amends. "I hear you are the new whiz kid at Tuesday night badminton, Ned."

He visibly brightened. "I'm enjoying the games. I haven't played in years and I must admit, rusty as I am, I still think I have the old touch."

"Next tournament, we'll let you prove it." Having ventured onto safer neutral territory, Phyllis let him hold her gaze longer.

"Good. I love a challenge," he told her, and his pointed look made it clear he was referring to more than badminton.

Suddenly Shanna heard the familiar stirring on the monitor. Alicia had awakened from her nap in her portable playpen upstairs. Shanna excused herself, but her father barely noticed as he took charge of what he jokingly termed, "The Sale of the Century."

Undoubtedly he was a more spirited man around Phyllis, although Shanna prayed he wasn't setting himself up for a heartbreak. She had to credit his persistence, however. It seemed to be a quality she shared with him.

She'd been seeing Derek steadily since their reunion during Alicia's illness. Most of the time she felt he gave his whole heart to her, but at other times she sensed he was hiding something from her. He'd made some mysterious trips out of town—"conducting business," he'd told her in an odd, disquieting voice. She couldn't escape the fear that he wasn't being entirely truthful with her, especially when his business usually fell on a Saturday or Sunday. Perhaps he was making excuses because he needed time alone, away from her.

She'd asked him once if he thought they saw too much of each other—most weekend evenings and once or twice during the week. He'd said he'd let her know when that time came, making love to her so tenderly that she was in no doubt that the sparks were still very much alive, despite the number of times they'd been lit lately. But she continued to sense disturbing undercurrents from him, and she didn't know how to approach him about her fears without appearing paranoid.

SWEAT TRICKLED DOWN Derek's face as he lunged toward the corner. At the last possible moment his racket connected, sending the tiny squash ball forward with a powerful force, but knocking himself off balance. His shoulder slammed into the wall. He quickly recovered in time to return Ray's next shot. He put everything he had left into that low hard drive and the ball dropped beautifully at the front end of the court.

Ray must have anticipated exactly where it would land because he was cutting across the court and swinging before Derek himself had even moved. The ball grazed the wall, then dribbled to a halt. Ray had won the critical point . . . and the final game.

Slowly Derek pushed his safety goggles onto his forehead, then he bent to retrieve the ball. He hit it one last time, needing to react to the sour aftertaste of defeat. "Good match," he said, still breathing hard.

"Thanks."

Ray, who was leaning against the side wall, catching his breath, didn't move for the customary procedure of shaking hands after a game, so Derek decided not to force the contact. Ray had been sullen ever since the talk about the proposed title changes. At least he'd shown up for work, although he'd made it clear that he wasn't ready to discuss anything yet. Leo had left him alone for the time being. Derek had withheld his own decision, too.

Derek reached outside the small door of the court for two club towels and the plastic bottle sticking out of his gym bag. After throwing a towel to his brother, he rubbed his damp head vigorously and wiped his face. With the towel draped over his neck, he unscrewed the lid and swallowed a few mouthfuls of lukewarm water. "Want some?"

At Ray's nod he threw the bottle his way. While Ray drank, Derek glanced at his sports watch. They'd been playing for an hour and fifty minutes, but when Ray had surprised him by asking for a match after work, he'd said he'd reserved the court for two hours.

"So how have you been?" Derek asked, leaning against the back wall, one leg up.

"Not so good." Ray threw back the empty bottle, which Derek dropped. They watched it roll away.

"That game wasn't about squash, was it, Ray?"

"I guess not."

"I didn't think so. I hope there's no blood on my racket."

Lowering himself to sit up on the scuffed hardwood surface, Ray faced him across the brightly lit, white-washed room. "Maybe I had to see us playing the game, each in our own way," he said slowly, then added in the same tight voice, "It's strange. Winning, being on top, matters for a moment, and then it doesn't matter anymore. The importance passes. So maybe it shouldn't have mattered so much to begin with. There are so many more important things...."

"Like what things?"

Ray stared at his hair-covered knees, absently rubbing at a red patch where he'd fallen earlier. "About ten days ago. Brenda told me she wanted to separate," he stated flatly. "She said I was married to myself and she couldn't be a third wheel anymore. It's been a rough time for me, what with that news Dad sprung on me, but I always thought she'd be around...."

Stunned, Derek stared at him. Ray had been going through this and he hadn't known. "What about the boys?"

"She said she couldn't protect them forever, but she didn't want them to know yet, not until she and I could work out new arrangements. She took them out of school and they all went down to Florida. By the time they returned, I was supposed to have moved out of my own home." His voice cracked from pain and disbelief.

"You can stay at my place for a while, if you need to—"

"I'm not going anywhere," Ray retorted with the same force with which he'd been smashing the ball around. His voice echoed off the room's high ceiling. "I spent a week alone in that house, remembering the confusion and the accusations on my sons' faces as they left. I'm sure they sensed what was going on. I kept reliving the way Brenda walked out that door, suitcase in hand, looking back with none of the agony that was ripping me apart. I was afraid I'd stupidly killed what I'd always taken for granted." He stopped, drew a deep breath, met Derek's eyes for the first time. "I've been going crazy, which you'd probably say is nothing new." He attempted a weak smile.

Derek looked at his older brother, concerned. "I want to help. Any way I can. Where's Brenda now?"

"She came home two days ago, and she was upset that I was still there. After the boys went to sleep, we talked. A long time. I think I finally convinced her to give me another chance. Not a second chance, but about my tenth one. She's threatened to leave me before, but she's never meant it. She means it now. Knowing what I stand to lose, I really believe things can be different this time. She doesn't believe it yet, but she will. By God, she will. I can't blow it.''

The small room grew perfectly still. ''Well, for what it's worth, *I* believe you, Ray. If you want something badly enough, you'll do what's needed and get it.''

''That's not how it worked with the top rung at Morgan's.''

Derek's leg moved down the wall as he shifted uncomfortably. ''I'm sorry, Ray. It was Dad's decision.''

''You could have backed me up, not him. Or if you didn't have your own interests at heart, you could have fought to divide the position.''

''I could have. But we both know only one of us should do the job.''

As Ray distractedly twirled his racket, he didn't deny Derek's claim. In a subdued voice he said, ''Since it really hit home to me that Brenda and the kids are the most important things in my life, everything else seems to be falling into place.'' He gave Derek a long steady look. ''I think, I hope, I can handle what Dad is proposing. You *are* going to take the job, aren't you?''

Derek finally voiced what had been ripening inside him. ''Yes.''

''You'd be a fool not to. And I think we've worked together long enough to know how far to push each other and when to back away.''

''Agreed—with a few new boundaries.''

Ray nodded. ''You should know that I don't intend to shirk my duties at Morgan's, but I intend to cut down on some of my grueling hours so that I can spend more time at home. That's the main reason I won't mind being second-in-command. As the boys get older, they'll need me more that ever. And Brenda, well, let's just say my campaign to win her back is going to be a long uphill struggle. Got any suggestions? You're still out there on the singles circuit where all that romantic stuff really counts.''

Derek had a swift mental picture of Shanna's warm smile when he'd picked her those wildflowers. He thought of all the times he'd failed her, all the ways he wanted to please her now. "I may need a few pointers myself in that department. I'm back with Shanna.''

"Really?''

Derek was about to elaborate when an impatient, loud knock sounded on the door of their court. The next players had arrived. Ray jumped up, while Derek, reluctant to end the discussion, stood more slowly, then began to flex a sore ankle. Because his brother had been so fiercely determined to play right away, Derek hadn't warmed up as much as usual.

Ray watched him, a slow smile breaking across his face. "You know, you may be the business buff of the family and I'm the troubleshooter, as Dad said, but my reflexes are a hell of a lot sharper on the squash court. It sure feels good to know I can still whop you there.''

Derek grinned back at him. "Come on. You've just been visited by Lady Luck a lot lately.''

"The last four matches? Looks like a rematch is in order. But if I lose it'll be because I don't want to beat my future boss.''

"Excuses, excuses. But you're on!''

Even as they challenged each other in the familiar competitive way, Derek realized that certain barriers had been lowered between them. Somehow they had learned to have more respect for each other's strengths, weaknesses and choices.

They shook hands, belatedly, before they left the court.

CHAPTER SEVENTEEN

SUMMER SKIPPED INTO AUTUMN amidst the parade of changing leaves. On the afternoon of the Thanksgiving holiday, Derek insisted on taking Shanna for a country drive along the rural highway between Kitchener and Guelph. He seemed to be filled with nervous energy. He said he'd been under considerable pressure at work lately since he'd finally accepted his father's offer of president.

"It's pretty out here, isn't it?" he asked her rather impatiently.

The crimson and gold colors were past their prime, already browning, and clouds were casting a gray pallor over the farms, fields and houses they passed. "It's okay," Shanna murmured, thinking of how much she had to do when she got home. She'd invited the Hartlys for turkey dinner, along with her father. What's more, Alicia had fallen asleep in her car seat behind them, which would throw off her nap schedule for the day.

"Don't sound so enthusiastic."

"I'm sorry, but the potatoes aren't going to peel themselves, and everyone will be there in a few hours...."

He turned the car around at the next driveway, screeching the tires so testily that she didn't speak to him the rest of the way, thinking he was better left alone.

To make matters worse, her father arrived early in a miserable mood. He cornered her in the kitchen as she was scrambling to fix her vegetables. "Phyllis has been tied up the whole weekend with her family. She didn't even try to accommodate seeing me."

"I thought you two were just friends."

"Who knows? She showed up at the garage sale in time to help me clean up. She's been like Miss Congeniality at our badminton games, but there's always so many others present. I thought maybe we should spend some time alone."

"Can't you tactfully arrange it?"

"She goes to great lengths to avoid just that, as if she's afraid of me."

"Give it time." Shanna smiled consolingly, but she didn't really believe her own words. Maybe Phyllis would never accept her father's romantic overtures. At least he'd met a whole new circle of friends through her. "How about venting some of that frustration on this turnip, Dad?" Without waiting for an answer she left the knife, cutting board and unpeeled vegetable on the counter and dashed into the dining room to finish setting her table.

Miraculously she had dinner under control when Kim, Roger and Teddy arrived twenty minutes later. While Derek greeted them, she ran upstairs to change into dressy black pants and a silky tunic-style top in emerald-green, adding a gold chain around her neck. Thankfully, by the time she returned, Derek seemed less distracted, more like his usual sociable self.

When they finally all sat down at the table adorned with her best china and crystal, Derek offered a toast, wine glass in hand. "To Roger," he began fondly. "Morgan's big loss and Redding's even bigger gain." As the others followed, Roger raised his own glass in modest acknowledgment.

"You're looking great, Roger," Shanna added, amazed at the transformation. His eyes, his posture, his whole body seemed more relaxed.

Kim winked. "He discovered he likes to be boss. But only at work, I have to keep reminding him."

Roger pretended to sigh heavily. "Such harassment..."

"Soon I hope to meet Roger's parents," Kim added slyly.

Roger threw her an uneasy look. "I told you, maybe in time."

"Soon," she insisted, and Shanna knew that the determined Korean woman would not give up on this delicate matter until she had her way.

"And here's another toast to one of my star pupils," Shanna suddenly thought to offer. With the pressures at home relieved, Kim was thriving in the school environment, her English already rapidly improving.

Kim interrupted her with a wave of her hand. "Thank you, but at the same time we must also toast you, Shanna, my favorite teacher and my friend, too."

"Hear, hear," Derek said quietly, drawing Shanna into the blue depths of his eyes.

"Why don't we just toast everyone at the whole darn table before the food gets cold?" This time a jovial Ned led an all-round, practical toast, then started to pass around the platters.

Before long, however, Teddy, who was running a slight fever, started fussing, which provoked a sympathetic response in Alicia, whose nap time had been cut short by their drive earlier. The Hartlys ended up eating quickly, then leaving early. Ned soon followed, mumbling something about a pressing phone call, and Shanna was fairly certain to whom. She put Alicia to bed, then returned to the kitchen to face the piles of dishes. They looked infinitely less appealing, however, than the solid male physique around whom she slipped her arms.

Derek gently moved out of her embrace, kissing her on the forehead. "Shanna...I'd love to stay, but I have some important tax documents to go over tonight. I'm meeting with our accountant tomorrow. I'm sorry," he added with what seemed like sincerity.

Her mouth tightened in disappointment. "You were tied up Saturday, I was over at Talia's yesterday. Today is our only time together—"

"I'll make it up to you next weekend," he hastened to say. "I promise. But as I told you, what with expanding our service to the States and Dad finally relying on me to handle the major details now that Ray and I have worked everything out, I've been swamped. Next weekend, okay?"

"Okay," she echoed.

"I love you," he said as he always did now before he left.

"You, too," she replied as she always did, as well.

The point was finally driven home to her, however, that her love for him was causing her a lot of pain. She felt torn in two every time he walked out the door. She didn't want to keep wondering if he'd ever come back. She wanted so much more.

As she was scrubbing pots and pans, she decided that she would make next weekend special indeed. It was time to face reality. On his own, Derek might never take the final step toward commitment. He needed help. Her help. To steer him in the right direction. In fact, he needed something more. She'd been offering her help for months now. The only thing left to do was to propose to him. She froze at the thought. Yes, the only thing left to do was to propose to him. As she repeated the words, she felt certain it was the right thing to do.

But how? Just blurt out the words? Set up a traditional candlelight dinner with seduction in the air? Surprise him with something more zany?

The worst that could happen was a refusal. At least, she'd know where she and Alicia stood in his life. She wasn't prepared to throw any ultimatums at him . . . yet. And she knew in her heart such threats would only defeat her purpose, considering Derek Morgan's unstable emotional history. Maybe she was taking a serious risk with their relationship, but she had to do it. She loved him and she wanted their lives to merge fully, for all time. She wanted to marry him.

And after the night he'd spent by Alicia's side in the hospital, she had faith that he would make a caring stepfather for her child, even if he still had doubts about his own capacity for responsibility. Love had a way of growing, spreading, like branches of a tree, once the roots were firmly planted . . . .

She slept little that night as she mulled over several approaches and acted out various scenarios in her head, trying to predict how he'd react. Finally she gave up. She would simply have to follow her instincts.

After school the next day, she dropped into a department store to pick up some panty hose. As she was rushing out, she saw them—a huge furry pair of slippers, bootie-style, emblazoned with the colorful face of a clown. No one in their right mind would ever wear such monstrosities. Without a second thought Shanna bought them for Derek—in case he ever got cold feet about their relationship again.

That night she sat down at her kitchen table with a pile of magazines and a pair of scissors in front of her. The slippers had inspired her. Humor was the magnet that had drawn her and Derek together and the tool she would use to keep them together.

She searched diligently for the right pictures and captions, and by Thursday night she had finally designed her proposal card. On the cover page, she'd pasted the perfect caricature of a "browner" with carrot-red pigtails. Her young look-alike was kneeling on a pile of books with such titles as Marriage 202, *As We Like It,* A Funny Thing Happened on the Way to the Hospital . . . .

On the opposite side of the cover page was an overdressed super-jock, ready for action. He wore a football helmet; pads covered most of his body. He carried an assortment of rackets, sticks and gloves. He was perched precariously but confidently, judging by his cocky smile, on a pile of balls of every shape and size.

However, a baby with a sweetly devious grin had crawled between the two, about to topple the books and balls with each hand.

Shanna had cut out words and letters that read "We may have our differences . . ." The card opened to finish the statement. "But I love the ways we balance each other." An attractive man and woman had landed upon each side of a giant weigh scale that Shanna had drawn herself; the scale trays were actually replicas of a familiar rubber dinghy.

The last page showed a couple on the hood of a giant Morgan's truck. They were dancing under a bright full moon. "Let's ride ahead to a wonderful life together. Will you marry me?" She signed her name and left a blank line for his answer.

The lighthearted card was the most serious gamble Shanna had ever taken in her life.

Derek called her once during the week to tell her he would be in Buffalo until late Friday evening, but he was counting on seeing her Saturday night. Afraid of losing her nerve, Shanna asked her father to baby-sit Saturday morning, but she withheld the real reason. She would surprise Derek at his condominium, where there would be no interruptions or distractions. Chances were high he'd be there, sleeping in.

She broke down and confided in Talia, who gave her full support to the plan. Shanna gamely followed through with it, arriving at Derek's place in downtown Kitchener by eleven. She was stopped by a security guard in the lobby.

"May I help you, ma'am?" he asked, suspiciously eyeing her bulky parcel as if it were a bomb.

She'd naively thought she could buzz Derek's unit directly. Suddenly she felt like a burglar who'd been caught in the act of breaking and entering, instead of a gutsy woman taking her life into her own hands. "Derek Morgan, please," she said, clutching her bag with dignity, having the uncanny sensation that he could see through it to the gaudy slippers. "Tell him it's Shanna."

After what seemed like an eternity, Derek answered his intercom and quickly gave his permission for her to enter. He was waiting for her at his doorway as soon as she got off the elevator.

"Is everything okay? Are you all right?"

"I'm fine," she said, except for the fact that her heart beat against her chest like a paddle.

"Come in, come in."

Black jogging pants hugged his muscular legs, sitting low on his hips, as if he'd pulled them on hurriedly. With a heated awareness she stared at his unruly hair and the dark sprinkling on his bare chest and forearms. "I'm sorry if I woke you up."

"Don't be. I—I just didn't expect company." She smiled as he bustled around, picking up old newspapers, empty glasses and discarded clothing. "Have a seat while I make myself presentable."

She refrained from telling him he looked more than presentable. He was the sexiest creature she'd ever seen. He kissed her lightly, then disappeared into the bedroom, leaving her to wonder why he appeared more disoriented than she.

Dropping her parcel, she looked around his ample living space. It was contemporary, simple, masculine. A black leather sectional couch dominated the room, all the more striking against a white carpet upon which children had surely never trod, she thought wryly. Ironically she was wearing the same colors—black corduroy slacks, a drop-shouldered white cashmere sweater. Her glance swept past the modern ceramic-based lamps, the tasteful placing of silk plants, the framed prints of gallery showings by unknown artists. Feeling like a voyeur, but needing to know as much as possible about the man she loved, she walked past the fireplace and the wet bar, then stepped up to the dining room.

A sleek smoked-glass table was untidily covered with papers and official-looking documents. She turned away, then looked back. Her second scrutiny confirmed what she'd thought she'd seen. Blueprints. House plans.

Derek rounded the corner, tucking the tails of his shirt into dark pants, and met her startled eyes. "Hey, you're not supposed to be catching a sneak preview of my big surprise," he said, closing the distance between them.

"What surprise?"

His arms encircled her, and he turned her to face the table, resting his chin in the slope of her shoulder. "My new house."

His new house. She swallowed. "Where?" she asked, half expecting it to be somewhere on the other side of the country or out of the country entirely, what with Morgan's expansion plans.

"The property, a couple acres, is off the highway between Kitchener and Guelph. I almost showed it to you last week, but I-I decided to wait."

"Why?"

He didn't answer her question. "It's in the country, but close enough to be accessible to both cities. The house I'm having built will be set back from the highway enough for privacy. There's an existing cedar grove and creek thrown in for good measure." His breath was warming her cheeks, making her ears tingle. "Here's a walk-out from the family room to the sun deck. There's windows everywhere and all kinds of levels inside. The architect and I have tried to keep the rooms as open as possible. Look, the kitchen is huge with a bay window, looking out to a stand of trees, which I'm hoping to keep. Those squiggles are supposed to be trees. What do you think?"

"It seems...lovely." She tried to face him, but he wouldn't let her. He took her hand, placed it upon the blueprint. "Here's the master bedroom, even bigger than the kitchen. But I want a lot of space if I'm going to share it with a special woman for the rest of my life." His hand continued to guide hers, which had started to tremble. "And over here is a nursery, big enough for a growing toddler. There's two other bedrooms for future needs— offices, guest rooms, maybe more little ones...." This time he didn't resist as she turned around, their eyes colliding. "Shanna, will you marry me and make my house a home?"

"I—I didn't expect this," she sputtered, suddenly feeling light-headed.

"I just finalized the deal on the land a few days ago and I've been scrambling to get some rough house plans drawn up. I wanted to present them to you tonight, in a more formal, special way. But here you are, jumping the gun on me..."

Shanna laughed out loud then, a short laugh of incredulity. He misinterpreted it. "I've never done this before, but I would have handled it better tonight. Really. Please don't laugh. This is the most serious moment of my life. I—"

Her lips silenced him. "No, no. You're doing fine. I'm just overwhelmed. You are the most amazing man I've ever known."

"You can make any changes to the house. It's not cut in stone."

"That's good to know."

"What would be even better to know is your answer."

"Just like that?" she couldn't resist asking, drawing out the wonderful joy spreading inside her. "Without a word, a hint, of what you've been up to?"

He sighed. "I wanted everything to be perfect." His eyes searched hers, trying to fathom the complexity of emotions there. He set out to convince her of his seriousness. His voice grew somber. "Shanna, after that long night at the hospital with you and Alicia, everything changed for me. I had two choices. I could flee again, at the mercy of all my fears, or I could act on my love. Then I realized I really only had one choice. I wanted to give you something as permanent and as solid as my love. Marriage and a home."

"I never guessed. I was too busy thinking the opposite. I—"

"Even the presidency at Morgan's seemed meaningless," he added hastily, "unless you could be by my side." His eyes continued to probe hers. "Is it Alicia? Is that why you look so bewildered, so thrown off? I'm trying to fit her into all this. I really am. I understand

how important that is for you. And I do care for her, too.
But it all has to start with you and me. Right?''

Knowing she would relieve the questioning, sweetly
pained look on his face in a few moments, she drew back
from him. "Wait here. I have something to show you,
too."

She returned, carrying her large bag. Keeping her
expression deadpan, she handed it to him. Slowly he
opened the slippers, wrapped in tissue.

"Beautifully tacky," he murmured appreciatively.
"But I won't be needing them, after all." And she knew
he'd instantly understood their purpose.

"Maybe you will, for those cozy nights at home . . ."

But he wasn't listening as he read the enclosed card. He
didn't respond as quickly as he had to the message of the
slippers. His mouth twisted into a crooked smile as he
turned the pages, and when he finished he looked at her
speechlessly, shaking his head.

"It looks as if we're both ready to negotiate the same
deal," Shanna finally murmured. "I'll accept yours if
you'll agree to mine."

"Done," he returned, his voice hoarse with emotion.

The card dropped as their hands linked firmly and they
began to kiss each other, tiny kisses of amazement and
happiness.

"Soon you're going to make me forget one more very
important matter," Derek said when the kisses started
lengthening, deepening, building in intensity. He led her
to his bedroom, and Shanna barely noticed the heavy oak
furniture or the four-poster bed as she watched him root
through his sock drawer with increasing impatience.

"Some enticing new sexual aid?" she asked devil-
ishly.

"Don't need that with you." He pulled out a striped pair of sports socks, then unrolled them to cup a black velvet box in his hand. "I didn't want to risk losing this."

"Don't you know thieves always look in socks?"

"Then it's high time I put this where it belongs." A large solitaire diamond stared back at them, its prism-like shape reflecting the light magnificently. "It reminds me of our love," Derek said, suddenly shy, struggling to find the right words. "How we are separate yet joined. Not only through destiny but through our own wills, too."

"Oh, Derek, it's beautiful. And *that* was beautiful." There would be plenty of time to tell him she'd thought similar sentiments so long ago at Maple Lake.

He slipped the engagement ring onto her finger. "We can get it sized."

"It fits perfectly." And by now Shanna wasn't even surprised.

"There's one more thing I have to tell you," he said, his eyes feasting on the moist happiness in hers as he gently pushed her backward.

"What?" Her knees bent when the firmness of the bed touched them. He eased her down.

"I love you—"

"That's old news," she said, her eyes merry.

His finger touched her lip with a delicate caress. "I love you, *but* I'm not threatened by that love anymore. And that feels so fantastic. The real issue, my love, isn't one of domination but of completion, between two equals...more or less."

She playfully punched him in the arm for his teasing addendum. "And how did you discover that?"

"I don't know. Maybe a big birdie in my heart told me the time was right, that you are the only woman in the world for me."

"Maybe..." But Shanna knew that Derek Morgan had finally allowed her into that deep loving core of himself that he'd shut off at such a young age. He had so much love to give and she had so much to give back and only a lifetime to do so.

Briefly she remembered how she'd lost Michael prematurely, and her arms tightened around Derek. Fate had given her a second chance at love, and such a love at that. She wasn't going to waste a moment of that precious gift.

Derek seemed to share that belief and they made love with a power greater than words or symbols.

DEREK KEPT STEALING glances at the woman beside him in his car, as if his brain hadn't yet caught up with the reality of their engagement. "What'll I call you? My fiancé? No, sounds too pretentious. My wife-to-be? That's even worse."

"My name will do."

"No, I'll just have to marry you quickly to avoid the whole problem. Then I could get used to 'the little missus.'"

"You wouldn't dare!"

He laughed. "Okay. Wife. That has a nice solid ring to it. Wife. I like that. Unfortunately it's not very original I'll have to think of a few ways to show you how origina I can be...."

Her fingers brushed the back of his neck in a care lessly intimate gesture, remembering the one-of-a-kind lovemaking they'd just shared. "I have no doubt you'l keep doing just that." She leaned back. The refreshing crispness of the late autumn air slapped at her through the partly opened window. "When will you tell you family about us?"

"Maybe tomorrow. We'll talk to my dad first. When tell him I'll be the first president of Morgan's who i going to master the fine art of delegation, he'll instantly know why.''

"Thanks a lot. It'll be like watching dynamite explode, volcanos erupt, the way he feels about me."

"He likes you. Thinks you're spunky. Like a fencer might enjoy a good sparring partner." She stared over at him, unconvinced. "My dad has been coming around in lots of ways. He may surprise us both and even give us his blessing, a handsome wedding present, or both."

"Mercenary!"

"So we'll give it away to charity and live on love in our big, heavily mortgaged house. At least Ray is delighted I finally took his advice to invest in property. Sometimes, though, I've questioned the wisdom of confiding in him about it. He keeps razzing me about the swamp out back."

"I thought you said it was a creek . . ."

"Would I lead you astray, my love?"

"Oh, yes," she said, and they laughed together. "How are Ray and Brenda doing?" He'd told her about their latest troubles and Ray's heartfelt attempts at a reconciliation.

"Fine, but there's one problem. They're going away for another weekend together and they've run out of sitters. Apparently we're next on the list. At the end of the month. Is that okay with you?"

"Of course . . ."

"In return, Brenda said she'd help you with the catering and flowers and all that stuff—"

"What? Did everyone know about your plans but me?"

"I let it slip to Ray when we were talking about the house, and apparently he blurted it out to Brenda, who swore she wouldn't tell another soul, *after* Terry over-heard her and Ray talking about it . . .''

Shanna shook her head, more amused than anything by his sheepish grin. ''Was it so obvious that I would accept your proposal?''

''Probably to everyone except me. Terry thinks the wedding will be a perfect chance for everyone to meet his new lady friend. Oh, and he wants to be the deejay at the bash after the ceremony. Okay?''

''As long as he doesn't make us do the Slosh. I *hate* that dance.'' As they tossed words back and forth in their lighthearted way, Shanna felt an immense excitement building inside at her upcoming marriage. ''Derek, could you stop the car? Please?''

He shot a panicked look her way, then down at the upholstery. ''Are you feeling sick?'' The car ground to a halt.

''No, I just need to move.'' She stepped out and started running, a slow steady pace that reddened her cheeks and blew her hair back against the raw October wind. Derek's Porsche was delayed at an intersection. She waved back at him as she rounded a corner, a few blocks from her house where they were heading to share their news with her father. Her own car was at Derek's; they would pick it up later. All that mattered at that moment was the incredible happiness bursting inside her. She speeded up.

Derek's vehicle pulled up alongside her. ''You're crazy, lady,'' he shouted, then parked the car and leaped out.

''That's okay. I've just been committed, anyway.''

In a few long strides he caught up to her, grinning. ''Sounds like my kind of institution. As long as you're there, too.''

''Oh, I'll be there all right.''

The smiles they flashed at each other made a passerby they hadn't even noticed stare at them in bemused wonder. Panting, they finally burst through the door of Shanna's house.

Ned rushed into the entrance hall in alarm. "What on earth—"

"We're been running," Shanna said.

"We're engaged," Derek added on the same breathless note.

"We wanted you to be the first to know."

"And Alicia, too."

Stunned, Ned looked from one to the other as if following a tennis volley. "I thought you were doing some extra work at school this morning," he muttered to Shanna.

"Sorry. A little white lie. In case Derek turned me down."

"I asked her first, though, as it turned out."

"You know what they say about great minds..."

"By the way, Shanna, where did you get those pictures?"

"*National Lampoon, Mad Magazine,* your cronies."

"I told you, I'm a *GQ* man."

Ned didn't pretend to understand this exchange, nor mind that the lovers had unintentionally excluded him. His face creased into a giant delayed smile of delight. "Well, well, well. Congratulations. Let me just catch up a minute here. This isn't as sudden as it appears, is it?"

"Yes...no," they said simultaneously.

He extended his hand to Derek. "I couldn't be happier for my daughter. And I mean that."

"Thank you, Ned."

"And for myself, too. I'll be gaining not only a son-in-law, but a fellow sports fan."

They wandered into the living room where the progress of a car race was blaring on the television. But Shanna was more interested in the cookbooks spread out on the coffee table, which Ned immediately closed and shoved to the side.

"What were you doing, Dad?"

"Oh, just looking up a few recipes." Her gaze grew even more curious. "Actually Phyllis is coming to dinner tomorrow," he admitted reluctantly. "And I can't remember a single thing I learned at those cooking classes."

She smirked. "You could always call Helen."

"No thanks."

"So, how did you...ah, persuade Phyllis to join you?" Shanna persisted. "Surely not your culinary expertise?"

"I may have stretched the truth about that just a little," he confessed. "I decided I needed to take more...initiative with her. After badminton night, I...well, I managed to kiss her." He was flushing charmingly. "We're all adults here. It seemed, I, ah, gave her more to confront than her fears. She's a stubborn woman, but not as set in her ways as she likes to pretend. Still, it may take more than a few dinners to get through to her."

"Well, I can give you a few pointers in the menu department," Shanna offered.

"And I'll volunteer as a consultant in the...post-game encounters." Derek's eyes glittered mischievously. "I've run across a stubborn woman or two who've taught *m* a lot."

Shanna shot him an amused glance of warning.

"Anyway, I think it's time I started taking the reins of my own life," Ned asserted in a quiet voice. "I can't just hitch a ride on yours forever, Shanna. Especially now that there will be a new man around the house."

"Hey, you'll always be welcome at our place," Derek hastened to say.

But Shanna knew her father wasn't feeling abandoned. He was finally ready to be more independent. "The important thing is you were there for me when I needed you," she told him softly.

"And maybe sometimes when you didn't. But thank you for putting up with me when I wanted to feel needed."

"That's what families are for." He simply nodded in agreement as they shared a deeply fond look.

Derek waited a few seconds, then addressed Ned. "And whenever you feel so inclined, we'll be living in a new house on a few acres that may need some professional puttering, particularly gardening expertise."

Ned's eyes immediately lit up. "I may be able to fit you in, between playing badminton, refinishing furniture and pursuing Phyllis."

"And catering to Alicia," Shanna added. They all glanced in the direction of the cackling monitor as Alicia joined in the conversation from her nursery.

"I'll get her," Derek volunteered before running up the stairs.

Shanna was left alone with her father, who gave her a long tight hug of approval. Any questions he might have had about her engagement were answered by the joy shining on her face.

Suddenly they heard the fuzzy voice of Derek speaking to Alicia through the nursery monitor, which neither of them felt inclined to turn off at their end....

ALICIA HAD PROPELLED herself via her tummy, knees and elbows into a corner of the crib and she had just managed to roll onto her back when Derek entered the room. She looked up at him, quite pleased with her accomplishment, but not quite sure how to react to him. Lately she'd been making strange.

"You're going to be a lively one, aren't you, kiddo?" he said soothingly in order not to frighten her so soon after she'd woken up.

She kicked vigorously in acknowledgment. Carefully he picked her up, doing his best to engage her in conversation, telling her what a big girl she was getting to be, how pretty she was, how much like her mother. The flattery seemed to win her over and she responded with her favorite sounds as he supported her in the cradle of his arm.

"You know, Alicia," he went on more seriously, but, keeping his voice as softly modulated as possible, "I may be new at this, but I intend to be the best dad I can for you. If you'll have me, that is."

She blinked up at him with familiar green eyes, neither objecting nor giving her full consent.

"There'll be lots of time for you to think it over," he said, undeterred. "I really want to take care of you and your mom. I'm having a big house built for you both, but most of all, I want to give you my love."

Alicia thought about that a second, then her mouth curved into a wide sunny smile that lit up her eyes. Derek smiled back at her, feeling a wonderful, natural lift.

"Hey, you two," he heard Shanna say in a choked voice behind him.

His other arm pulled her close, too, and he held her in a loving embrace. Shanna pulled Alicia's hand away from his hair, they laughed, and his circle of love was finally complete—only he knew now that it would always keep widening....

Everyone loves a spring wedding, and this April,
Harlequin cordially invites you to read the most
romantic wedding book of the year.

With This Ring

ONE WEDDING—FOUR LOVE STORIES
FROM OUR MOST DISTINGUISHED
HARLEQUIN AUTHORS:

BETHANY CAMPBELL
BARBARA DELINSKY
BOBBY HUTCHINSON
ANN McALLISTER

*The church is booked, the reception arranged and the
invitations mailed. All Diane Bauer and Nick Granatelli
have to do is walk down the aisle. Little do they realize that
the most cherished day of their lives will spark so many
romantic notions....*

Available wherever Harlequin books are sold. HWED-1AR

GREAT NEWS...

HARLEQUIN UNVEILS NEW SHIPPING PLANS

For the convenience of customers, Harlequin has announced that Harlequin romances will now be available in stores at these convenient times each month*:

Harlequin Presents, American Romance, Historical, Intrigue:

> May titles: April 10
> June titles: May 8
> July titles: June 5
> August titles: July 10

Harlequin Romance, Superromance, Temptation, Regency Romance:

> May titles: April 24
> June titles: May 22
> July titles: June 19
> August titles: July 24

We hope this new schedule is convenient for you.

With only two trips each month to your local bookseller, you'll never miss any of your favorite authors!

*Please note: There may be slight variations in on-sale dates in your area due to differences in shipping and handling.

HDATES

HARLEQUIN'S WISHBOOK
SWEEPSTAKES RULES & REGULATIONS
NO PURCHASE NECESSARY TO ENTER OR RECEIVE A PRIZE

1. To enter the Sweepstakes and join the Reader Service, affix the Four Free Books and Free Gifts sticker along with both of your Sweepstakes stickers to the Sweepstakes Entry Form. If you do not wish to take advantage of our Reader Service, but wish to enter the Sweepstakes only, do not affix the Four Free Books and Free Gifts sticker; affix only the Sweepstakes stickers to the Sweepstakes Entry Form. Incomplete and/or inaccurate entries are ineligible for that section or sections of prizes. Torstar Corp. and its affiliates are not responsible for mutilated or unreadable entries or inadvertent printing errors. Mechanically reproduced entries are null and void.

2. Whether you take advantage of this offer or not, on or about April 30, 1992 at the offices of Marden-Kane Inc., Lake Success, NY, your Sweepstakes number will be compared against a list of winning numbers generated at random by the computer. However, prizes will only be awarded to individuals who have entered the Sweepstakes. In the event that all prizes are not claimed, a random drawing will be held from all qualified entries received from March 30, 1990 to March 31, 1992, to award all unclaimed prizes. All cash prizes (Grand to Sixth), will be mailed to the winners and are payable by check in U.S. funds. Seventh prize to be shipped to winners via third-class mail. These prizes are in addition to any free, surprise or mystery gifts that might be offered. Versions of this sweepstakes with different prizes of approximate equal value may appear in other mailings or at retail outlets by Torstar Corp. and its affiliates.

3. The following prizes are awarded in this sweepstakes: ★ Grand Prize (1) $1,000,000; First Prize (1) $25,000; Second Prize (1) $10,000; Third Prize (5) $5,000; Fourth Prize (10) $1,000; Fifth Prize (100) $250; Sixth Prize (2,500) $10; ★ ★ Seventh Prize (6,000) $12.95 ARV.

   ★ This Sweepstakes contains a Grand Prize offering of a $1,000,000 annuity. Winner will receive $33,333.33 a year for 30 years without interest totalling $1,000,000.

   ★ ★ Seventh Prize: A fully illustrated hardcover book published by Torstar Corp. Approximate Retail Value of the book is $12.95.

   Entrants may cancel the Reader Service at anytime without cost or obligation to buy (see details in center insert card).

4. Extra Bonus! This presentation offers two extra bonus prizes valued at a total of $33,000 to be awarded in a random drawing from all qualified entries received by March 31, 1992. No purchase necessary to enter or receive a prize. To qualify, see instructions on the insert card. Winner will have the choice of merchandise offered or a $33,000 check payable in U.S. funds. All other published rules and regulations apply.

5. This Sweepstakes is being conducted under the supervision of Marden-Kane, Inc., an independent judging organization. By entering this Sweepstakes, each entrant accepts and agrees to be bound by these rules and the decisions of the judges, which shall be final and binding. Odds of winning in the random drawing are dependent upon the total number of entries received. Taxes, if any, are the sole responsibility of the winners. Prizes are nontransferable. All entries must be received at the address printed on the reply card and must be postmarked no later than 12:00 MIDNIGHT on March 31, 1992. The drawing for all unclaimed Sweepstakes prizes and for the Bonus Sweepstakes Prize will take place May 30, 1992, at 12:00 NOON at the offices of Marden-Kane, Inc., Lake Success, NY.

6. This offer is open to residents of the U.S., the United Kingdom, France and Canada, 18 years or older, except employees and their immediate family members of Torstar Corp., its affiliates, subsidiaries, and all other agencies and persons connected with the use, marketing or conduct of this Sweepstakes. All Federal, State, Provincial and local laws apply. Void wherever prohibited or restricted by law. Any litigation within the Province of Quebec respecting the conduct and awarding of a prize in this publicity contest must be submitted to the Régie des Loteries et Courses du Québec.

7. Winners will be notified by mail and may be required to execute an affidavit of eligibility and release, which must be returned within 14 days after notification or an alternative winner will be selected. Canadian winners will be required to correctly answer an arithmetical skill-testing question administered by mail, which must be returned within a limited time. Winners consent to the use of their names, photographs and/or likenesses for advertising and publicity in conjunction with this and similar promotions without additional compensation.

   For a list of our major winners, send a stamped, self-addressed envelope to: WINNERS LIST, c/o MARDEN-KANE, INC., P.O. BOX 701, SAYREVILLE, NJ 08871. Winners Lists will be fulfilled after the May 30, 1992 drawing date.

ALTERNATE MEANS OF ENTRY: Print your name and address on a 3″ × 5″ piece of plain paper and send to:

In the U.S.
Harlequin's WISHBOOK Sweepstakes
3010 Walden Ave.
P.O. Box 1867, Buffalo, NY 14269-1867

In Canada
Harlequin's WISHBOOK Sweepstakes
P.O. Box 609
Fort Erie, Ontario L2A 5X3

1991 Harlequin Enterprises Limited   Printed in the U.S.A.

LTY-H491RRD

This April, don't miss #119, CHANCE OF A
LIFETIME, Barbara Kaye's third and last book in the
Harlequin Superromance miniseries

A powerful restaurant conglomerate draws the best and brightest
to its executive ranks. Now almost eighty years old, Vanessa
Hamilton, the founder of Hamilton House, must choose a succes-
sor. Who will it be?

Matt Logan: He's always been the company man, the quintessen-
tial team player. But tragedy in his daughter's life and a
passionate love affair made him make some hard choices....

Paula Steele: Thoroughly accomplished, with a sharp mind, perfect breeding and looks to die for, Paula thrives on challenges
and wants to have it all...but is this right for her?

Grady O'Connor: Working for Hamilton House was his salvation
after Vietnam. The war had messed him up but good and had
killed his storybook marriage. He's been given a second
chance—only he doesn't know what the hell he's supposed to
do with it....

Harlequin Superromance invites you to enjoy Barbara Kaye's
dramatic and emotionally resonant miniseries about mature men
and women making life-changing decisions.